D0610987

French Kissing

Lynne Shelby

Published by Accent Press Ltd 2015

ISBN 9781783758135

One

Chère Alexandra,

Je m'appelle Anna Mitchel. J'ai onze ans. J'ai une sœur. My French teacher says we have to write to our penfriends in French but I do not know many French words yet because I have only been learning it for one term at my new school. French is hard. I live in London.

Á bientôt,
Anna

Dear Anna,

My name is Alexandre. Alexandra is a girl's name. I am a boy. I am eleven years old like you. I have one sister like you. My father is French but my mother is English. I speak English because my mother taught me so it is easy for me. I live in Paris.

Yours sincerely,
Alexandre Tourville

Cher Alexandre,

J'espère que tu as aimé ta visite à Londres ... I hope you enjoyed your visit to London. I'm sorry that I left you on your own so much. Thank you for not telling my parents that it was

1

my fault you got lost on the underground. Thank you for saying I was with you the whole time at the disco. Do your parents really let you drink wine? … *boire du vin*?

Á bientôt,
Anna

Dear Anna,

I enjoyed my visit to London very much. I took some great photos. The best is the photo of you in Regent's Park. I showed it to my sister and she said that you are very pretty and look older than thirteen. I told my parents that the reason I got lost was because I do not have a mobile phone and I could not call anyone, and at last they have agreed to buy a phone for me!! All French teenagers drink wine.

Best wishes,
Alexandre

Cher Alex,

I passed my A Levels – and got the grades I need to go to university! For French I got an A!!!! In September I'm off to study the History of Art for three years. I can't wait to be a student and live away from home.

On Saturday my friend Beth and I went clubbing and met these two really hot guys. We're going back to that club next weekend!!

Ciao,

Anna

Dear Anna,

2

My first term as a photography student has been amazing and has gone unbelievably fast. I thought I was a good photographer, but now I know I have so much to learn.

I am sad for you that you broke up with Daniel. But not <u>very</u> sad, because he sounds like a total jerk.

I am still dating Francine, but all we seem to do is argue – even when we are in bed. She wants us to move in together, but for me it is far too soon to make that sort of commitment.

It is good to hear that you are enjoying your studies of art history. One day I hope you will come to Paris, and I will show you my favourite paintings in the Louvre and the Musée D'Orsay.

Best,
Alex

Cher Alex,

I have a job! Tomorrow, I start work as an account executive at Nova Graphics, a small graphic design company in Camden. It's not exactly the gallerista job I had in mind when I graduated, but Oliver and Natalie (partners in life as well as professionally), who own the studio, are lovely, and the money is good enough that my friend Beth and I can afford to rent a flat together!! Which I'm *really* pleased about, because moving back home to live with my parents after uni has certainly *not* been easy!

The other big event in my life is that Tom and I have decided we should stop seeing each other. There are no hard feelings – we've just drifted apart. Actually, several of my friends recently split up from the people they were dating at uni.

Maybe one day, if the invitation still stands, I'll just jump on the Eurostar and come and visit you in Paris. I would love to see Paris, and you of course.

Ton amie,

3

Anna

Hi Anna,
I have my first commission! It has taken months of trudging round photography agencies with my portfolio and pitching for work, but I am finally booked on a fashion shoot. Caroline is a great photographer, and I have learned more in the year I have been working as her assistant than I learned in college, but it is time I struck out on my own ...

Your friend,
Alex

Cher Alex,

Nick wants me to meet his parents! He has invited them to join us for lunch at his golf club. I don't mind admitting that I'm terribly nervous, but I guess that's normal when you meet your boyfriend's mother for the first time. I so want his family to like me ...

Ton amie,
Anna xx

From: alexandretourville@alexphotographie.com
To: annamitchel@webmail.co.uk
Subject: London

Hi Anna,

Just a quick email to let you know that I've taken a six-month contract with an English magazine, and from next week, I'm going to be based in – cue drum roll – LONDON. We will finally have a chance to meet up again! I won't have time to sort out my accommodation before I arrive in England, so can you recommend a hotel for me, preferably near where you live?

4

Alex

From annamitchel@webmail.co.uk
To alexandretourville@alexphotographie.com
Subject: London

Cher Alex,

I know you're used to living out of a suitcase, but there's really no need for you to book into a London hotel. You're very welcome to come and stay in my spare room until you find a place of your own.

Anna xx

I listened with growing impatience to the voice on the other end of the phone. Alex's train was due to get in at 6.00 and it was already gone 5.30.

'I'm afraid Oliver has left for the weekend,' I told the client, 'but I'll have him telephone you first thing Monday morning ...'

Finally, the client was happy, and I was able to end the call.

Natalie came out of her office, already wearing her outdoor coat.

'Coming for a drink, Anna?' she said.

'I can't tonight. I'm meeting Alexandre off the Eurostar.'

For a moment, Natalie looked puzzled, but then she said, 'Oh, yes, your Frenchman.'

'Well, Alex is French, and male, but I don't know that he'd like being described as "my Frenchman".'

'I guess it does sound a little proprietorial.'

Natalie waited while I put on my coat and picked up my bag, and we walked downstairs and through the revolving doors that led onto the street. Outside, it was dark, cold, and just starting to rain. February was certainly not the best time of year for Alex to be coming to London.

'Goodnight, Anna,' Natalie said. 'I'll see you and Nick tomorrow, at the party my husband has so kindly arranged to "celebrate my fortieth birthday".'

'Your fortieth! The big Four-O.'

Natalie grimaced. 'Tomorrow I'll be forty. I'll be embarking on my fifth decade. And I'm *absolutely fine* about it.'

I glanced at my watch. 5.45. From Camden Town to St Pancras was only two stops on the tube, but I was going to be late.

I said, 'Nat, I really have to shoot off. I'll see you tomorrow.'

'You can bring your Frenchman, if you like,' Natalie said. 'I'm worried Oliver hasn't invited enough men.'

'I'll bring Alex, then – if he hasn't made other plans.' I couldn't resist adding, 'The French appreciate an older woman's charms.'

'Not helping, Anna.' Natalie headed off to the pub (where Oliver and the rest of my co-workers were no doubt already making inroads on the wine) and I hurried to the station.

As always in central London on a Friday night, the underground was crammed with commuters returning home from work (or an after-work drink with their colleagues) and revellers making their way into town. By the time I'd queued to get through the ticket barriers and down the escalators, battled my way on and off the packed train, and followed the signs to the Eurostar terminal, it was nearly 6.30. I was hideously late. I scanned the crowds milling around the arrivals gate. There was no sign of Alexandre. He'd been in London for less than half an hour, and already I'd managed to lose him. Again. Just like the last time. My heart started thudding in my chest, but then I realised that there really was no need to panic. Alex was no longer a shy thirteen-year-old schoolboy on his first trip abroad, but a twenty-eight-year-old man and a successful professional photographer, whose work had taken him all over the world. And he had a mobile phone.

I fished my iPhone out of my bag. I had one missed call and

a text.

Hi Anna. Cannot find you at arrivals. Will wait for you by bronze statue of man and woman. Guidebook tells me it is called The Meeting Place, so it seems appropriate! Alex xx

Being unfamiliar with the layout of St Pancras, I looked around wildly for the famous statue of the embracing couple. As it was about ten metres high, and situated under the clock, I saw it immediately, even though it was on the upper level of the station. I pelted across the concourse and leapt up the stairs two at a time. Reaching the top, I dodged past the people heading the opposite way, and tried to spot someone near the statue who could be the adult version of a boy I'd last seen fifteen years ago. Most men of the right age were either with a girl or a group of friends. There was a guy in a leather jacket, standing with his back to me, who seemed to be on his own, but his hair was too dark for him to be Alex. Another lone man, with lighter hair, was reading a newspaper, holding it up so I couldn't see his face. I really can't start accosting strange men in a train station, I thought.

Realising that I was still clutching my mobile, I scrolled through my address book and called Alex's number.

The dark-haired guy reached into his jacket for his phone.

'*Bonjour*, Alex,' I said, when he answered.

'Anna. Hi. Where are you?'

'I'm standing right behind you.'

He turned around.

'Alex?'

The last time I'd seen Alexandre, he'd been a head shorter than me, a scrawny boy, with a pale face and thin, bony shoulders. The man striding towards me, carrying a holdall and a camera case, was well over six feet tall, and his shoulders were broad. His brown hair had grown so dark it was almost black, he was tanned, and his jaw was covered in stubble. And he was *gorgeous*. I stared at him, not quite able to believe that

7

anyone's physical appearance could change so much. Deep within me, I felt the unmistakable stirring of desire. I reminded myself *very* firmly that I had a steady boyfriend.

'Anna? Is that really you?' Alex bent his head to greet me the French way, with a kiss on either side of my face. I breathed in a deliciously masculine scent of leather and cologne.

'Don't you recognise me?' I'd never thought about it, but obviously I also looked somewhat different to my gawky teenaged self. For one thing, I'd long ago stopped slouching in an effort to appear less than 5' 8" tall. These days, I was very rarely seen in public without my high heels.

'I didn't recognise you at first. But I do now.'

'I'm so sorry I was late meeting you,' I said.

'Not to worry, it gave me a chance to admire the statue.'

I looked up at the bronze man and woman towering above us. They were gazing into each other's eyes, standing so close together that their foreheads were touching. His arms were about her waist, and her hands were reaching up to his face.

'Maybe, like me, the man has just arrived from France on the Eurostar.' Alex smiled, and suddenly I caught a fleeting glimpse of the boy who had somehow turned into this extraordinarily handsome man. '*Je suis content de te voir*, Anna.'

I said, 'It's good to see you, too, Alexandre.'

Two

I unlocked the front door to my flat, and led Alex into the narrow hall.

'That's my bedroom,' I said, pointing. 'Bathroom, kitchen, living room. And this is your bedroom while you're here. It's quite small ...'

Alex followed me into the spare bedroom and looked around. The room was in fact tiny, with barely enough space for the double bed, wardrobe, and dressing table with which it was furnished. It seemed even smaller now that Alex was in it.

'I don't need a massive bedroom,' Alex said. 'I just need somewhere to sleep.'

It occurred to me that the pink floral duvet cover, cushions, and matching curtains would most likely not be a guy's first choice of decor.

'I'm sorry about the colour scheme.'

'Anna, it's fine,' Alex said. 'I'll only be here as long as it takes me to find my own place to rent, and most of the time I'll be out working.'

'Right. Well, I'll leave you to get settled. Are you hungry? As you know, I'm not much of a cook, but I do have pizza.' When Alex had stayed with my family when he was thirteen, he'd always been hungry.

'Pizza would be great.' He rummaged in his holdall. 'And here's a bottle of wine to go with it.'

Leaving him to get unpacked, I went to the kitchen, put two pizzas in the oven, and made a salad (my culinary skills may be limited, but I can at least slice a cucumber and chop up a tomato). I opened the wine, poured myself a glass, and took a sip …

It's the last night of the French children's visit to England, and my school's enthusiastic PTA has arranged a farewell party: a disco for my class and our visitors. It's the usual dire affair, held in the school hall (the girls dancing, the boys lounging against the wall), and supervised by our teachers from both sides of the Channel. And, as always happens at such events, some of the boys have smuggled in alcohol.

We leave the hall separately. Beth and I, and Beth's penfriend Fabienne, go first, and shortly afterwards Sean and his penfriend, Gérard, follow. I like Gérard. I like him a lot. He's taught me some interesting French swear words, and he's the only boy my age I've met who's taller than me. And I know it's wrong of me to go off with him and leave Alexandre on his own again, but I don't care.

We meet up in the library. Sean and Gérard produce the cans of beer and bottle of wine that they'd hidden earlier that day in the boys' changing rooms. Whispering and giggling, we sit in a circle on the carpet between the stacks. I sit next to Gérard, who unscrews the wine, drinks, and passes it to me. I put the bottle to my lips, and tip it up so that the warm red liquid fills my mouth. It tastes strange, but not unpleasant. I swallow some more. The others are gulping down the beer.

We all freeze as the library door swings open and someone comes in, and then relax when we see that it's only Alexandre.

By way of greeting, he says, 'I thought you'd like to know that Monsieur Bernard and Miss Crawford are patrolling the corridors. And they're coming this way.'

We all look at each other in terror, and then as one we leap to our feet and run to the library exit. We hear voices coming from the stairwell, so we pelt in the opposite direction, our footsteps agonisingly loud on the wooden floor. Gérard sprints ahead of the rest of us, and vanishes around a corner. I'm falling behind the others. Despite my long legs, I'm not a fast runner, and I'm slowed down even more by my tight skirt.

'Quick, Anna, in here.' Alexandre seizes my arm, and drags me into an empty classroom.

I gasp, 'We can't stay here. They'll find us.'

'Get behind the desk.'

Alexandre and I crouch down under the teacher's desk at the front of the classroom. Almost immediately, someone opens the classroom door and switches on a light. My heart is hammering. Alexandre takes hold of my hand and squeezes it. He raises a finger to his lips.

I hear my French teacher, Miss Crawford, say, 'There's no one in here, either.'

'Then we are alone.' That was Alexandre's teacher, Monsieur Bernard.

'Oh, Alain, I ... We can't ... We shouldn't ...'

'Jennifer ... ma chérie ...'

This is followed by a number of gasps and sighs.

Alexandre and I stare at each other in disbelief. Cautiously, he peers round the side of the desk.

He whispers, 'Ils s'embrassent.' And, in case I haven't understood, he adds, 'They are kissing.'

I think, But they can't be – they're our teachers.

I also look round the desk.

Miss Crawford and Monsieur Bernard, entwined in each other's arms, are kissing on the mouth.

Miss Crawford says, 'Alain, mon chéri, *we have to go back to the hall. The children ...'*

Monsieur Bernard replies in French, speaking too rapidly for me to follow. There are some more sighs, and then one of them switches off the light. The classroom door opens and closes again.

Alexandre and I wait a few minutes, and then crawl out from under the desk.

'I thought they'd search the classroom,' I say.

'For a moment so did I, but they had other things on their minds.' Alexandre puts his hand over his heart. 'Oh, ma

11

chérie …'

'Ooh, Alain … What was that last thing he said to her?'

'"Tu me rends fou"? That means "you drive me crazy".'

I start giggling, and suddenly both of us are doubled up with laughter. I laugh so hard that it hurts. It occurs to me that I've not been very kind to Alexandre this week he's been in England. It's not that I've been mean to him, not exactly. But I've been trying so hard to get Gérard to like me that for most of the time, Alexandre has been ignored.

'Merci, Alexandre,' I start speaking in French, but it's too much of an effort, so I switch to English. 'Thank you for coming to the library to warn us …'

Alexandre shrugs. 'That's OK. You were all making such a racket you were easy enough to find.'

'If we'd been caught with the wine, we'd have been suspended for sure. My parents would have gone ballistic.'

'My parents allow me to drink wine with meals – but they too would be angry if I drank it in school.'

I think how much nicer a boy he is than Gérard, who is very good-looking, but so up himself. And who ran off and left me to get caught.

'Alexandre,' I say, 'Miss Crawford said that after this year, we won't be writing letters to our penfriends in lessons any more. Can you and I still write to each other anyway?'

'Mais, oui,' Alexandre says. 'Bien sûr. Of course. Shall we go back to the disco now?

'Anna?' Alex's voice jerked me back to the present.

'I'm in here,' I called out.

He came into the kitchen.

'I was just thinking about your first visit to London,' I said. 'Do you remember the disco?'

'I remember hiding with you under the desk. And that we were the only kids that didn't get caught.'

Having fled the crime-scene, Gérard and the others had been apprehended climbing out of a downstairs window by Madame

Lefevre (another of the French teachers, and a very scary woman), and my school's headmaster, Mr Walsh (whose sole mission in life was to catch students red-handed doing something they shouldn't). Gérard had still had the half-empty wine-bottle, Beth was clutching a can of beer, and Sean was more than a little drunk. There followed much furious shouting in French (Mme Lefevre) telephone calls to parents (Mr Walsh), and a thorough search of the whole school building which discovered the empty beer cans in the library and three boys drinking vodka in the science lab. As one of the teachers thought that they'd seen me leave the hall with Beth, I was hauled into the headmaster's office and interrogated as to my part in 'this disgraceful incident', but Alex (his dark brown eyes wide and innocent) had insisted that I'd been with him the whole evening, so I was allowed back into the disco. Beth's parents had grounded her for a month.

'You were my hero that night,' I said.

Alex laughed. 'I thought you liked Gérard.'

I rolled my eyes. 'I had a huge crush on him, but my excuse is that I was only thirteen.'

'I hated being thirteen,' Alexandre said. 'I was such a little runt.'

'No you weren't.' He was, but he certainly isn't now, I thought. 'When I was younger, I hated being tall. I was convinced that I would never ever find a boyfriend.'

'Who'd be a teenager?'

'Not me.' I checked the oven. 'The pizzas are ready.'

Alex helped me carry everything through into the living room. When I ate on my own, I just balanced a plate on my knees in front of the TV, but as it was Alex's first night in London, we sat at the dining table. He told me some more about his new job as a staff photographer for *The Edge* magazine, how it would still leave him time for freelance work, and how he was hoping to explore (and photograph) England while he was here. I knew so many intimate details about his life, and I'd told him things in my letters that I'd told no one else, not even

Beth or Nick, but it still felt strange to be chatting to him over the dinner table. He was both familiar and unfamiliar at the same time.

'I suppose you'll be going back and forth between London and Paris quite often,' I said. 'It's so easy to get to the continent with the Eurostar.'

Alex shook his head. 'No, I've no plans to visit France in the next six months.'

I raised my eyebrows. 'And what does your girlfriend think about that?'

'I've no idea. Cécile and I split up three weeks ago.'

I gaped at him. 'Oh, no, Alex, I'm so sorry. What happened?'

'She finished with me.'

'But why? I mean, the last time you wrote, you said your relationship was going so well. Was it because you took this job in England?'

'No, I took the job because I'd broken up with Cécile. I wanted a fresh start away from Paris – and her.' He drank some wine and poured himself another glass. 'We were together almost a year, and then she ... met someone else. I since found out that she was sleeping with him while she was still with me.'

She sounds like a right slut, I thought. Aloud, I said, 'I really am sorry, Alex. That's awful.'

'When she told me we were over, I was devastated, but now ... It still hurts, but I'm getting there, you know?'

'Yeah, I know. When Daniel dumped me, I cried for a fortnight, but then I just didn't feel like crying any more.'

'Remind me which one was Daniel?'

'The boy I dated in my first term at uni.'

'Oh, yeah. The jerk.' Unexpectedly, Alex smiled. 'It's odd talking to you like this. We've written so many letters to each other, and I know so much about your life, and yet, I keep getting the feeling that you're someone I've just met. Does that sound crazy?'

'No, it's the same for me.'

14

Alex was studying my face. 'Can I photograph you?'

'What, now?'

'No, not right now.' Alex leant across the table, and tucked my dark blonde hair behind my ears. Then he put a finger under my chin, and turned my head from side to side, so that he could see my profile. 'I'd like to photograph you in a studio, with proper lighting. Some of my best pictures have been of beautiful women.'

Did he just say I was beautiful? Absurdly, my face grew hot.

To cover my confusion, I said, 'I'm not a model.'

'No, but you have very good bone structure.' He gave me a quizzical look. 'It's fine if you'd rather I didn't photograph you. Some people get very self-conscious when they're in front of a camera.'

'It's not that I mind having my picture taken, but I never look great in photos. You might be wasting your time.'

'A photoshoot with a professional photographer is a little different to having your most embarrassing moments preserved for posterity on a friend's iPhone.'

I laughed. 'OK, Alex, I'll pose for you. Now, how about coffee?'

We drank our coffee in a companionable silence, listening to the rain pattering against the living-room windows.

Eventually, Alex said, 'I thought I'd go into central London tomorrow, maybe do a bit of sight-seeing – if the weather improves.'

'Would you like some company?'

'I would – if you're free. I don't want you altering your plans because of me.'

'Oh, I'm not doing anything tomorrow. Not during the day. In the evening Nick and I are going to a fortieth birthday party – to which you're invited, by the way.'

'I'm invited?'

'When I told Natalie – the birthday girl – Nova Graphics' Creative Director – that you were arriving in England today, she said to bring you along. Will you come?'

'Are you sure you want me there.'

'Why wouldn't I?'

'Anna, just because I'm staying in your home, please don't feel that you have to entertain me.' His dark eyes glinted with amusement. 'I'm no longer that puny teenage boy who got lost on the London underground. These days, I'm pretty good at finding my way around a foreign city.'

'We've both changed since we were thirteen,' I said. 'But we're still friends. And I would very much like it, *mon ami,* if you would come with me and Nick to Natalie's party. Besides, Natalie needs you there. Her guest list is short on good-looking men.'

Alex's mouth lifted in a lop-sided grin. 'In that case, how can I refuse the invitation?'

Three

The doorbell rang. That would be Nick. Stopping to put on a bathrobe before I left my bedroom (Alex knew a lot about me, but he didn't need to know the colour of my underwear), I went and opened the front door.

'Hey, Nick.' I tilted my face up and he dropped a perfunctory kiss on my lips. 'I'm not nearly ready – I still have to do my make-up.'

'That's OK, Anna. I'm early.' Nick stepped past me into the hall. 'So where's this French house-guest of yours? Do I get to meet him tonight?'

'You'll get to meet him when he's finished taking a shower. He's coming with us to Natalie's.'

'You spent the entire day with him, and now you're taking him to your boss's party?' Nick frowned. 'You're not planning to cart him about with you all weekend, are you? Because I was hoping you and I could spend some time together tomorrow. Just the two of us.'

'Tomorrow, I'm all yours,' I said. 'But Alex is only going to be staying with me a few weeks, and I would like to spend some time with him while he's here.'

'A few weeks? I thought you said he'd only be staying a few days?'

'It's however long it takes for him to find a place of his own. Don't sulk, Nick, we can always go to your place if we want some time alone.'

I put my arms up around my boyfriend's neck, intending to draw down his head and kiss away his bad mood, but at that

17

moment, Alex, naked except for the towel around his waist, came out of the bathroom. His hair was still wet from his shower, and rivulets of water ran over the smooth planes of his chest and the hard ridges of his superbly toned abs, to vanish amongst the dark hair on his stomach. My gaze travelled over his gleaming torso, past the towel hanging low on his hips, to his muscular legs, and back up to his face, and I thought: his body is amazing.

Removing my arms from Nick's neck, I said, 'Alex, this is my boyfriend, Nicholas Cooper. Nick, this is Alexandre Tourville. The guy I've been writing to all these years.'

'Hello, Nicholas,' Alex said.

Nick said, 'Bong-joo-er, Alexandreh. Common ally voo?'

I smothered a smile. Nick remembered very few French phrases from his schooldays, and his pronunciation was appalling.

'*Je vais bien, merci* ...' Alex said, once he'd worked out that Nick was asking how he was doing. '*Je ne sais pas* ... I didn't know you spoke French, Nicholas.'

'*Il ne fait pas,*' I said. 'He doesn't.'

'Then tonight we must speak in English,' Alex said. He added, 'I should go and put some clothes on.'

Must you? Really? I thought.

Alex went off to his bedroom. Nick followed me into mine, shut the door, and sat down on my bed.

'That was kind of you to speak to Alex in French,' I said. 'I'm sure he appreciated it.'

'I was just being polite,' Nick said. 'Though I needn't have bothered. He obviously speaks excellent English.'

'He does. He's totally fluent.' Like I told you. Many times. When Nick made no further comment about Alex's linguistic abilities, I said, 'Alex and I had a really good time today. He wanted to go sight-seeing, so we started out at Buckingham Palace. Then we cut through St James' Park –'

'Rather a cold day for a stroll in a park, I'd have thought.'

'It was freezing, but it was beautiful by the lake – the air was

18

so clear and crisp. After we left the park, we went down to the river, and walked along the Embankment to Waterloo Bridge. Alex loved the view from the centre of the bridge as much as I do. He took some great photos.'

'What's so wonderful about the view from Waterloo Bridge?'

'You can see so many famous landmarks – St Paul's Cathedral, the Shard, the Houses of Parliament, the London Eye … You get a real sense of history …'

Nick raised one eyebrow. 'You sound like a tourist guide. Did you and Alex spend all day trekking round London?'

'Pretty much. Apart from when we had a very late lunch in Covent Garden, listening to the buskers singing opera. After that, we went to Trafalgar Square.' The memory of Alex talking me into climbing on the lions, an activity he'd missed out on the first time he'd visited London, made me smile. I tried to imagine Nick sitting on a lion, and failed.

'You must have walked miles,' Nick said.

'It was fun. You and I should have a day out in London.'

'I commute into central London Monday to Friday. I don't feel the need to go there on a Saturday.'

'Oh. Well, we don't have to.' I took a sequinned dress out of my wardrobe and held it up against me. 'Is this too formal for Natalie's party, do you think?'

'How would I know?' Nick said. 'She's your boss not mine.'

I gave him a long look. 'Nick, is something wrong?'

'You told me Alex was shorter than you.'

'He was the last time I saw him, but naturally he's grown since then.'

Nick's face flushed. 'I don't know that I'm entirely comfortable with your sharing your flat with him.'

'What?' Where was this coming from, I wondered.

'You know what I'm getting at. You and I don't spend every night together. There'll be times when you're alone here with him …'

Seriously? 'Nick, we've been together over a year now. Are

19

you telling me that you don't trust me?'

'It's not that I don't trust you, not exactly, but Alex is ...' Nick's voice trailed off.

'Alex is what?'

'He's the sort of man that girls find attractive.'

'And you think I'm going to jump into bed with him, just because he's sleeping down the hall?'

'When you put it like that ... I'm being ridiculous, aren't I?'

'You are, actually.'

'There really is no need for me to worry?'

'Absolutely not.' I stepped into my dress and turned around so that Nick could zip me up. 'I like Alex, but I don't like him in *that* way. And you'll like him, once you get to know him. I'm sure you will.'

Looking far from enthralled at the prospect of getting to know Alex, Nick got out his phone and scrolled through his messages. I sat at my dressing table and began applying eyeliner.

My boyfriend was jealous of my friendship with another man. However ludicrous it was, there was a part of me that was just a little pleased by his outburst of possessiveness. At least it showed he cared. There had been times lately, when Nick's assumption that I would always fall in with his plans, his routines, and his ghastly mother's demands for our attendance at family gatherings had made me feel rather taken for granted.

The journey across London to Natalie and Oliver's tastefully renovated Victorian house in Fulham took over an hour on the tube. Alex and I talked non-stop the entire time. A sullen Nick, who had evidently not changed his opinion of Alex as a potential rival for my affections, barely said a word. Alex telling me how lovely I looked when he first saw me in my sequinned splendour hadn't helped. After standing the whole way, wedged between them in the unbearably hot, crowded carriage, I was very glad to come up out of the underground, even though it was a bitterly cold night.

'The pavement's icy,' Alex said, as we started walking. 'Are you going to be OK in those high-heels, Anna?'

'I'll be fine,' I said.

We'd only gone a few paces when I slipped on a patch of ice, and would have fallen if Alex hadn't caught me. I righted myself, smiling my thanks. Alex offered me his arm. Without thinking, I slid my arm through his, and then, when I saw the glowering expression on Nick's face, I clutched his arm as well. The three of us resumed walking. Fortunately, Natalie and Oliver's place was only a few minutes from the station.

It was Oliver who answered the door when I knocked, welcoming me to his home with his habitual warm smile.

'Anna. Come on in. Natalie's around somewhere ...'

We all trooped into the hall. From further inside the house, I could hear music, laughter, and the clink of glasses.

'Hi, Oliver,' I said. 'You've met Nick, my boyfriend ...'

'At the office Christmas party,' Oliver said. 'Hello, Nick.'

'And this is Alexandre Tourville.'

'Welcome – to – England – Alexandre,' Oliver said, shaking hands with Alex. He spoke with exaggerated slowness and his voice was extremely loud, almost a shout. 'I – am – Oliver – Heywood. Natalie's – husband. Am – I – Speaking – Too – Fast – For – You?'

'No, not at all,' Alex said. 'It's good to meet you, Oliver. And I must thank you for including me in the invitation to your wife's birthday celebrations. Anna often writes to me about her work, and I'm very glad to have the opportunity to meet her colleagues.'

'You speak such good English,' Oliver said, impressed. As Nova Graphic's Accounts Director, dealing with clients on a daily basis, he was necessarily a good communicator, but like so many Brits, he'd never learnt a foreign language. My ability to speak French amazed him almost as much as my talent for chasing up printers and invoices.

Natalie came into the hall, holding a glass of wine. At work, like the rest of the creative team, she usually wore jeans and a

T-shirt, but tonight she was wearing a red maxi-dress with spaghetti straps which clung to her in all the right places, and looked absolutely stunning.

'Happy birthday, Natalie,' I said.

'Anna! Nick!' Natalie hugged me and Nick, and then turned to Alex. 'And you must be Anna's Frenchman.'

Inwardly, I groaned. Nick wouldn't like her calling him that. I glanced at my boyfriend, but his face was expressionless.

'*Enchanté, madame.*' Alex took hold of Natalie's hand and kissed it. His dark eyes locked on hers. 'I am Alexandre Tourville. I wish you *un joyeux anniversaire.*'

What's with the French and the hand-kissing? I shot Alex a look, but his attention was focused on Natalie.

'Thank you, Alexandre,' Natalie said, rather breathlessly. 'Oliver, would you take everyone's coats upstairs? And Anna, would you mind helping yourself and Nick to drinks? And get one for Alexandre? I'd like to introduce him to some friends of mine.'

After a brief hiatus while Oliver relieved us of our outdoor wear, Natalie spirited Alex off into the living room. Nick and I found our way to the kitchen, where other guests were also helping themselves to drinks from an extensive array of wines, beer, and spirits. I introduced Nick to the people I knew, and he was soon discussing that afternoon's football results with a copy-writer, a freelance illustrator, and Natalie's father. I poured myself a glass of wine, and as there was no sign of the conversation turning from sport to a subject in which I had the slightest interest, I poured a second glass for Alex, and went and joined the party in the other room.

Natalie and Oliver's long through living room (think white walls, white voile curtains, pale wooden floor) was overflowing with people, music, and conversation. The first person I recognised was Alfie Lennox, a designer who'd been working at Nova Graphics for almost a year. For once, he didn't have earphones clamped to his head (claiming that he needed to hear music at all times to inspire his artwork, Alfie was rarely without his iPod), and he'd combed his unruly hair and had a shave. And he was wearing jeans *without* holes in the knees, together with a neatly ironed shirt.

'Hey, Mr Lennox,' I said. 'You're looking very dapper tonight.'

'Yeah, well, got to make an effort for Natalie's *fortieth*,' Alfie said, with a grin. 'You scrub up pretty well yourself, Ms Mitchel.'

'Thank you, kind sir,' I said. 'You haven't seen a tall, dark French guy anywhere around, have you? I was supposed to be fetching him a drink.'

'I saw Natalie leading a tall dark man in the direction of the conservatory. I don't know if he was French.'

'I'll try in there, then,' I said.

I edged my way through the crowd in the living room, stopping to talk to Natalie's mother, and one or two other people, and went into the conservatory at the back of the house.

There were fewer people out here, and I spotted Alex straight away. He was standing in the middle of the room, leaning casually against a table, surrounded by women. At least half a dozen of them. Apart from Natalie, I didn't know any of them. Alex was talking, and the women were hanging on his every word, smiling at him, tossing their hair, practically salivating. Not that I blamed them. He was *ridiculously* good-looking.

Natalie detached herself from the back of the group and came and stood beside me.

I said, 'I see that you've helped Alex make some useful new contacts.'

'Oliver isn't the only one who's good at networking,' Natalie said. 'Not that your Frenchman needed much help from me to raise his profile.'

'I guess his Unique Selling Point is instantly recognisable.'

'I'm a happily married woman, but when he kissed my hand, I swear my legs turned to jelly.' Natalie fanned her face with her fingers. 'He is *so* hot, Anna. Why didn't you tell me?'

23

'I didn't know,' I said. 'The last time I saw him, he was thirteen and a bit of a geek.'

'But surely you've seen him in photos since then?'

I shook my head. 'Alex photographs other people. He's not into selfies.'

'Haven't you ever Googled him? What about Facebook?'

'There aren't any pictures of *him* on the internet. He has a website, but that's for his work. I'd no idea that he'd grown up into such an attractive guy until yesterday, when I met him off the Eurostar from Paris.'

'Natalie! Happy birthday!' Izzy Drake, Nova Graphic's most recent recruit, rushed up to Natalie. A petite brunette, Izzy had joined the creative team as a graphic designer six months ago, soon after she'd graduated from college.

'I'm so sorry I'm late,' Izzy said. 'I decided to drive, but my car wouldn't start. And then there was a delay on the tube …' Her voice trailed off as she caught sight of Alex. 'Who is that simply gorgeous man?'

'That,' Natalie said, 'is Anna's French penfriend.'

'*Pen*friend? You mean you *write* to him?'

'We've been writing to each other since we were eleven years old,' I said. 'My French teacher had once worked in Paris, and knew his English teacher – actually, now I look back, I'm pretty sure they were having a torrid affair. They arranged for their students to exchange letters. Everyone else gave up after a while, but Alex and I carried on writing.'

'You *write letters* to him?' Izzy sounded incredulous. 'Actually *write? On paper?*'

'Yep. By hand. On notepaper.'

'But nobody actually *writes* letters any more,' Izzy said. 'If you wanted to keep in touch, why not just phone him? Or text?'

'I guess we both like getting letters,' I said. 'We do email each other occasionally, but even that's not the same as receiving an envelope with a foreign postmark.'

At that moment, Alex glanced across the room, and saw the three of us staring at him. With a smile, he extricated himself

24

from the group of women he'd been talking to (their sighs were audible), and joined Natalie, Izzy and myself.

'I brought you a drink,' I said, handing him the wine I'd been holding all that time.

'*Merci.*' Alex's dark eyes met mine, and even though he was a friend, and I was in a steady relationship, my whole body shivered deliciously. Firmly, I told myself to get a grip.

'Alex,' I said, 'you've not met my colleague, Izzy Drake. She's a very gifted graphic designer. Izzy, this is Alexandre. He's a photographer, and also very gifted.'

Alex raised Izzy's hand to his lips, '*Enchanté, mademoiselle.*'

Izzy looked as though she was about to swoon. 'Alexandre … Sorry, how exactly do you say your name?'

Alex repeated his name, exaggerating the French pronunciation, drawing out the last syllable by rolling the 'r'.

'Alexandrrr,' Izzy cooed, looking up at him from under her long lashes. 'Alexandrrr.'

'*C'est parfait,*' Alex said.

'I do wish I spoke French,' Izzy laughed. 'I find it so irritating having to read the subtitles whenever I watch a French film.'

'You like French films?' Alex said.

'Very much.'

Natalie broke in, 'I see that my in-laws have just arrived. I must go and say hello to them.'

She hurried off. Sensing that neither Izzy or Alex were particularly anxious for my company at that precise moment, I left them discussing the delights of the French cinema, and went in search of another drink.

The evening went on. Oliver produced a cake (Natalie swore there really was no need for him to have put *forty* candles on it), and pink champagne (Natalie decided turning forty wasn't so awful if you got to drink champagne), and after she'd blown out the offending flames, and we'd all sung 'Happy Birthday', there was dancing. Or what passes for dancing among the mildly inebriated. I danced with Oliver, Alfie, and some of the other guys from work (and with Nick, of course). Alex danced with Izzy, and I saw that he was a remarkably good dancer, one of those rare men who moves easily with the music, rather than flailing about. I'd have liked to dance with him myself. Annoyingly, he'd led Izzy off the improvised dance floor and vanished back into the conservatory before I got the chance.

Towards midnight, the party quietened down. People lounged on sofas and floor-cushions, drinking coffee and 'maybe just one more glass of wine'. Several older couples (not *old*, but older than me) left, citing the need to 'get back to drive the babysitter home'. I was talking to one of Natalie's school-friends (who was very interested to discover that Alex didn't have a girlfriend pining for him back in Paris), when Nick appeared at my elbow, and said that we should also be making a move. I'd have happily stayed longer at the party (no need to rush home before dawn when you're not a parent), but I could see that Nick was determined that we were leaving. The clue was that he already had his coat on. And he was holding my faux fur and Alex's leather jacket.

'Where's Alexandre?' Nick said, passing me my coat.

'Well, he's not in here,' I said, gesturing towards the people scattered about the living room, 'so he must still be in the conservatory. I'll get him. You go and start saying goodbye to Natalie and Oliver.'

I took Alex's jacket from Nick, and went out into the conservatory. Alex and Izzy were sitting on a wicker bench, twisting towards each other, so that their heads were very close together. He was talking, too quietly for me to hear what he was saying, and she was smiling, laughing softly at something he whispered in her ear. He reached up his hand and brushed a strand of hair out of her eyes.

I thought, this, I do not need to see. It was one thing reading about Alex's amorous exploits in his letters, but it was quite another watching him in action. Feeling excruciatingly awkward, I cleared my throat. Loudly.

Alex turned his head towards me. 'Hey, Anna. You ready to go home?'

'Er, yes.' I said. 'Are you coming with us?'

Alex looked at Izzy, and his mouth lifted in a lazy smile. 'I think I'll stay a while longer. But you and Nick head off, Anna. Don't worry about me. I'll make my own way back – I've got my key.'

Alex had a key to my flat, and Nick didn't. I realised I really should give Nick a key.

'I'll see you later, then, Alex,' I said. 'Bye, Izzy.'

I don't think she heard me.

Four

Alex and I are alone in a capsule on the London Eye, looking out over the city. I am wearing the dress I wore to the party, but he is naked except for a towel slung around his hips. I point out various landmarks, Buckingham Palace, the O2, the Gherkin, and the Shard. He reaches up and unzips my dress. I shrug it off my shoulders so that it falls to the floor. When Alex sees that I'm not wearing any underwear, he smiles, and cups my breast with his hand ...

I awoke with a start, my heart beating furiously. Nick, lying next to me, muttered something in his sleep and rolled over onto his side, taking the duvet with him. Guilt washed over me. I was in bed with my boyfriend and I was having erotic dreams about Alex.

But it was just a dream. It didn't mean anything. And if Nick had made love to me last night, instead of falling asleep as soon as we were in bed, I probably wouldn't have dreamt about another man. I glanced at the clock on my nightstand. 8.00 a.m. Way too early to be getting up on a Sunday, but I knew I wasn't going to be able to get back to sleep. Careful not to disturb Nick, I slid off the bed, pulled on a sweatshirt over my pyjamas, and padded out of my bedroom, closing the door quietly behind me.

In the kitchen, I found Alex making coffee. For a moment, my dream still vivid in my head, I was acutely embarrassed to be in his presence. Then I reminded myself that he couldn't possibly know I'd been dreaming about him.

I said, 'You're up early.'

'I've only just got in.'

I realised that he was dressed in the same shirt and jeans he'd worn last night. He still looked jaw-droppingly gorgeous.

'Oh, so you've not been to bed yet ...'

'I stayed at Izzy's,' Alex said.

'Ah.'

'I saw her home after the party.'

'And you stayed over.'

'Yeah. Do you want coffee?'

'Tea. I'll make it.' Alex had slept with Izzy. The thought of the two of them together left me feeling oddly disquieted.

Alex said, 'Don't you trust me?'

'What?'

'To make you a pot of tea. I may be French, but I do know how. My English mother made sure of that.'

Alex had slept with Izzy. 'OK. You make the tea. I'll make toast.'

'French toast?'

'Absolutely not. You're living in England now, monsieur. You'll have toast and Marmite and like it.'

Grinning, Alex filled the kettle, and I shoved two slices of bread in the toaster.

I said, 'So are you going to see Izzy again? Are you going to ask her out?'

'You mean, am I going to ask her on a date? No I'm not. I've just been through the break-up of a serious, long-term relationship. I've no intention of getting involved with anyone else right now.'

So it was just a one night stand. Did Izzy know that, or was she sitting at home, wondering when – if – Alexandre was going to call?

Aloud, I said, 'Alex, do me a favour. Try not to break anyone's heart while you're in London. At least, not any of my friends' hearts.'

'I'll do my best.'

30

'I'm serious.'

Alex gave me a quizzical look. 'You're in a strange mood, Anna. Have I done something that's upset you?'

He'd slept with my friend. And it shouldn't matter. But it did. And I wasn't sure why. 'Of course not.' I forced myself to smile. 'So. What are your plans for today?'

'I thought I might do some more sight-seeing –'

'There you are, Anna.' Nick stepped into the kitchen, yawning and rubbing his eyes. Seeing him standing there in his boxers and crumpled T-shirt, I felt a surge of affection for him. OK, maybe we didn't have sex as often as we used to, but I suspected that was true of most couples who'd been together as long as we had.

'Good morning, Nicholas,' Alex said.

'Morning, Alexandre,' Nick said. 'Did you enjoy the party?'

'Very much,' Alex said.

I'll bet he did, I thought.

Further conversation was interrupted by the ping of the toaster.

'Toast,' I said, somewhat unnecessarily, rooting in the fridge for butter.

'Tea,' Alex said, colliding with me as he reached for the teapot.

I ducked under his arm and retrieved jam, peanut butter, and Marmite from a cupboard.

Nick hovered for a moment, watching us as we dodged around each other in the confined space of the kitchen, and then he said, 'I'm going back to bed. There isn't enough room in here for three people.'

Left on our own, Alex and I quickly assembled breakfast.

'I'll take this in to Nick,' I said, putting two mugs and plates on a tray.

'Valérie always used to bring me bed in breakfast on a Sunday morning,' Alex said.

'Valérie? Is she the dancer at the Moulin Rouge?'

'No, that's Monique. Valérie is a singer.'

31

'You'll forgive me if I don't remember the name and profession of every woman you've dated.'

I thought about the letter Alex had written to me when he was about fifteen, telling me how difficult he found it to walk up to a girl and ask her to dance. A couple of years later, and he was dating a different girl almost every time he wrote.

Hi Anna,

I met a girl. Her name is
Thérèse ... Francine ... Monique ... Camille ... Valérie ...
Solange... Maxine ...

For the last year, his letters had only mentioned Cécile.

Alex said, 'Valérie threw a plate of croissants at me the last time we ate breakfast together.'

'She threw a plate at you?'

'Well, if I'm honest, she threw it at the wall,' Alex said. 'She was always throwing stuff. She's a very passionate woman.'

'I don't think smashing crockery has much to do with passion.' It sounded more like she was crazy.

'That's because you're English.' Alex picked up his tea and a mountain of toast, and headed out of the kitchen. 'I'll see you later, Anna.'

I went and joined Nick in my bedroom.

'Alexandre's looking somewhat worse for wear today,' Nick said.

'You think? I can't say I noticed.' I set the breakfast tray down on the bed between us.

'Did he tell you what time he got in? It must have been very late.'

'More like very early this morning.'

'Really? Did he get lucky last night?'

'If you're asking, in an Unreconstructed Male sort of way, if he spent the night with a woman, then yes.'

Nick chuckled. 'He's only been in London for two days. He doesn't waste much time, does he?'

'Apparently not.'

Nick said, 'Who was she? Anyone I know?'

'Izzy Drake.'

'Pretty dark-haired girl who works in your office?'

'Yes. Izzy works in the same design studio as me. Could we talk about something – anything – other than Alex's sex life, please.'

'I guess he's less likely to hit on you if he's shagging your friends.'

'Would you stop?'

'Sorry.'

We ate and drank, and when we'd finished, Nick leant back against the pillows. I put the tray on the floor and lay down next to him. He put his arms around me, and bent his head so that he could kiss me.

Well, I may be an English rose, but I'm just as passionate as some crazy Frenchwoman.

I said, 'Nick, what you said about spending the day together, just the two of us … It seems like a plan to me.'

'Good. What would you like to do?'

'Something … passionate.'

Smiling in what I hoped was a seductive manner, I peeled off my sweatshirt, and just to make sure that Nick knew exactly what was expected of him, I took off my pyjamas as well. He caught on pretty quick. It wasn't his fault that his mobile rang just as he was stripping off his boxers. Though he really shouldn't have answered it.

'Mum. Hi.' Nick pulled up his boxers and sat on the side of the bed. 'I'm very well, thank you. How are you?'

That woman's timing is impeccable, I thought. How does she do it? With a sigh, I covered myself with the duvet, and reached for the paperback on my bedside table. I knew from experience that any call from Nick's mother was likely to last long enough for me to read several chapters. To be fair, it wasn't entirely unknown for me to have hour-long conversations on the phone with my mother or my sister, Vicky, but not at a time that would irritate Nick.

Nick said, 'No ... Well, yes ... I'd like that too, but ... Oh, well, if they're going to be there ... No. No, that's not too soon ... Yes, we'll see you then.' He ended the call.

'Nick,' I said, 'What have you just agreed to do for your mother?'

And why didn't you check with me first?

'Matt and Georgina and the boys are going to Mum and Dad's for Sunday lunch. I've said we'll join them, that's all.'

'So what happened to us spending the day together, just the two of us? One phone call from your mother and we're rushing off to eat lunch with your entire family.'

'Aw, don't be like that, Anna. I've not seen the boys in weeks. I don't want them to forget they have an uncle. It's a good opportunity for us all to be together.'

I felt bad when Nick said that, because I knew he was very fond of his elder brother's five-year-old twins (who were, I had to admit, adorable).

'You're right,' I said. 'I'm being selfish. It's important that you spend time with your nephews.' Even if it meant that I had to spend time with his mother – who had known me for over a year, and still expected me to call her Mrs Cooper. I pushed back the duvet. 'So when is your mum expecting us?'

'I said we'd be there in an hour.' Nick's gaze strayed to my breasts. 'There's time for us to have sex. If you still want to.'

So much for passion. Maybe I should start throwing the odd bit of china. Starting with Mrs Cooper's dinner service.

'Oh, why not?' I said.

Five

Mrs Cooper said, 'You'll never guess who I ran into yesterday, Nicholas.'

'You'd better tell me, then,' Nick said.

'Melissa.'

'Really?' Nick said. 'I haven't seen her in years. I thought she relocated to New York.'

'She did,' Mrs Cooper said. 'But she's back in England now.'

'Who's Melissa?' Matt said.

'Surely you remember Melissa,' Mrs Cooper said. 'Melissa Harrington.'

'Oh, you mean Nick's ex,' Matt said.

'Such a delightful girl,' Mrs Cooper said. She looked directly at me. 'There was a time when I hoped that Nicholas and Melissa would marry. Sadly, it wasn't meant to be.' She sighed. 'I was very fond of Melissa.'

Unbelievable. I glanced round the dining table. Nick and Matt were systematically working their way through the port and the stilton. Matt's wife, Georgina, was languidly sipping her coffee. Mr Cooper was leaning back in his chair, arms folded across his ample stomach, an expression of benign contentment on his face. I wondered if I was the only one who thought what Nick's mother had just said was plain bad manners.

Mrs Cooper continued. 'It's so hard to keep in touch with people who live in another country.'

'Not always,' I said. 'Alexandre, my French penfriend, has

35

recently come to London and is staying with me for a few weeks. Alex and I have been writing to each other since we were eleven years old.'

'How charming,' Mrs Cooper said. 'Though it must be frightfully difficult having another person living in your tiny little flat. What with your having only one bathroom.'

I thought of how hard I'd worked so I could afford to buy my little flat, and how much I loved it. In my lap, under the cover of the snowy white tablecloth, my hands clenched so hard that my nails dug into my palms.

Don't say anything to her. Just don't say anything.

From outside the house came the shouts and laughter of the twins, who'd been released from the torments of Mrs Cooper's lunch table before the rest of us, and were playing in the garden.

Mrs Cooper said, 'Have you put Charlie and Joshua's names down for Gade Court yet, Matthew?'

'No, not yet,' Matt said.

'Well you should do it as soon as possible. There's no guarantee that they'll get places just because you and Nicholas are former pupils.'

'We may not be sending them to Gade Court,' Georgina put in.

'Why ever not?' Mrs Cooper asked. 'It's an excellent school.'

'I'm sure it is.' Georgina' said, 'but it may not be right for Josh and Charlie.'

Mrs Cooper pursed her mouth. 'Well, you must do what you think best …'

'Nothing's been decided,' Matt said.

Georgina drained her coffee cup. 'Talking of my sons, they've suddenly gone very quiet, which usually means they're up to something. I should go and check on them. Come with me, Anna? I want to hear all about this penfriend of yours.' She pushed back her chair and stood up.

'Sure.' The afternoon was too grey and overcast to make the Coopers' back garden an enticing prospect, but I wasn't going to turn down a chance to get away from Nick's mother.

'I'll come out and give the boys a game of football once I've finished my port,' Nick said.

I hurried after Georgina, who was already striding from the room. Snatching my coat off the peg in the hall, I followed her through the house and out onto the patio. Josh and Charlie were chasing other around the apple trees at the far end of the garden. They waved to Georgina and me, and we waved back.

'They don't seem to be doing anything too terrible,' I said.

'I didn't think they were,' Georgina said. 'But I needed a break from Mrs C and I thought you could probably do with one too.'

I gaped at her.

'If I have to listen to any more of her snide remarks about the way I'm bringing up my own children, I swear I won't be responsible for my actions. I put up with her for Matt's sake, but – Why are you staring at me?'

I said, 'I'd no idea that you felt that way about Mrs Cooper.'

'I can't stand the woman.'

Before I could stop myself, I blurted, 'Neither can I. She doesn't seem to like me much either. I don't know why.'

'It isn't *you*. No girl will ever be good enough for her sons.'

'Except for Melissa Harrington.'

'Apparently. Although, strangely, I don't recall Mrs C being particularly eager for her company when Nick was dating her.'

I smiled at that, and Georgina smiled back.

'That's quite enough talk about my dear mother-in-law,' she said. 'Do tell me about this penfriend of yours. Have you really been writing to each other since you were children? I didn't think anyone actually wrote *letters* any more …'

I was telling Georgina about Alex's first trip to London when, much to Charlie and Josh's delight, Nick appeared in the garden carrying a football. The three of them spent an energetic half-hour kicking it round the lawn, while Georgina and I cheered them on from the patio, before the light began to fade and we were forced to retreat inside. Matt and his family left almost immediately (Georgina told Mrs Cooper that she'd have loved to have stayed longer, but she really couldn't keep the boys out late on a school night), and not long after, Nick decided that we too should be getting off home. Mr Cooper roused himself out of his post-prandial stupor to tell me that he hoped he'd see me again very soon. Mrs Cooper said goodbye, without expressing any particular hope that I would be present in her near future.

Outside, it was now fully dark, and the streetlamps made halos of yellow light between the skeletal branches of the trees lining the road. Shivering in the night air, I took Nick's hand and we walked quickly along the pavement to where he'd parked. He handed me his keys, and we got in.

'Thanks for saying you'd drive,' Nick said. 'I'd have hated to miss that rather good bottle of Cabernet Sauvignon that my father produced to go with the beef.'

'Oh, I don't mind being the designated driver when we visit your parents. I can't tell the difference between the expensive stuff they like to drink and the wine boxes I buy in the supermarket.'

Nick laughed.

'Where do you want to spend the night?' I said. 'Mine or yours?'

'Mine, I think. I'm worried that I might not be able to get a decent drink at your place.'

I pulled away from the kerb.

'You had a long chat with Georgina this afternoon,' Nick said.

'Yes. I've never really had the chance to talk to her before. We've more in common than I realised.'

'We really should try to see my family more often.'

I see quite enough of your mother, thank you very much, I thought.

'Mum is always so pleased when we visit,' Nick said.

Choosing my words carefully, I said, 'Nick … sometimes … I'm not sure that your mother … approves of me.'

'Why ever would you think that?'

I took a deep breath. 'Just … a couple of things she's said. Like today, when she was talking about meeting your ex-girlfriend, I got the impression that she'd rather you were still with Melissa, and not with me.'

'Are you jealous of Melissa Harrington?'

'What? No, I'm not jealous of Melissa Harrington.'

'You *are* jealous.' Nick sounded incredulous. 'You're upset because my mother mentioned one of my exes? That's crazy.'

'You're totally missing the point –' I broke off. If Nick had no idea what I was getting at, if he hadn't see anything objectionable in his mother's comments, then there was not much use in my picking a fight about it.

'I haven't seen Melissa for at least five years,' Nick said. 'I don't even have her number in my phone.'

My hands gripped the steering wheel more tightly.

'I'm thirty-two years old,' Nick said. 'It would be odd if I didn't have a couple of long-term relationships behind me, don't you think?'

I gave up. 'You're right. I'm being unreasonable.'

'We've both dated other people, but we're together now, and that's what matters.'

'I know that – in my less crazy moments.'

Mollified, Nick switched on the radio and was soon humming along to a piece of classical music.

I drove on through the empty night-time streets. Not for the first time after I'd spent a Sunday afternoon in Mrs Cooper's company, I wondered how my boyfriend could have such a total blind spot when it came to his mother.

Six

Monday morning began in its usual chaotic way, with my arriving home from Nick's with just enough time to shower and change before I had to dash off again to get to work. I was already half way out the front door, when Alex, wearing just a pair of jeans, emerged from his bedroom.

Step away from the candy, I thought.

Averting my gaze from Alex's muscles, I wished him good luck for his first day in his new job, and hurried on my way.

At Nova Graphics, I'd barely sat down and switched on my computer before Izzy came bounding up, and perched on the front of my desk.

'Alexandre Tourville is such a lovely guy,' she said.

'Yes,' I said. 'He is.'

'I can't believe that you've been writing to him all these years and you'd no idea that he was so utterly lush.'

The image of a shirtless Alex floated into my mind.

'Well, it's true.' I said. 'Actually, the first time I wrote to him, there was some confusion over his name, and I thought he was a girl. I was horrified when I found out that my penfriend Alexand*ra* was a boy named Alexand*re*.'

'But why?'

'I was eleven. To me, at that age, boys were just annoying, noisy creatures who talked about football all the time.' We both glanced towards our male colleagues who were grouped around the water cooler, animatedly discussing the weekend's sporting highlights.

'Point taken,' Izzy said. We exchanged smiles.

41

'I found it really hard to write to Alex at first,' I said. 'What with him being a boy. And because I had to write in French, which I wasn't very good at. It was only after his school came on a visit to England that he and I became friends. We started writing to each other so often that my French improved dramatically.'

'That's what Alex told me at the party. He said that you were both thirteen the last time he came to London. I'm guessing your opinion of boys had changed by then?'

'Well, yes … Did Alex tell you what happened on that school visit?'

'Only that he stayed with you and your family.'

'I wasn't very nice to him. He was very shy, and I thought he was a geek.'

'This is the same Alexandre Tourville you're talking about? The guy you introduced met to on Saturday?

'Yes. He's changed –'

'I'll say he has.' Izzy smiled dreamily.

I said, 'Day one of the French children's visit, we were all taken on a coach outing to Madame Tussauds. Afterwards, we had a picnic in Regent's Park, and then we were given some free time. We were supposed to stay in the park, but a group of us sneaked off and took the tube to Trafalgar Square. I was too busy flirting with a French boy called Gérard to notice that Alex had got separated from the rest of us …'

We're standing on the platform at Marylebone Station. Gérard is telling me his family owns a gîte in the Dordogne. I've no idea what a gîte is (or where the Dordogne is either – presumably somewhere in France?), and I can only understand about half the words he says, but I smile up at him (he is so tall!) and wonder if he'll kiss me before he goes back to Paris. I've never kissed a boy. The thought of kissing Gérard is thrilling – and just a bit scary.

The chittering of the rails announces the arrival of the train. The doors open, the crowd on the platform surges forward, and we go with it. It's only when I'm sat next to Gérard, with Beth and Fabienne sitting opposite, and Sean standing precariously between us, all of us laughing as he tries to keep his balance as the train jolts along, that I realise Alexandre isn't with us.

'Where's Alexandre?' I say

Gérard looks at me blankly.

'Où est Alexandre?' I say more urgently, looking up and down the carriage.

Gérard shrugs, unconcerned.

Beth looks worried. 'I think he must still be on the platform.'

I groan. 'We'll have to get off at the next stop and go back for him.'

It takes a while for Gérard to understand this (his English is even worse than my French), but he refuses to go back for Alexandre. And because he's put his arm around my shoulders, I decide to stay on the train as well. And when we get to Trafalgar Square, we're too busy clambering on the lions to think about Alex, who must be the only teenager in France whose parents won't let him have a mobile phone ...

'... so it was only when he wasn't at the coach when it was time for us to go home that the alarm was raised. A couple of teachers stayed in town in case he turned up, and the rest of us were taken back to the school, where our parents were waiting to collect us. We'd just got off the coach, when the school secretary got a call from the police –'

Izzy put her hand over her mouth.

'I was terrified that something dreadful had happened to Alex and it was all my fault, but he arrived back at the school in a police car, terribly apologetic, claiming that he'd got lost in the park, and couldn't find the coach. Eventually, after wandering the nearby streets, he'd gone up to a policeman. Everyone was so glad he was safe, that the question of how he'd come to be on his own got overlooked.'

'He didn't grass you up for abandoning him on the underground?'

43

'Of course not. Don't you remember what it's like being thirteen?'

'Not really,' Izzy said. 'So, after Alexandre lied to the police, that was when you and he became friends?'

'No. We were friends after the underage drinking incident.'

'Your schooldays were certainly a lot more interesting than mine. But then I did go to an all-girls private school.'

'You poor deprived child.'

'And did Gérard kiss you before he went back to France?'

'No. But I didn't care. I decided I didn't really like him that much.'

'Did Alex kiss you?'

'No. Back then, he was much too shy.'

'You missed out, meeting him so young. Now, he's a really great kisser.'

'Who's a great kisser?' Alfie, having tired of the discussion by the water cooler, came and sat on my desk next to Izzy.

'Alexandre,' Izzy said, 'It's not just the way he kisses. He really knows how to –'

I said, 'Too much information.' I was well aware that Alex must be pretty good in bed – no guy could sleep with as many women as he had and not pick up a few ideas along the way – but I had no desire to discuss his sexual expertise with my co-workers.

Izzy grinned, completely unabashed. 'Have you seen much of Alexandre since Saturday?'

'I saw him yesterday morning. And for about two minutes this morning before I left for work.' Although I did see quite a lot of him in that short time.

'Did he say anything about me?'

I hesitated. What should I tell her?

Before I could frame a tactful answer, Alfie said. 'Are you going to see him again?'

'Yes I am,' Izzy said. 'Even if he hasn't realised it yet.'

'Listen, Izzy,' I said. 'Alex is a very attractive guy, but you need to know that he just broke up with his long-term girlfriend,

44

and he isn't looking to get into a relationship right now.'

'Oh, he told me about Cécile. I reckon I'm exactly what he needs to make him forget her. So if he asks you for my mobile number, Anna, you have my full permission to give it to him. Actually, would you just text him my number now? Make it clear it was my idea that he should have it.'

'I hate to break it to you, Izzy,' Alfie said, 'but if he didn't ask *you* for your number, he's not interested.'

'Oh, he's interested,' Izzy said. 'He just needs a bit of encouragement.'

'So you're planning on having a casual fling with this French guy?' Alfie said.

'I don't do *flings*,' Izzy said. 'Alexandre may not think he wants a girlfriend, but I'm sure I can change his mind.'

'Just be careful you don't get hurt,' Alfie said.

'Alfie! I didn't know you cared,' Izzy said.

Oliver put his head around the partition which separated his and Natalie's office from the rest of us.

'Morning all,' he said. 'Anna, could you come in here, please. We need to go over the brief for the hotel brochure.'

'Be right with you,' I said.

Oliver ducked back into the inner sanctum.

'See you guys at lunch.' Izzy slid off my desk, and went to her own work station.

'I do care,' Alfie said. 'I care about Izzy a great deal.'

'Friends should care about each other.'

'I don't want to be her *friend*.' Alfie leant forward over my desk, and lowered his voice, so that only I could hear him over the buzz of conversation and the ringing of phones. 'I was planning to ask her out. I was just waiting for the right moment.'

I gaped at him. 'Alfie … I didn't know …'

'Well, I was. And you are so not going to tell her that.'

'I won't,' I said. 'Not if you don't want me to,'

'Because it really doesn't matter how I feel about her. Not now she's fallen for your Frenchman.'

I started to protest that Alexandre was not *my* Frenchman, but Alfie put his earphones in his ears and stomped away to his desk, next to Izzy's, on the other side of the office.

I stared after him. Unlike Alex, whose emotional outpourings in his letters left very little to the imagination, Alfie had never regaled me with tales about his love life. I'd never once suspected that he had *feelings* for Izzy.

I spent the rest of the week cringing each time Izzy mentioned Alex in front of Alfie. Which seemed to be every time the three of us happened to be together, whether it was in the lunchroom, in the pub after work, or when I was giving them the brief for a new account. In Nova Graphic's daily staff meetings, I noticed that Alfie sat as far away from her as possible (which made me realise that in the past he'd always sat next to her). He'd also taken to staring at her from behind his computer screen, while looking thoroughly miserable. She spent an inordinate amount of time googling *les photographies d'Alexandre Tourville* and drifting round the office with a vacant smile on her face.

'It's unbearable,' I said to Beth, when I telephoned her on Saturday morning. 'It's like working with two hormonal adolescents. I've told Izzy that Alex isn't going to call her – he didn't want her phone number when I offered it to him – but she won't listen.'

'Who'd have guessed that weedy Alexandre would grow up *hot*,' Beth said. 'And cause such havoc.'

'Not me,' I said, and added, 'He really is stupidly good-looking. His body is incredible.'

'Anna Mitchel! How exactly are you in a position to know anything about Alex's body?'

'He has this habit of wandering around my flat without his shirt.'

'You fancy him, don't you? Admit it.'

'No, I don't. I do find him attractive, but only in a purely objective way. You'll have to meet him, Beth, and see for yourself. Maybe you and Rob could come round to my place for supper one night next week?'

'I'd like that,' Beth said, 'but it's always so difficult to find a babysitter. If only my parents hadn't moved so far away from London …'

'Forget babysitters – bring Jonah and Molly with you.'

'No, Molly's actually been sleeping through the night the past couple of weeks, and I don't want to upset her routine. Why don't you and Alex – and Nick – come to us?'

'Great. I'll talk to Alex, and find out when he's free. Nick's away at a conference next week, so it'll be just the two of us.'

Beth sighed. 'I do miss the days when I could leave the house without having to plan every outing like it was a polar expedition.'

'Babies do seem to need an awful lot of stuff when they travel.'

'You have no idea, Anna – Oh, Molly's awake.'

Beth's phone wasn't on speaker, but I could still hear Molly's wails.

'I'll have to go,' Beth said.

'Yes, of course –'

'Let me know which night you and Alex want to come round.' She ended the call.

Beth and I'd been sharing a flat for almost two years when she'd met Rob at a party. Six months later, he'd asked her to marry him. And now they had two-year-old Jonah and seven-month-old Molly. My best friend, the girl who used to spend every weekend in clubs and wine bars, and her summer holidays at beach parties in Ibiza, was a mother. She had a husband, and children, and a life of domestic bliss. And I didn't get to see her nearly as often as I'd like.

I went and knocked on Alex's bedroom door, and he called out for me to come in. He was sitting on his bed, his laptop balanced on his knees. And once again, as he wasn't wearing a shirt, I was confronted with his naked torso.

I would not stare at my male friend's body. It would be inappropriate, disrespectful, and just plain wrong.

Keeping my gaze firmly on Alex's face, I said, 'Are you working?'

He shook his head. 'I'm looking at flats to rent. I've arranged to go and view one this afternoon. If it's any good, I'll be out of your way early next week.'

'You're not in my way.' It had been good to arrive home, on the nights I wasn't seeing Nick, and find Alex there, eager to tell me about that day's shoot (his new job seemed to be going really well), and to hear about my own working day. 'I like having you around.'

'You're not such bad company yourself.'

It was then that a bit of a thought struck me.

I said, 'Alex, do you particularly want to get your own place while you're in England?'

'I'm not desperate to get away from you, if that's what you're asking.'

'Good. Because there's no reason for you to move out of my flat, if you're happy to carry on living here with me.'

Alex closed his laptop and regarded me thoughtfully. 'I would like that, Anna. But … are you sure you want me as a flatmate?'

'Yes, I am. Unless you turn out to have one of those habits that drives flat-sharers insane, like using up the last of the milk or borrowing shoes without asking.'

'I promise that I'll always ask before I borrow your high heels.'

'That's OK, then.'

'I'll pay rent, of course. That's only fair.'

'Well, all right. I'll check what the going rate is for a rented room in this area, and we can sort something out.'

'And if you change your mind about my staying here, you must tell me.'

'It's a deal.'

We smiled at each other.

I said, 'I mentioned to my friend Beth that you were in London, and she's invited you and me over for dinner one day next week. When – if – you're free.'

'That's kind of her. I won't know my schedule 'til Monday, but I'd like to meet Beth again. You wrote that she has a child now, I think.'

'She has two, a boy and a girl.' I added, 'Nick won't be able to come with us, unfortunately. He's away the whole of next week.'

'Your boyfriend is leaving you all alone?'

'It's only a few days. I'm sure I'll survive.' I sat down on Alex's bed. 'Nick and I aren't the sort of couple who need to be together 24/7.'

'How often do you see each other?'

'Oh, I don't know … Two or three times a week, maybe.'

'Wouldn't you like to see him more often?'

'I've never really thought about it.'

'Have you talked about living together?'

'No.'

'Why not? Most couples in their late twenties who've been dating more than a year have that conversation, and end up moving in together.'

'I don't think that's true. I've loads of friends who live on their own or flat-share.'

'Perhaps it's different in England. Most of my Parisian friends in their late twenties are living with a partner.'

'Nick and I are happy enough as we are.'

Alex said, 'Do you love him, Anna?'

Did I love Nick? My heart didn't beat faster when he came into a room, I didn't feel the need to wake up next to him every morning, but I couldn't imagine not being with him. Our relationship was serious.

I said, 'Yes, I do.'

'You've never written that you love him in your letters to me.'

'I'm sure I have.'

'No, I'd remember,' Alex said. 'Does he love you?'

'Yes …' Not that he'd told me lately, but then he'd never

49

been one for romantic declarations of undying love, not even in the early days of our relationship. 'But that doesn't mean that we're ready to move in together.'

It occurred to me that the only time I told Nick I loved him was when we were having sex, so I could hardly complain if he wasn't very forthcoming about his feelings for me.

Alex said, 'I was going to ask Cécile to move in with me.'

'You never wrote *that* in any of your letters.'

'I did, actually, but I tore the letter up. It felt disloyal to tell you about my plans before I'd said anything to her. Which is ironic, considering that she'd been cheating on me for weeks.'

To my consternation, pain flickered over Alex's face. He hung his head and put his hand over his eyes.

'I loved her so much,' he said. 'She was my life.'

Other than telling me that he'd broken up with her, and wasn't interested in getting involved with anyone else, Alex hadn't mentioned Cécile. She'd hurt him, I knew that, but he'd said that he was doing better, and for the past week, since he'd been in England, he'd seemed fine. I'd no notion until then, that he was still so cut up inside.

He said, 'When she told me we were finished, I thought I was going to die. It was as though someone had stuck a knife in my chest. I couldn't breathe –' He took his hand away from his face, and his eyes fastened on mine. 'You must think I'm pathetic.'

'No, I don't.' I decided it would be very easy for me to hate Cécile, a girl I'd never met, because of the hurt she'd caused my friend.

'I know I have to forget her,' Alex said, 'but sometimes – I have moments when I just can't get her out of my mind.' His mouth lifted in a sad smile.

He was still in love with her.

Alex visibly pulled himself together. 'That's enough of my feeling sorry for myself. Thanks for listening, *mon amie.*'

'*De rien,*' I said. 'You're welcome.'

Instinctively, I put my arms round Alex's bare shoulders and hugged him, and he put his arms around me and hugged me back, so that I was pressed tight against the hard muscles of his chest, his skin smooth and cool, against my face. To my disquiet, desire for him, a purely physical reaction, shot through me. Hastily, I let go of him, and stood up.

'I should ...' I was completely unable to think of anything that required my attention.

'Yeah, I need to cancel that flat-viewing.' Alex reached for his laptop. 'Anna, do you want to do something this afternoon? Maybe go to the Tate?'

'Oh, I'd have loved that. I've not been to an art gallery in ages.' Not since I've been dating Nick. 'But Nick and I are going shopping. To buy a new washing machine for his flat.'

'Not to worry. I don't mind going on my own.'

And while he was looking at paintings, I'd be looking at electrical appliances.

'I'll see you later, Alex.'

'It'll probably be tomorrow that we'll see each other,' Alex said. 'Tonight, I'm going to a record launch party with some people from work. I've been warned that it's going on until the early hours.'

'Tomorrow then. Have a good time.'

'You too, Anna.'

I left the room, went into my bedroom, and flung myself down on my bed. A sentence from one of Alex's recent letters floated into my head ...

... Sometimes, after we have made love and Cécile is asleep, I lie awake beside her, watching her all night, and think how fortunate I am to love her, and to be loved by her.

I wondered if Nick ever watched me while I slept. Somehow, I doubted it.

Seven

I sat cross-legged on Nick's bed. 'So what's this conference you're going to about?'

Nick placed five neatly folded white shirts in his suitcase. 'Process Management – the alignment of strategy and services.'

AKA watching paint dry. 'Is it going to be … fun, do you think?'

'I doubt you'd find it much fun, but for those of us who work in business assurance, it should be extremely interesting.'

'Right.' I had very little idea of what Nick did all day at work – despite my best intentions to be a supportive girlfriend, my eyes glazed over whenever he talked about his job – but as he was head of a department of thirty people, I assumed he must be very good at it.

Nick counted out five pairs of grey socks, and added them to his case. 'Have you got much on next week, while I'm away?'

'I've not got a whole lot planned. Tomorrow, I'll probably call in on my parents. And Alex and I are going to dinner with Beth and Rob on Thursday, but that's about it.'

'Why would Beth invite you and *Alex* over for dinner?'

'She met him the first time he came to England, don't forget. You were invited as well – but you'll still be at the conference.'

'Oh.' His packing finished, Nick zipped up his suitcase, leaned it against the wall next to his briefcase and his laptop, and headed off to the bathroom. While he was gone, I sprayed myself liberally with perfume, before climbing between his white Egyptian cotton sheets. He came back into the bedroom and undressed down to his boxers, carefully placing his shirt

53

and his socks in his laundry basket, and hanging up his jeans in his wardrobe. He switched off the light, and got into bed next to me. His hand slid under my nightdress, and absently stroked my thigh. I waited for him to suggest that I should take the nightdress off.

He said, 'How's Alex's flat-hunting going? Any chance he'll have moved out of your place by the time I'm back from Manchester?'

'Oh … I didn't tell you. Alex isn't moving out. I've said he can stay with me 'til he goes back to Paris.'

'You've done what?'

'It's only for six months.'

Nick sat bolt upright and switched on his bedside lamp. 'You've invited Alex to live in your flat for the next six months without asking me what I thought about it first?'

'I didn't realise I needed to ask your permission to have a friend to stay.' I also sat up.

'You know I've never been comfortable about your relationship with Alex.'

'Are we seriously going to have this discussion yet again? Alex is my friend. Get over it.'

'Even if you are just *friends*, that doesn't mean I want him hanging around you all the time.'

'I don't see that much of Alex –'

'I hate the way you talk to him in French so that I don't know what you're saying –'

'I don't –'

'You don't even realise you're doing it half the time – it's so frickin' annoying.'

Taken aback by the anger in Nick's voice, I said, 'If it's such a big deal, I'll make sure I only speak to him in English when you're around.'

'I want you to ask him to leave.'

'I can't – I won't do that.'

'So what I want doesn't matter to you?'

'Of course it does, but right now you're being totally

unreasonable.'

'We're a couple. I should come first with you.'

'You do.' I put my hand on Nick's arm but he shook it off. 'Let's not fight. Please.'

'Oh, whatever.' Nick switched off the lamp. The mattress creaked as he lay down and rolled onto his side with his back to me.

I said, 'Nick?'

'What?'

'When I said Alex could stay on in my flat, it honestly never occurred to me that you'd mind.'

'Just leave it, Anna. I've got a long drive ahead of me in the morning. I need to get some sleep.'

I turned away from him and lay still, staring at the dark. My thoughts tumbled over one another. Should I have checked with Nick before I invited Alex to stay on in my flat? I didn't see why. If he was still jealous of Alex, then it was his problem, not mine. Yes, I thought Alex was an attractive guy, but so what? Nick was my boyfriend, but that didn't mean he could tell me how to run my life.

It was a long time before I finally fell asleep.

Eight

Beth answered her front door with one hand, holding Jonah on her hip with the other. Dressed in jeans and a loose shirt, and wearing no make-up, her hair caught up in a ponytail, she didn't look nearly old enough to be the mother of two children. In the red shift dress and heels I'd worn to the office, I felt very over-dressed for a quiet supper with friends.

'Anna.' Beth's face lit up in a brilliant smile. 'It's so good to see you.'

'You too.' I smiled at Beth's little son. 'Hello, Jonah.'

Jonah smiled shyly back at me.

Alex had been standing a little way behind me, but now he stepped forward into the light spilling out from the hall.

'Alexandre?' Beth's eyes widened in surprise. '*C'est toi?* You're so tall ...'

'*Oui, c'est moi,*' Alex said, amused. 'It's really me. Hello, Beth.'

'*Bonsoir,*' Beth said. 'See, Anna, I haven't forgotten all my schoolgirl French.'

'These are for you.' Alex handed Beth the flowers he'd bought for her.

'Ooh, *merci*, Alexandre,' Beth said. 'They're lovely.'

Rob, Beth's husband, appeared from the direction of the kitchen, and I introduced him to Alex. While Beth went off to put her flowers in water, and to get Jonah into bed, Rob led us into the living room, and poured us each a glass of wine. I sat down next to Alex on the sofa, only to yelp and jump up again as something hard dug into my rear. I looked down to see a

57

plastic tyrannosaurus staring back up at me.

'Did it bite you?' Alex said.

I grinned. 'I'm sure I'll survive.'

'Sorry, Anna.' Rob tossed the offending dinosaur into a brightly coloured toybox. 'We do try and tidy up after Jonah, but he only gets his toys out again.' He turned to Alex. 'Beth tells me that you're a photographer.'

'Yes,' Alex said. 'I've been based in Paris, working freelance, travelling wherever the job takes me, but now I'm in London on a six-month contract.'

'Are you a famous photographer? Should I have heard of you?'

'No, you really shouldn't. I'm well enough known in Paris to make a living from my photography, but I'm not famous.'

'He's being modest,' I said. 'He's more than a jobbing photographer. He's an artist. People hang his photos in art galleries.'

'That has happened only once,' Alex said. 'As you know very well, Anna.'

To Rob, I said. 'One of Alex's photos won an extremely prestigious competition, and I wrote to congratulate him. Unfortunately, my French vocabulary let me down. Instead of telling him I was excited to hear of his success as I thought I'd done, I'd told him I was turned on by it. *Je suis excité* ... In French, *excite* has a sexual connotation.'

'I was flattered,' Alex said.

Beth came into the living room and threw herself down in a chair. 'Jonah went out like a light, thank goodness. Some nights, I have to read him his favourite story over and over again for about an hour before he drops off. I've been known to fall asleep before he does.'

'Looking after small children can be very tiring,' Alex said.

'Not everyone realises that.' Beth gave Alex an appreciative smile. 'Anyway, enough of the joys of parenthood, what were you talking about before I came in?'

'Alex's work,' I said. 'He's photographed ever so many

well-known people, politicians, actors, writers … and not just in Paris. He's worked in New York, in LA, Japan …'

'Anna, you are embarrassing me,' Alex put in, although he didn't sound particularly embarrassed.

I put my hand on his arm. 'I'm proud of you, *mon ami.*'

'I used to travel for work,' Beth said.

'What do you do, Beth?' Alex asked.

'I gave up my job when I had Jonah,' Beth said. 'But I was a buyer – a trainee buyer – for a chain of department stores. Knitwear. I got to go to fashion shows in Milan.'

'Not Paris?' Alex said.

'No, I never made it to Paris.'

'Paris is top of my list of cities that I'd like to visit,' I said.

'I hoped to come back to London after my first visit,' Alex said, 'but my life took me to other places.'

Rob frowned. 'Can I smell burning?'

'Oh, no!' Beth said. 'The lasagne!'

At that moment, the door to the living room swung open to reveal a pyjama-clad Jonah holding a teddy bear.

'Story?' he said, hopefully.

'Not right now, sweetheart,' Beth said. 'You take him back to bed, Rob. I need to rescue our dinner.' She hurried off to the kitchen.

'Come on, you.' Rob swept Jonah up into his arms. 'You two go through to the dining room. Help yourself to more wine.' He went out, and I heard him telling Jonah he needed to 'be a good boy and go to sleep now' as he carried him up the stairs.

I showed Alex the way to the dining room, and we sat down opposite each other. He poured us each another glass of wine. There were candles on the table, and as Beth had left out a box of matches, I lit them.

Alex said, 'I will show you Paris one day, Anna.'

'I'm holding you to that. It's ridiculous that I speak French and I've never been to France. Not even a daytrip to Calais. When Beth and I used to go on holiday together, before she was married, we just chose somewhere hot with lots of nightclubs.'

'My beautiful city just couldn't compete with Malia or Ayia Napa.'

'Exactly.'

'There's something I'm going to hold you to.' Alex leant forward, and put his hand under my chin.

'What's that?' I said, suddenly conscious of the touch of his cool fingers on my skin.

'Your promise to let me photograph you.' As he had done on his first night in London, he turned my head from side to side.

'I'm looking forward to it.'

'Good. So am I. These candles have given me an idea for lighting –' He broke off as Beth and Rob came into the room, and took his hand away from my face.

'Dinner is served,' Beth said. 'The bits of it that haven't been incinerated.' She and Rob set down plates of lasagne (unburnt, but miniscule portions), hunks of bread, and a huge bowl of salad, and joined us at the table.

'Can I fill your glass, Beth?' Alex said, holding up the wine bottle.'

Beth shook her head. 'No wine for me, I'm afraid. I'm still breastfeeding Molly.'

As if she'd heard her name, Molly started crying, her heart-breaking sobs relayed from her cot to the dining room by a baby alarm.

Beth shovelled a mouthful of lasagne into her mouth, and stood up.

'Leave her a few minutes,' Rob said. 'She may go off again.'

'No she won't. And she'll wake up Jonah if I don't go to her. Excuse me, Alex, Anna.' Beth swallowed another mouthful of lasagne and left the room.

The baby's cries continued for a few moments more, and then Beth's voice came over the alarm, hushing her, and telling her 'It's all right, Mummy's here.' Molly stopped yelling.

Alex, Rob and I carried on eating (even if the portions were tiny, the lasagne was delicious). Rob (just like Izzy and Georgina) expressed amazement that Alex and I actually *wrote letters* to each other. Alex asked Rob what he did for a living, and then asked a lot of intelligent questions about his work as a solicitor, and the differences between the English and French legal systems. Rob opened another bottle of wine. The remains of Beth's lasagne grew cold and congealed on her plate.

Rob said, 'Alex, do you have any recommendations on what might be a good camera for an amateur? I have a very basic model, and I'm thinking of upgrading. I'd really appreciate your advice.'

'It depends on the sort of pictures you want to take,' Alex said.

I sensed the conversation might be about to get very involved. 'Beth's been a while. I'm going to go and see if she'd like some company.'

'Oh. Yes. Right. Good idea,' Rob said, distractedly.

I left the two men talking photographic equipment, and went upstairs.

The door to Molly's bedroom was open, so I put my head around it. Beth was sitting in a rocking chair, cradling Molly, who was blissfully suckling on her left breast.

'Want some company?' I whispered.

'Oh, yes, please,' Beth whispered back. 'The childcare books never tell you this, but breastfeeding is incredibly boring.'

'Isn't it supposed to help you bond with your child?'

'Molly and I are plenty bonded, thank you. I'd like some adult conversation.'

I sat on the cushioned window-seat.

'This room is so pretty,' I whispered, my gaze travelling over the delightful wall mural of fairies, elves, and unicorns, the bluebird mobile, and the white cot with its stencilled pink flowers. 'I don't know how you found the time to decorate it so beautifully.'

'Neither do I.' Beth looked down at her daughter. 'She's

asleep again. At last.'

She shifted Molly onto her shoulder, gently rubbing her back.

'She's getting so big,' I said.

'She is,' Beth said. 'It's time I gave up feeding her myself.'

'Is it?' I said. 'I mean, I wouldn't know anything about it.'

Beth laid Molly down in her cot, and buttoned her shirt. I went and stood next to her, and we both gazed down at the sleeping child.

'I can't imagine what it must be like to have kids,' I said.

'Do you want children, Anna?'

'One day,' I said. 'Maybe. Not right now.'

Beth stroked her daughter's mop of brown curls.

'So what do you think of Alex?' I asked.

Beth put her finger to her lips. For a moment, I thought I'd spoken too loudly and she was worried I'd disturbed Molly, but then she pointed to the baby alarm. Which was carrying my whispered words downstairs. Where Alex and Rob were still sitting at the dining table.

I put my hand over my mouth. Beth grinned, and gestured towards the door. She blew a kiss at Molly, and went out onto the landing. I followed her, closing the door behind me.

Still grinning, Beth said, 'What do I think of Alex? Oh, my goodness, it can't be legal for a man to be that attractive.'

I laughed. 'He does have a certain Gallic charm.'

'And he's living in your flat! I don't know how you can keep your hands off him. Nick had better watch out.'

'I'd never cheat on Nick,' I said, more sharply than I'd intended. 'I'd never hurt him like that.'

'I was joking, Anna.'

'Oh. Sorry. I didn't mean to snap. It's just that Nick's not too happy about Alex staying with me. We had a row about it.'

'But you and Nick are OK now?'

'I think we are.' The morning after we'd argued, Nick had been a bit subdued, but he'd kissed me when he dropped me off at my flat on his way to the motorway, and he'd texted that he'd arrived safely at his hotel. And signed his text, 'Love Nick xx'. 'We'll be fine once he's back in London.'

'After all, what possible objection could your boyfriend have to your moving a hot guy like Alex into your flat?'

I rolled my eyes.

'Seriously, Anna. I can understand if Nick's feeling a little insecure.'

'He needn't be.'

'Well, maybe make sure he knows that – when he gets back to London.'

'He tries to tell me which of *my* friends I can invite to *my* flat, and you think I should be *extra nice* to him?'

Beth laughed. 'If you want a successful relationship, then you have to be prepared to make sacrifices.'

I said, 'Nick and I are good together. But Alex's friendship is important to me. And Nick needs to understand that.'

A small voice said, 'Mummy?'

Jonah came out of his bedroom, clutching his teddy bear, a toy elephant, and a toy dog.

'Oh, for goodness' sake, Jonah,' Beth said. 'You've been charging around the house since 6 a.m. Why aren't you asleep? You go on downstairs, Anna. Tell Rob to make some coffee. I'll be down in a minute.' She led Jonah and his menagerie back to his bed.

I went downstairs and being familiar with Beth's kitchen, made the coffee myself and took it through to Alex and Rob. Beth joined us just a few minutes later. Suddenly, she looked very tired, which was, I supposed, unsurprising, if she'd been up since six o'clock running after Jonah. I wondered what time Molly woke up in the mornings. I knew very little about babies, but I suspected that they started the day fairly early.

'Both of them sleeping now?' Rob said.

'Finally,' Beth said, picking at the remains of her lasagne, before deciding it was no longer edible. She yawned, and then smiled at Alex. 'You know, it's remarkable how you and Anna have become such good friends through your letters. It makes me wish I'd kept writing to Fabienne, my French penfriend. I don't suppose you know what she's up to these days?'

'No, I don't,' Alex said. 'As far as I remember, she wanted to become a doctor, but I've no idea if she went to medical college. I've lost touch with most of the people I was at school with. Though, I do hear from Gérard occasionally.'

'Gérard?' Beth said.

You must remember Gérard,' I said. 'He was arrogant and wild, and I fancied him like crazy. Whatever happened to him, Alex?'

'He went into the *gendarmerie*.'

'That bad boy became a policeman?'

'He's been promoted several times,' Alex said. 'He's very respectable these days. He's engaged to a teacher.'

'It's so strange how people's lives turn out,' Beth said. 'I never expected to become a stay-at-home mother in my twenties. More coffee, anyone?'

'Not for me, thank you,' I said, aware that Beth was having difficulty keeping her eyes open. I looked pointedly at Alex. 'You and I should probably make a move.'

Alex nodded. 'I'm on a shoot tomorrow, and I have an early start.'

'Me too,' Beth said. 'An early start, I mean. Not a photoshoot.'

We all stood up, and made our way into the hall. Alex helped me on with my coat.

'Thank you so much for tonight, Beth.' he said. 'It's been wonderful to see you again.' He bent down and kissed her on both sides of her face. '*Au revoir.*'

'*Au revoir*, Alexandre,' Beth said, smoothing her hair. Alex's goodbye kiss appeared to have left her rather flustered.

Alex shook hands with Rob. 'Good to meet you. Call me if you have any more questions about that camera.'

'I will,' Rob said. 'And I'll email you the contact details for my gym.'

I hugged Beth and Rob. With promises that we'd all meet up

again very soon, (and with Nick too, of course), Alex and I left the house, and headed off to the station.

We were on the train, hurtling homewards along the Piccadilly line, when Alex said, 'So what does Beth think of me?'

I groaned. Stupid baby monitor. 'You weren't meant to hear that.'

'But I did.'

'She thinks you're an attractive guy.'

'Good to know.'

'As if you didn't know that already.'

Alex's teeth flashed in a grin. 'I had a good time this evening, although I think we were right to leave when we did. Beth looked exhausted.'

'That's exactly what I thought.'

'It's only just gone 10.30. Do you fancy getting off the train and going for a drink?'

'Don't you have to get up early?'

'Not that early.'

'OK, then.'

We jumped off the train, and went out of the underground into the bright lights of Piccadilly Circus. Even though the night was chill, the area was thronged with people staring at the illuminated advertising screens, and taking photos of the statue of Eros on their mobile phones. In front of the statue, a crowd had gathered to watch two boys perform a gravity-defying breakdance. Further along the pavement, a busker was playing a saxophone.

'I like London at night,' Alex said. 'There's so much going on, so much energy.'

'Where shall we go?' I said. 'Is there a particular bar you want to try?'

'Not really. Shall we just wander for a bit until we see somewhere we like the look of?'

'Sure.'

We linked arms, crossed the road, and started walking down

Shaftesbury Avenue, stopping now and then to examine the posters outside the theatres. Turning a corner into a side road lined with bars and restaurants, we almost collided with another couple coming the opposite way. And I found myself face to face with Mr and Mrs Cooper. Eight million people in London, and I had to run into Nick's mother.

'Hello,' I said. 'This is a surprise.'

'Indeed,' Mrs Cooper said.

Mr Cooper cleared his throat and said, 'Good evening, Anna.'

'Is Nicholas not with you?' Mrs Cooper said.

'No, he's away this week,' I said. 'A work thing. He won't be back 'til Saturday.'

'I see.'

There was an awkward silence, during which I realised, to my horror, that what Nick's parents were seeing was their son's girlfriend out on the town with another man.

Quickly, I said, 'Mr and Mrs Cooper, this is Alex, my flatmate. The penfriend who I've been writing to since we were children. We're looking for a bar – to have a drink –' I broke off. Why did I sound so guilty? I'd not done anything wrong.

Mrs Cooper frowned. 'I was under the impression that your penfriend was a girl. Alexandra.'

'It's an easy mistake to make' I said. 'I made it myself. Alex's full name is Alexandre. It does sound like Alexandra.' Rather desperately, I added, 'He's French.'

Mrs Cooper drew in her breath.

Alex chose that moment to put his arm around my shoulder and say, 'I'm taking very good care of Anna while Nick's away.'

Thanks for that, Alex. Spotting a theatre programme in Mr Cooper's hand, I said, brightly, 'Have you been to the theatre? Which show did you see?'

'*A Tale of Two Cities*: the musical,' Mr Cooper said.

'Now that's a show you and I should see together, Anna,' Alex said.

'Oh, yes, the two cities being London and Paris,' I said.

Mrs Cooper said. 'Well, we do have a train to catch, so ...'

'Er, yes, we must dash,' Mr Cooper said.

'Goodnight,' I said.

Mrs Cooper was already striding around the corner. Her husband hastened to follow her, his customary wish that he would see me 'very soon' for once unspoken.

'So that's Nick's mother,' Alex said. 'She's just as I imagined her from your letters.'

'Those things I wrote about her,' I said. 'They're all true. Her default mode is disapproval.'

Mrs Cooper would no doubt take great delight in telling Nick how she'd met me out with Alex, and exactly what she thought of girls who hung around West End bars with attractive Frenchmen. She was probably on the phone to him already.

Nine

'Anna, are you awake?' Alex rapped loudly on my bedroom door.

I opened my eyes and raised my head from my pillow.

'Anna, it's half past seven.'

What? I should be leaving for work round about now. I checked the alarm clock on my nightstand. Which had failed to wake me up. Because, coming in so late last night, I'd forgotten to set it. My head pounding from lack of sleep (OK, I admit it, and from the amount of wine I'd drunk), I forced myself out of bed, stumbled groggily across my bedroom, and flung open my door.

An unshaven Alex met me in the hall with a cup of black coffee. 'I thought you might need this.'

'I do. I feel terrible.'

'Yeah. Me too. Can't think why.'

I managed a weak smile. After our encounter with Nick's parents, Alex and I'd shared a bottle of wine in a piano bar, before making the (rash) decision to go clubbing. Even on a week night, the queue to get into ultra-fashionable Club Attitude stretched around the block, but a flash of Alex's white teeth and a few words in French to the hostess on the door, and we were ushered past the bouncers and inside. I'd dragged Alex straight out onto the dance floor (well, now I finally had the chance to dance with him, I wasn't going to let him decide that what he really wanted to do was sit at the bar and gape at the celebrities in the roped-off VIP area), and the next couple of hours passed in a blur of flashing lights and pulsating music. It was only the thought of having to get up for work the next morning that made us leave the club before it closed.

'I feel ghastly now, but I had fun last night.' I said.

'So did I,' Alex grinned. 'We should do it again, but maybe when we can sleep in the next day – sorry, Anna, I really need to get going. Not that they can't start the shoot without me, but it looks just a bit unprofessional if I arrive late. *Salut.*'

Stopping only to pick up his camera case, Alex let himself out of the flat.

I swallowed a mouthful of black coffee, hoping that the bitter taste would clear my head. It didn't. Neither did the shower, the aspirin, or the pint of water I drank, before I too headed off to work. I was well and truly hungover. But last night had been great. It'd been far too long since I'd danced 'til dawn (or 'til I'd missed the last train home and had to get the night bus), and I wasn't about to start regretting my night out, even if I was paying for it now.

By *not* blow-drying my hair, and doing my make-up on the train, I managed to arrive at Nova Graphics more or less on time, and with the assistance of several more black coffees, I got through the emails, phone calls, and meetings that made up my working day. Several of my colleagues said that they liked my new hair-do ('Those waves really suit you, Anna'), which made me wonder why I ever bothered to get up in time to straighten my hair. I was still very relieved when 5.30 arrived, and I was able to switch off my computer, slip out of the studio unnoticed (before anyone tried to rope me into an after-work drink), and head for home.

I was almost at the station when I heard Izzy calling my name.

'You look ever so pale, Anna,' she said, falling in beside me and matching her stride to mine. 'Are you OK?'

'I'm just tired,' I said. 'I didn't get much sleep last night.'

'Was Nick staying over?' Izzy said, with a giggle.

'No, he wasn't,' I said. 'He's out of town. At a conference.'

'Were you lying awake pining for him? That is so sweet.

When does he get home?'

'Tomorrow.'

'So how are you planning to welcome him back?'

I looked at her blankly.

'Anna! You must let Nick know how much you've missed him. I recommend the traditional candlelit dinner for two, with champagne on ice and classical music, followed by mind-blowing sex.'

Oh, for goodness sake, the man had only been gone a week.

'I'll give it some thought.'

We came to a bus stop. 'This is me,' Izzy said.

'I'll see you Monday, then,' I said.

'Before you go,' Izzy said, 'there's something I want to ask you. About Alexandre.'

My heart sank. I'd only had four hours' sleep, was still hungover, and had spent most of the day in front of a computer screen. I really couldn't deal with Izzy's unrequited passion right now.

Izzy said, 'I was thinking that you could invite me round to your place sometime, when he's there …'

Give me strength. 'Alex isn't interested in dating you,' I said, heartlessly, 'and throwing yourself at him isn't going to make any difference.'

'I wouldn't be throwing myself at him. I'd just be reminding him of my existence.'

'Izzy, you can't *force* Alex to like you.'

'I can try,' Izzy said. 'Oh, there's my bus –'

'Have a good weekend, Izzy,' I said, making my escape while she was scrabbling in her bag for her Oyster card.

I didn't manage to get a seat on my train journey home, and by the time I let myself into my flat, the headache I'd had on and off throughout the day had returned with a vengeance. Half an hour later, lying in a hot bath, with half a bottle's worth of bubbles, sipping a cup of camomile tea, and I was feeling a whole lot better. And hungry. Actually, I was starving. Probably because I'd had nothing but black coffee and dry biscuits all day (which was all I'd felt able to stomach). I'd make myself some cheese on toast, I decided, and then I'd go to bed and watch a rom com on my laptop, before having an early night.

The doorbell rang. I ignored it. It rang again. It occurred to me that Alex might have forgotten his key.

With a sigh, I got out of the bath, wrapped myself in a towel, trotted into the hall, and picked up the intercom.

Nick's voice said, 'Anna. Hi.'

'Nick? I thought you were in Manchester 'til tomorrow.'

'I decided to drive back tonight. I thought I'd surprise you.'

I felt a stab of annoyance. Nick never came to my flat without phoning first, unless I invited him. Why did he have to choose tonight to turn up unexpectedly on my doorstep, when all I wanted to do was relax.

'Anna? Can you let me in?'

I buzzed him in, and a few minutes later, let him into my flat.

'How come you're back early?' I said.

'I was missing you.' Nick set his laptop case down carefully on the hall table. 'I couldn't face another night in a lonely hotel room. So I skipped the end-of-conference dinner, and drove straight here.'

Nick never did anything on the spur of the moment, but he'd come back to London a day early just to be with me. My irritation at his arrival faded. Suddenly I was riven with guilt that I hadn't flung myself into his arms the moment he'd stepped inside the door.

Nick said, 'You're not dressed.'

'No, I was in the bath –'

I remembered what Beth and Izzy had said about welcoming Nick home. I didn't have any champagne in the fridge, and there was no classical music on my iPod, but I could still be *extra nice* to him tonight. I smiled, and lowered my towel.

'The water's still hot,' I said. Come and join me.'

Nick's eyes widened and his mouth actually fell open. Clutching my towel with one hand, I reached up and unknotted his tie with the other. Then, with a glance over my shoulder and another smile, trailing my towel behind me, I walked slowly along the hallway to the bathroom, and climbed back into the bath.

After about five minutes, Nick came into the bathroom in his boxers.

'Sorry I was so long,' he said. 'I had to hang up my suit.'

So much for spontaneity.

Nick pulled off his underwear, stepped over the rim of the bath, and cautiously lowered himself into the water, so that he was sat facing me. I leant forward, and we kissed. Somewhat chastely, I felt, considering we sitting in a bath together, naked.

'So how was your conference?'

'It was useful,' Nick said, 'How was your week? I hear that you and Alexandre met my parents last night.'

Despite the warmth of the bath water, I suddenly felt cold. Was this why Nick had decided to come home a day early? Because he wanted to check up on me and Alex? Unbelievable.

'Yes, we did,' I said. 'We'd stopped off for a drink on our way home from Beth and Rob's, and ran into your parents in Piccadilly Circus.' Keep it simple, Anna. No need to mention that you stayed out half the night dancing in a club.

'Oh, yes, you said you were going to Beth and Rob's.'

'We had a good evening,' I said. 'Shall I wash your back?'

Nick shook his head. Then he grabbed hold of my shoulders and kissed me again. Evidently, he'd decided that Alex and I could be trusted to visit an old friend – whatever his mother had said to him. I slid forward so that I was sitting with my arms around his neck, my legs around his waist, and his erection against my stomach. We kissed until the bathwater grew chill.

'I think we should go into the bedroom now.' Nick said.

Ten

I lay on my side on my bed, resting my head on one elbow, Nick lying close beside me, his hand straying over my rear. My empty stomach rumbled accusingly, but Nick didn't appear to notice. He rolled me onto my back, and I opened my legs so that he could position himself on top of me. He shoved himself into me, and then he was pounding away, eyes shut, breathing hard, and I was holding him, my arms tight around him, noticing a new crack in the ceiling plaster, hoping that Alex's working day had been better than mine, wondering what he was doing now, hearing Nick groan as he came –

Nick sighed contentedly, and clambered off me.

'I hope that was as good for you as it was for me,' he said.

'It was lovely,' I lied. He'd only feel bad if I told him I didn't come.

While Nick relaxed back onto the pillows, I found myself unable to lie still. Restless and hungry, I got out of bed and put on an over-sized T-shirt.

'I'm going to fix myself some cheese on toast,' I said. 'Would you like some?'

'No, thanks, I've already eaten,' Nick said. 'I stopped at a service station on the motorway.'

'I won't be long.'

Nick yawned. 'Take as long as you like. I'm going to sleep.' He turned onto his side and pulled the duvet up over his shoulders.

I went to the kitchen, grilled a couple of slices of cheese on toast, and carried my plate into the living room. Alex was

75

sitting on the sofa, texting on his mobile.

I said, 'Hey, Alex.'

He started. 'Anna. I thought you'd gone to bed.' His gaze strayed to my legs. Belatedly, I realised that my baggy T-shirt barely covered the top of my thighs. He said, 'Is Nick here?'

'Yes, he is.' I sat at the dining table, pulling the T-shirt down as far as it would go.

'I thought he must be,' Alex said. 'I saw his boxers on the bathroom floor. At least, as they're not mine, I assumed they're his.'

'Yes, they'll be Nick's,' I said, thankful that Alex hadn't come home while Nick and I were in the bath, as I didn't recall either of us locking the bathroom door. 'Shall we discuss something other than my boyfriend's underpants? How was your shoot?'

'It was good – once the aspirin kicked in and I got over my hangover. I was photographing a writer. Verity Holmes.'

I paused in the act of taking a bite of toast. 'She's my favourite author. I adore her books.'

'I know.' Standing up, Alex passed me a paperback, which had been lying on the sofa. 'She gave me a copy of her latest novel, so I had her sign it for you.'

I opened the book at the title page and saw the words, 'To Anna Mitchel. I hope you enjoy reading my book as much as I enjoyed writing it. With best wishes, Verity H.'

'Thank you *so* much. This is the first time I've ever owned a book signed by the author. *Merci beaucoup.*'

'You're welcome, *mon amie.*'

He was standing next to the dining table, looking down at me, his dark hair falling over his forehead into his eyes, a soft smile playing about his full, sensual mouth. I smiled up at him, and found myself wondering what it would be like to kiss him, to feel his lips on my lips, his tongue …

What was wrong with me? My boyfriend, with whom I'd just had sex, was in the next room, in my bed.

'I'm glad you're pleased with the book,' Alex said.

Abruptly, he turned away from me, and sat back down on the sofa.

'I – I'll start reading it tomorrow.'

Alex didn't answer. He was studying his phone, apparently absorbed in whatever was on the screen.

I swallowed my last few mouthfuls of cheese on toast, and said, '*Bonne nuit*, Alex.'

'Goodnight.'

Hugging my book against my chest, I went to the kitchen and deposited my plate in the dishwasher, before returning to my bedroom. The light from the street lamp outside, shining through a gap in the curtains, was enough for me to see that Nick had pushed the duvet down to his stomach and was now lying on his back, his arms flung wide. His eyes were shut, and his heavy, even breathing told me that he was asleep. Placing my new novel on top of my books-to-be-read pile, I sat on the side of the bed, and watched Nick's chest rise and fall. I had a sudden compelling need to wake him up and tell him that I loved him, but contented myself with kissing his forehead very gently. Then I slid into bed.

I hadn't kissed Alex. I had no intention of ever kissing Alex. And even if I'd wanted to kiss him – if the thought of how it would taste and feel to kiss Alex had been anything more than just a momentary fantasy – he'd given no indication that he was interested in kissing me. Nick had nothing to worry about.

Eleven

Nick stopped his car outside my flat.

'You can still change your mind and sleep here,' I said.

'Not tonight, Anna. If I'm getting up at four a.m to drive my parents to the airport, it makes sense for me to stay at their place.'

When, a couple of weeks after he'd come back from Manchester, Nick had told me that his parents were going on a month-long Caribbean cruise, I'd been ecstatic. A whole month without his mother's incessant demands for our presence at some dire gathering. I shouldn't have been surprised when, the night before they were due to fly out to Antigua, Mrs Cooper decided that she couldn't trust a minicab to turn up on time, and that Nick would have to drive them to Gatwick. Nick and I had been in a restaurant when she'd called. I'd assumed that my touching his thigh under the table would encourage him to make an excuse as to why he couldn't just abandon his own (and my) plans for the night in order to act as her chauffeur, but as usual, he wouldn't refuse a request from his mother. Even when she was leaving the country, that woman managed to irritate me.

Through gritted teeth, I said, 'Tell your parents I hope they have a wonderful holiday.'

'I think you and I should book a holiday,' Nick said. 'A couple of weeks in the sun. Just the two of us.'

'Really?' Last year, he'd gone on a golfing holiday in Spain with some business associates ('It's such a good networking opportunity, Anna') and I'd gone to Crete with a group of female friends.

'Would you like that?' Nick said.

I thought of palm-fringed beaches and olive-covered hillsides, blue swimming pools and long cool drinks, bikinis and sarongs, Nick and I lazing in the sun or exploring narrow cobbled streets.

'I would love to go on holiday with you.'

'Great. I'll see you on Saturday, and we'll take a look at some of the online travel sites.'

'You could come over tomorrow night, if you like.'

'I can't. I'm going out with the guys from my office.'

Of course he was. Like he did every Friday.

Nick kissed the side of my face, and then leant past me to open the passenger door. 'Goodnight, Anna.'

'Night.' I got out of the car.

He waited until I was inside my building's communal hallway before driving off.

I trudged up the stairs to my flat and let myself in. The lights were on and I could hear music coming from the living room, so I knew that Alex was home. Whatever Nick might think about Alex's continuing presence, I'd seen very little of him over the last two weeks – either he'd come in after I'd gone to bed or I'd been at Nick's – but now, because of Mrs Cooper's travel arrangements, I'd have the opportunity to spend some time alone with my friend. Just this once, Mrs Cooper was forgiven.

I opened the living room door and went in.

The first thing I saw was Alex's shirt and jeans lying in a crumpled heap on the floor, next to an equally crumpled dress. Alex was sitting on the sofa in his boxers, his eyes shut, his long legs stretched out in front of him, kissing a woman wearing just a bra and a thong, who was sprawled on his lap.

'Alex!' I gasped. I couldn't help myself.

Alex's eyes flew open, and he looked at me with an almost comical expression of surprise on his face. For what seemed like ages, but in reality was probably no more than a few

80

seconds, I just stood there, frozen, unable to move. Then I turned and ran, slamming the door behind me.

I went to my room and sank down shakily on my bed. I was hideously embarrassed to have witnessed a scene of such intimacy, and more than a little shocked that Alex had brought a woman back to the flat. Then I had to ask myself why I was shocked. A single, twenty-eight-year-old guy, especially one as attractive as Alex, wasn't going to be short of offers, and while he might not want a *relationship*, while he might still be carrying a torch for his ex, that didn't mean he'd taken a vow of celibacy. It wasn't like this was the first time he'd been with a girl since he broke up with Cécile. He'd already slept with Izzy. Not that it was any concern of mine who he hooked up with.

I realised that I could no longer hear music. A few minutes, later I heard the sound of an angry female voice in the hall, and the front door opening and closing. Then there were approaching footsteps, and a knock on my door.

'Anna? Can I talk to you?'

My face on fire, I said, 'Come in, Alex.'

He pushed open the door and leant against the frame. He was, I was relieved to see, fully dressed.

'Has she gone?' I said.

'Yes. I called her a cab.'

At least I wouldn't have to make polite conversation with her over the breakfast table. 'She didn't sound very happy.'

'She got it into her head that you were my girlfriend, and wouldn't believe me when I told her that you weren't.'

'I hope you're not expecting me to apologise for ruining your night.'

'I'm the one who should be apologising. It was wrong of me to invite someone into your home without asking you first.'

'It's your home too, for the next few months. You don't need my permission to … have a visitor. Though you might have gone into your bedroom before you ripped each other's clothes off.'

'That was my intention,' Alex said. 'I hadn't reckoned on

81

Chloe being quite so eager. We'd only been in the flat five minutes when she took off her dress and started unbuttoning my shirt.'

'You poor little innocent French boy. I should have warned you about English girls.'

'I like English girls.'

'Evidently. Who is she, anyway, this Chloe? Someone from your magazine?'

'No. I only met her tonight. We were both on the guest list for the launch of a new fashion label. She's a model. A very successful model. As you might expect, given her figure.'

Her figure wasn't that great, from what I saw of it. Far too skinny. 'Well, I'm sure her being a model and your being a photographer had nothing to do with her taking her clothes off.'

'Are you suggesting that girl only came on to me because she thought I'd shoot her a new Z-card?'

'Yes.'

Alex looked at me uncertainly, not sure if I was being serious. I wasn't entirely sure myself.

'You're wrong,' he said, eventually. 'She was after my body.'

I gazed at him standing there in the doorway, tall and broad-shouldered, and I thought, I can't blame her for that. I reminded myself of my resolve not to think about Alex's muscles.

'You are so up yourself.' I threw a pillow at him.

He laughed and threw it back.

'I don't know why you're laughing, Alex. I was *mortified*, walking in on you like that.' I tried not to smile.

'You weren't the only one who was embarrassed, I can assure you,' Alex said. He added, 'Is Nick not with you? Or is he so mortified that he's hiding in your wardrobe?'

I explained about Mrs Cooper's mistrust of minicab drivers.

'And how are you and Nick?' Alex said.

'We're great. Why wouldn't we be?'

'No reason.' Alex walked across the room and flopped down next to me on my bed, resting on his elbows. 'I only asked because I haven't seen much of you lately, and I don't know what's going on in your life.'

'I was thinking the same about you. What have you been up to?' Apart from picking up girls at fashion launches.

Alex thought for a moment and then he said, 'Dear Anna, Over the last couple of weeks, I've had some challenging assignments in interesting locations around London, and I've taken some shots I'm very pleased with. I also spent a day photographing furniture, which was somewhat less interesting. I've played squash with Rob a few times –'

'Who won?' I said.

'Ssh. No interrupting my letter.' Alex cleared his throat. 'I played squash with Rob, and I won, although it wasn't easy, as we're pretty evenly matched. Rob invited me to call in for a drink on my way home, and I saw your friend Beth –'

'How is Beth? I've been meaning to call her.'

'Ssh! Beth seemed tired, so I didn't stay very long. Yours sincerely, Alexandre Tourville. PS. Tomorrow, if you are free after work, would you like to come with me to the National Gallery? It stays open 'til 9 p.m. on Fridays.'

'Ooh, I do like getting letters,' I said. '*Cher* Alexandre, thank you for your kind invitation. I would very much like to visit the National Gallery with you. *Á bientôt,* Anna Mitchel.'

'It's a date, then,' Alex said. 'What time do you finish work?'

I told him, and we arranged that he would come and meet me at Nova Graphics, that we'd spend a couple of hours at the National Gallery, and then go for a meal, and possibly on to a club. We chatted for a while, and then, seeing as we were both yawning, decided to call it a night.

'I'll see you tomorrow, then,' Alex stood up in one sinuous motion. '*Bonne nuit.*'

'*Bonne nuit*, Alex.'

He headed out of my room. I lay back on my bed and thought how easy he was to talk to, how easy to be around. And easy on the eye, of course. I ran my hand over the dent on the duvet where he had been lying next to me. My friend. *Mon ami*. I would miss him when he went back to France.

84

Twelve

The following morning, I'd just come out of one meeting and was getting my notes together ready for another, when Beth rang my mobile.

'Hi, Anna,' she said. 'Are you at work? Can you talk?'

'Yes, I'm at work, but I can talk for five minutes.'

'Well, it's short notice, but I know you never see Nick on Fridays, and Rob's said he'll look after the kids, so I was hoping that you and I could have a girls' night out. Go to a bar, somewhere with live music, like we used to –'

'Beth, slow down. Do you mean tonight?'

'Yes. Sorry, I'm wittering. It's what happens when you're at home with small children all day. You forget how to talk to people over the age of five.

'I can't tonight.'

'Tomorrow?'

'I'm really sorry, but I'm seeing Nick tomorrow.'

'Oh, well, maybe some other time,' Beth said, sounding horribly disappointed.

'Any other Friday would be fine,' I said, 'but tonight I'm going to the National Gallery with Alex.'

'You're going out with Alex?' Beth said. 'Then why I don't I come with you? I'm sure he wouldn't mind.'

Maybe he wouldn't mind. But I did. I'd been looking forward to my night out with Alex, and really didn't want a third person tagging along, not even my oldest friend.

'You want to spend an evening looking at paintings?' I asked.

'Why not? I never went to university like you, but that doesn't mean I can't appreciate a bit of culture.'

'No, of course it doesn't, but when we shared a flat I was always asking you to come with me to art exhibitions, and you always said you couldn't imagine anything more boring.'

'Did I? I don't remember.'

I should just tell her that I don't want her to come.

Beth said, 'I'm going stir-crazy stuck here with the kids. It'd be great to get out of the house – Jonah! Be careful! Oh, no!'

'What is it?' I said. 'Is Jonah OK?'

'Oh, yes, he's fine. It's just that he's spilt blackcurrant juice all over the living room carpet. What time shall I meet you at the gallery?'

'Well, Alex is meeting me from work so –'

'I'll do the same. Text me the time and Nova Graphic's address.' Beth ended the call.

Nothing like inviting yourself somewhere you're not wanted, I thought, Then I was overcome with guilt. Beth sounded like she really could do with a break from the demands of motherhood. And it wasn't as if Alex and I were going on a date. There was no reason why I should feel so possessive towards him.

At 5.30 sharp, I headed out of the studio and down the stairs to Reception, where I was meeting Alex and Beth. They were both already there – as was Izzy, who had somehow managed to get away from her desk even earlier than I had, and was talking to Alex. She hadn't mentioned him in almost a week, but my hopes that she was over her unrequited infatuation were completely quashed by the way she was gazing up at him from under her long dark eyelashes. Beth, standing next to Izzy, saw me before the other two, and her face broke into a delighted grin. I noticed that she was wearing make-up for the first time in months, she'd straightened her hair, and she had on a new pair of boots. This night off from her family duties certainly seemed to be a big deal for her. I hoped that she wasn't going to be disappointed. And that she wouldn't want to stay out too late, so that I got to spend at least some of the evening alone with Alex.

'Hi, all,' I said, as I joined the three of them. 'You look nice tonight, Beth.' To Izzy, I added, 'We're off to the National Gallery.'

'I know,' Izzy said. 'I'm coming with you. Alexandre invited me.'

'Great.' I gave Alex a tight smile. Well that was really going to convince her that he'd no intention of dating her.

'Izzy tells me that she's particularly interested in the paintings of the Renaissance,' Alex said.

'Oh, me too,' Beth said. 'Nothing I enjoy more than a bit of Renaissance.'

I shot her a look. 'Let's get going then, shall we?'

'And after we've done enough looking at pictures,' Beth said, 'maybe we could go on to a bar?'

'Good idea,' Izzy said.

So much for my night out with Alex, just the two of us.

Alex said, 'So every element of *The Embarkation of the Queen of Sheba* – the light reflected on the water, the figure of the boy on the quayside shading his face against the brightness – draws your eye to the luminous horizon, where the queen's ship is about to sail off into the open sea, towards the rising sun.'

'Yes, I see that now,' Beth said, staring up at Claude Lorrain's painting of a seaport in the early morning. 'Now that you've explained it.'

'It's so great to go round a gallery with someone who knows so much about art,' Izzy said to Alex.

Did she really have to tell him how wonderful he was every five minutes? I was longing to discuss the masterpieces that hung in the National Gallery with Alex, but what with Izzy's flirting and Beth's asking him questions, I'd not had a chance to exchange more than a few words with him all evening.

'Anna knows much more about paintings than I do,' Alex said. 'I've always enjoyed visiting art galleries, and as a photography student, I did study other visual media, but Anna's the one with the History of Art degree.'

Izzy, apparently not much interested in my academic qualifications, was examining the gallery floor-plan she'd picked up at the information desk. Alex and Beth crowded around her, and after some deliberation as to which painting they wanted to see next, they all headed off to an adjoining room, which was hung with works by artists of the Italian Renaissance. I trailed after them, catching up as they came to a halt in front of Botticelli's *Venus and Mars*. Izzy and Beth gazed at the painting in silence, and then turned expectantly to Alex.

He said, 'The woman on the left of the picture, sitting upright, dressed in a white and gold nightdress, is Venus, goddess of love, and the naked man lying beside her is Mars, god of war. He has returned from the battlefield, removed his armour, and made love to her, kissing her and caressing her, taking her with him to the heights of ecstasy, *le petit mort,* as we say in France, the little death. And now, all passion spent, he rests, while she smiles serenely to herself, knowing the power she has over him. The meaning of the painting is that love conquers all.'

'Ooh, Alexandre,' Izzy sighed, 'I could listen to you talk about art for hours.'

Beth said, 'I never realised that an old painting could be so … could have so much in it.'

'Another way of describing *Venus and Mars*,' I said, 'is that the man and the woman have just had a quickie, and he's rolled over and gone to sleep. Take a closer look at Venus' face – she doesn't seem like a girl who's just had great sex to me.'

Izzy giggled. 'I prefer Alexandre's description.'

'So do I,' Beth said.

I gestured at the painting. 'Do you see the wasps flying round Mars' head? They symbolise the painful stings of love. Maybe the meaning of the painting is that the woman wants more than the guy is prepared to give.'

'There's usually more than one way of interpreting a great work of art,' Alex said. 'Even the experts don't always agree. It could be that it's the guy who gets stung.' He glanced at his watch, and then looked at me. 'The gallery closes soon, so we've probably only got time to look at one more painting. What'll it be?'

I shrugged. 'You choose. Since you know so much about art.'

Alex frowned.

'If the gallery's about to close,' Izzy said, 'I'd like to go straight to the gift shop and buy some postcards.'

'Fine,' I said.

'And then we need to decide where we're going to eat,' Alex said.

'Why don't we go to a French restaurant,' Izzy said. 'There's one in Covent Garden that's had great reviews.' She smiled at Alex. 'I simply *adore* French cuisine.'

I supressed the urge to slap her.

'Sounds good,' Beth said, 'but Alex will have to translate the menu for me.'

'Where would you like to eat, Anna?' Alex said.

'Oh, I don't know.' My evening was already ruined, so I didn't care. 'Why don't we just go home and order a takeaway?'

'OK,' Alex said. 'If that's what you want.'

I turned to Beth and Izzy. 'You two are very welcome to come back to ours.'

I'd so much rather they didn't.

'I'd love to come back to yours for a takeaway,' Beth said.

'Me too,' said Izzy. 'And we should pick up some beer and wine.'

'Yay!' Beth said. 'Mine's a sauvignon blanc.'

'I thought you weren't drinking alcohol while you're feeding Molly,' I said.

'Oh, didn't I tell you?' Beth said. 'I've given up breastfeeding. I can drink all I want!'

'So let's party,' Izzy said. 'Dance with me?' Izzy stood in front of Alex, who was lounging on the sofa, cradling a glass of wine.

'Not tonight,' Alex said.

'Aw, please dance with me.' Izzy lifted her arms above her head and started swaying from side to side in time to the music coming from my iPod speakers. Alex raised his wine glass to his lips, and watched her through hooded eyes.

I glanced at my watch. Gone midnight. And, despite me doing my domestic goddess act, clearing away the detritus of our Chinese takeaway and collecting up empty glasses, neither Izzy nor Beth were showing any signs of wanting to get off home. When I'd turned down the music, Izzy had turned it up again.

Beth, who'd drunk far more than her share of the white wine we'd bought and had now moved onto red, got up out of the armchair where she'd been sitting and came and joined me at the dining table.

'Your friend Izzy seems very young,' she said, pitching her voice so that only I could hear. 'How old is she?'

'Twenty-one.' Twenty-one going on sixteen. And apparently determined to make a fool of herself over Alex.

'I remember being twenty-one,' Beth said. 'You and I were sharing a flat. We'd go out every Friday night. Drink wine. Dance. Meet boys.' She drained her wine, picked up the bottle that was on the dining table and refilled her glass, spilling a fair amount.

'We had some good times.' I mopped up the spilt wine with a tissue.

'Izzy looks like she's having a good time too,' Beth's voice, I noticed, was becoming increasingly slurred.

Izzy, having failed to persuade Alex to dance with her, had kicked off her shoes, and was dancing alone, rolling her hips and tossing her hair. Still dancing, she undid a couple of buttons on her shirt and tied it up, revealing an enviably flat stomach. When her dance brought her close to Alex, she smiled at him and held out her hand. He shook his head, but his gaze continued to follow her as she writhed around the room. I didn't know which of them was annoying me more – Izzy for practically giving Alex a lap dance, or Alex for so obviously enjoying it. He's going to sleep with her again tonight, I thought. I swallowed a mouthful of wine. Not that his sex life was any concern of mine.

Beth said, 'It's not too late.'

'What? Sorry, Beth, what are you talking about?'

'I'm still young enough to strut my stuff on a Friday night.' Getting to her feet (and knocking over her chair in the process), Beth tottered unsteadily to the middle of the room, where she launched into a floundering parody of Izzy's dance.

Oh, my lord, she's completely pissed, I thought.

Abruptly, Alex stood up too. For a moment I thought he was going to dance with Beth and Izzy, but instead he walked over to me, and straightened up the chair.

In French, he said, 'You do realise that Beth's had way too much to drink?'

'Yes, I had noticed,' I said, in the same language. 'I'm thinking I should make her a coffee to sober her up before I send her back to Rob in a cab.'

'I'll say goodnight, then.'

'You're going to bed?' Alone?

'Your friends' enthusiasm for art has worn me out. I'll see you tomorrow.' Calling out goodnight to Izzy and Beth, he headed out of the living room.

Izzy stopped dancing. For a moment she stared after Alex, before flinging herself down on the sofa. Beth continued to lurch about.

With a sigh, I got up and switched off my iPod.

'What's happened to the music?' Beth said.

'Sit down, Beth.' I ushered her to an armchair.

'Is there any wine left?'

'No, but you can have a black coffee. What about you Izzy? Would you like a coffee before you go home?'

'Actually,' Izzy said, 'I was wondering if I could crash on

91

your sofa? I've missed my connecting train, and minicabs are so expensive.'

She'd never had any intention of catching her last train. She'd thought she'd be spending the night with Alex. Silly girl.

I forced myself to smile. 'No worries. I've a spare duvet.' Well, I could hardly turn her out onto the night-time streets, however much I was tempted.

Suddenly, Beth said, 'Alex isn't here. Where's he gone?' She peered round the room, as though he might be hiding behind the furniture. 'Alex? Alex?'

'He's trying to sleep,' I said. 'So keep the noise down. I'll make us some coffee.'

I went out to the kitchen, made one black and two white coffees, and put them on a tray. Thinking that Beth could probably do with something to soak up the alcohol, I added a packet of biscuits. Then I returned to the living room.

Izzy was sitting on the sofa, flicking through a copy of *The Edge* magazine that I'd bought because it had a double-page spread of Alex's photos. There was no sign of Beth.

I set the tray down on the table and handed Izzy a mug of coffee. 'Where's Beth?'

'She went to the bathroom,' Izzy said. 'I don't think she's feeling too good.' With an irritating giggle, she added, 'She's totally wasted.'

Memories surfaced of Friday nights out with Beth, when she and I were still sharing a flat. All too often, the evening would end with one of us holding back the other's hair while she threw up. 'I'd better check she's OK.'

Beth wasn't in the bathroom. And when I looked into my bedroom, thinking she might have collapsed in a drunken stupor on my bed, she wasn't there either. I glanced along the hallway. Alex's door was closed, but even as I stood there, it slowly swung open. And I saw him and Beth, standing next to his bed. Her arms were around his neck, and she was pressed close to his naked torso – he was wearing just his jeans. And he was kissing her.

I tore along the hall. 'What the hell are you *doing?*'

Without any apparent haste, Alex lifted his face from Beth's and removed her arms from his neck. Beth gaped at me in horror, clamped her hands over her mouth, and fled past me, back into the living room.

'How could you, Alex?' I was so angry with him, I could hardly speak. 'How could you kiss *Beth*?'

'She's very drunk –'

'Oh, well, that makes it all right, then. It's not like you took advantage of her.'

'Listen, Anna, whatever you thought you saw –'

'Shut up,' I said. 'Just shut up. And put a frickin' shirt on.' I turned on my heel and marched back along the hallway.

In the living room, I found Beth kneeling on the carpet, rummaging through her handbag.

'I can't find my phone,' she wailed. 'I have to call a cab, and I can't find my phone.'

'Beth, calm down,' I said. 'And get up off the floor.'

'I have to get home to Rob and Jonah and Molly. I want to go home.'

'I'll call you a cab,' I said. The sooner she went home the better. 'But first you need to sit quietly for a bit.'

From the sofa, Izzy said, 'She is going to have the most *awful* headache tomorrow.'

Thanks for that, Izzy. That really helped.

'I kissed him.' Beth said. 'I kissed Alex. I'm so sorry.'

'You and Alexandre …' Izzy's voice trailed off. Her face went very red.

'I want to go home,' Beth repeated.

Alex, wearing a shirt, came into the living room. He went straight to Beth, put his hands under her arms and raised her to her feet. She slumped against him, but let him walk her to an armchair and sit her down.

'I'm sorry, Alex.' Beth's eyes filled with tears. 'I just want to go home.'

'As you keep saying,' Izzy muttered.

'It's OK, Beth,' Alex said. 'We'll get you home.'

I said, 'The state she's in, we can't just put her in a cab –'

'Obviously not – I'll go with her.'

'I think you've done quite enough,' I said. 'I'll go with her.'

'I'd like to make sure she gets home all right.'

'I can do that.'

'Would you two stop?' Izzy said. 'I don't think Beth's going anywhere tonight.'

I spun around to see that while Alex and I had been squabbling about who'd take her home, Beth had fallen asleep, and was now half-sitting, half-lying in the chair, her head thrown back, her arms hanging limp, one leg draped over the other.

'She looks a bit like that Mars guy in the painting,' Izzy said. 'Maybe he hadn't just had sex – maybe he was drunk.'

Oh, for goodness' sake. I shook Beth's shoulder. 'Beth, wake up.'

Beth mumbled something unintelligible, and batted away my hand.

Alex said, 'It'd be better if she stayed here tonight, and slept it off.'

I knew he was right. However much Beth might want to go home, attempting to transport an unconscious woman across London in a cab in the early hours wasn't exactly practical.

'Do you want to put her on the sofa?' Izzy said. 'Because I can sleep on the floor.'

'No, it's OK,' I said. 'She can come in with me.' I wasn't going to be able to shift Beth to my room on my own, but I couldn't bring myself to ask Alex for help.

Alex said, 'I'll carry her.' He picked Beth up as easily as she lifted up Molly. Stifling the impulse to tell him to get his hands off her, I followed him as he carried her into my room, and laid her down gently on my bed.

'Is there anything else I can do?' he said.

'No,' I said.

He left without another word, almost colliding with Izzy in

the doorway. I heard his bedroom door open and shut.

Izzy said, 'I brought Beth's bag. Her phone rang. Your phone rang as well.'

'Oh, Lord, that'll be Rob wondering where his wife is. I'll have to call him back.'

'Beth's married?' Izzy's gaze flickered to Beth's left hand, where her wedding band gleamed softly on her ring finger.

'Yes, she's married,' I said. 'She has two children.'

I took off Beth's boots and her watch and covered her with the duvet. She moaned a couple of times, but then rolled onto her side and lay quiet. I located my spare duvet on top of my wardrobe, and handed it to Izzy who was still hovering in the doorway.

She said, 'Are Beth and Alexandre having an affair?'

'What? No. No, of course not. She's only met him a couple of times.' As far as I knew. 'Besides, she'd never – She and Rob are very happy.'

'Then what's she doing kissing Alex?'

'I've no idea. Goodnight, Izzy.'

'Night.'

I waited until Izzy had vanished inside the living room, and then I stormed into Alex's bedroom.

He was sitting on his bed, talking on his mobile, but he stood up when he saw me.

'She'll be fine,' he said. 'Anna will look after her … *Bonne nuit.*' He ended the call. 'That was Rob. He'd expected Beth to be home by now, and when he couldn't get hold of her on her mobile, he was worried. Especially as you weren't answering your phone either.'

'What did you tell him?'

'That she'd had too much to drink and was asleep in your bed. He's going to drive over in the morning with the kids, to collect her.'

'I presume you left out the part where you kissed her.'

'I didn't kiss –'

'I *saw* you.'

'I didn't kiss her. She kissed me.'

'Oh, *please*. Two days running, a girl makes a move on you? Seriously? Did Beth tear off your shirt like that model did? It's getting to be quite a problem for you, isn't it?'

'I was getting undressed for bed when Beth burst into my room and literally jumped on me –'

'It's bad enough that you sleep with Izzy and then discard her –'

'I've never slept with Izzy.'

'You told me you slept with her – the night of Natalie's party. I distinctly remember you coming in the next morning and saying that you'd stayed over –'

'I stayed at her house –'

'You *used* her, Alex. And now you're using Beth. Was tonight the only time you've kissed her? The first time? Or have there been others? Have you slept with her too?'

'I have not.' Alex's eyes flashed angrily. 'Is this what you think of me? That I go around seducing married women?'

'I don't know what to think.' By now, I was shaking with rage. 'You can have any girl you want, why would you hit on Beth? I invite you into my flat, into my *home*, and this is how you repay me.'

'If you want me to move out, you only have to say.'

'I do. I want you to go.'

'I'll leave first thing in the morning.'

'Fine.' I glared at him. 'You and I are no longer friends.' I strode out of his room, slamming the door behind me.

Thirteen

I woke with a start. Beth was lying next to me in my bed, her eyes closed. For a moment, I couldn't understand why she was there, but then the events of the previous night came flooding back to me. Izzy dancing. Beth getting drunk. Alex kissing her. Alex and I arguing …

I sat up and rubbed my eyes with the heel of my hand.

It was then that I noticed the white envelope that had been pushed under my door. I got out of bed, padded across the room, and picked it up. My name was on the front, written in Alex's familiar handwriting. I tore the envelope open, and pulled out the several sheets of paper that were inside. A letter. I sank down on the foot of my bed and read:

Dear Anna,

Last night you told me that we are no longer friends. That saddens me, but I am not going to beg you to change your mind. I will move out of your flat as soon I can. You also accused me of behaving badly towards Izzy and Beth. That, I cannot let pass.

When Cécile left me, I had a rough time, and I arrived in England feeling very low. Meeting a pretty girl like Izzy at your boss's birthday party, having her hanging on my every word and gazing up adoringly into my eyes, was flattering to my bruised ego, and made me feel a whole lot better, if only for a while.

Izzy is sweet and uncomplicated – the complete opposite of

Cécile – and I spent most of the party talking and dancing with her. When the party broke up in the early hours, it seemed only right that I should see her safely to her front door – or rather her parents' front door, as she still lives with them. And I kissed her. Standing there on the front step, outside her parents' house, I kissed her. But I did not sleep with her. I never had any intention of sleeping with her. She is a girl who wants a boyfriend, love, and romance, not casual sex with a guy she's just met. I did stay the night – at her suggestion, as the trains had stopped running and there was an hour's wait for a cab – but I slept in a spare bedroom. Alone, in a single bed. In the morning, I put my head round Izzy's bedroom door to say goodbye, and then I left, before the rest of the household woke up. I did not say that I'd call her, or ask to see her again, or make any promises that I knew I couldn't keep. Izzy has no reason to feel used. And no reason to think I'd want her to flaunt herself at me the way she did last night. It is true that I invited her to the gallery – but only after she'd hinted so strongly that she wanted to come with us that I really had no choice.

As for Beth – I have no idea what prompted her to come to my bedroom. All I can think is that she was so drunk she had no idea what she was doing. I certainly hadn't said or done anything that might encourage her to believe that I'd welcome her presence, but suddenly there she was, clinging to me and trying to kiss me. I was so amazed that I just stood there – which is when you came in.

I know you were shocked when you saw me with Beth, and I don't blame you for being angry if you thought I'd made a pass at her. What I can't understand is why you refused to listen to me when I told you that I was as shocked as you were. Instead, you immediately assumed that I'd already lured her into some sort of sexual liaison. You must have a very poor opinion of me if you seriously believe I would mess around with a woman who is another man's wife and the mother of two young children.

It seems to me that our friendship has run its course. Maybe it only ever existed on paper, in the letters that we wrote to one another, but to me, it felt very real.

This is the last letter I will write to you. I wish you well.

Alexandre Tourville

I thought back to the scene in Alex's bedroom. Beth's mouth on his, her hands clasped around his neck. Alex standing rigid, like a statue, his arms at his side. The calm, gentle way he'd loosened her grasp, and stepped away from her.

What had I done? I felt sick to my stomach. I'd been so furious with Alex last night, I hadn't stopped to consider that when he'd said Beth had burst in on him, he might have been describing exactly what had happened. Instead of hearing him out, I'd yelled at him, and told him to leave. I looked down at Beth, who was still sleeping soundly. Had she been drunk enough to lose all self-control and kiss a man who was not her husband? It would be totally out of character, and yet ... She wouldn't be the first girl to do something stupid when she'd had too much wine ... I bit my lip. I'd said some awful things to Alex last night. I had to talk to him.

Clutching the letter to my chest, I left my room and went and knocked on Alex's door. He didn't answer. I pushed the door open.

Alex wasn't there. His jacket wasn't on the back of the door where he habitually hung it. For one hideous moment I thought he'd taken me at my word and already moved out of my flat, but then common sense told me that he wouldn't go in the middle of the night, and certainly wouldn't have left his favourite camera and his laptop, which were on the dressing table that he used as a desk. Even so, I opened his wardrobe to check that his clothes were still there. Seeing his jeans and shirts reassured me that he hadn't walked out of my life forever.

I re-read Alex's letter. Last night, I'd been so certain that my outrage was entirely justified. Now, my anger had faded, and his version of events seemed far more likely. In the cold light of day, the idea that he and Beth had embarked on an illicit liaison was frankly ludicrous.

I didn't want those to be the last words he ever wrote to me. Whatever happened last night, I didn't want our friendship to end like this.

Stowing the letter in my pyjama pocket, I left Alex's room and closed the door behind me. The noise of someone moving about drew me into the kitchen. Instead of Alex, I found Izzy in the process of loading the dishwasher with wine and beer glasses.

'Thanks, Izzy.' I surveyed the empty cans and bottles on the kitchen counter. 'Did the four of us really get through all those?'

Izzy nodded. 'How's Beth?'

'Still asleep,' I said. 'I don't suppose you've seen Alex this morning? He seems to have gone out.'

'No, I haven't seen him.' Izzy leant against the counter. 'Anna, I – I think I made a bit of an idiot of myself last night.'

'No, you didn't –' I began. 'Well, maybe you did, just a little. But I wouldn't worry about it. You weren't the only one.'

'I'm so embarrassed. Alexandre must think I'm desperate, prancing around in front of him like that.'

'Forget it, Izzy. It's really no big deal.'

'It is to me. I'm mortified.'

Mortified but not heartbroken. She'd get over it.

'Izzy, can I ask you something? After Natalie's party, did you sleep with Alex?'

Izzy's eyes widened. 'No, I did not. I'm an old-fashioned girl. I want the first time I have sex to be with a man I love – and who loves me.'

'You've never been with a guy?'

Izzy shrugged. 'The right man hasn't come along yet. I did think that maybe Alexandre was going to be the one, but he obviously isn't interested.'

Well, I had told her.

'Anyway,' Izzy continued, 'I wanted to hang around until you got up – I couldn't leave without thanking you for putting

100

up with me last night – but I'd rather not face Alexandre. So I'll be getting off home now.'

'OK, Izzy.' I followed her out into the hall.

Izzy put on her coat and picked up her bag. 'I'll see you on Monday.'

'Yes, see you at work.'

Izzy left. I'd only just closed the front door, when a pale and bedraggled Beth staggered out of my bedroom.

'Morning,' I said. 'How are you?'

She burst into tears.

That bad. 'Oh, don't cry.' I went to her and led her back into my room. She slumped down on my bed. I sat beside her while she sobbed, and passed her a box of tissues when she stopped. She blew her nose, and wiped her tear-stained face.

'I kissed Alex,' she said. 'I went to his bedroom and I kissed him.

'*You* kissed *him*? He didn't kiss you back? It usually takes two.'

'He just stood there – and then he pushed me away.'

How had I got it all so wrong?

Beth said, 'He must think I'm such a slut.'

'You were drunk –'

'I'm a drunken slut.'

'No, you're not.'

'What am I going to tell Rob?' Beth's hands fluttered about her face. 'Did you call him? Does he even know where I am?'

'Alex spoke to him last night, after you passed out –'

'*Alex* spoke to him. What did he say?'

'Don't panic. All he said was that you'd had too much wine and were sleeping it off.'

'I love Rob, really I do. And now I've *betrayed* him. I'm so ashamed.' Beth started crying again.

I waited until she'd got herself under control, and then I said, 'I think you're making too much of this. You were drunk and you kissed Alex – for about two seconds. It's not like you had sex with him.'

'No, but I wanted to,' Beth said.

I stared at her.

'Not that it's any excuse, but I've been so tired lately. I'm alone with the children all day, and I'm up with one or the other of them half the night. And when Rob comes home from work he only ever asks about Jonah and Molly, never about me. I don't blame him – I've turned into a frump.'

'That's not true –'

'Yesterday, at the gallery, I kept thinking how fabulous you looked and how young and pretty Izzy is, how you both have careers, and social lives that don't involve talking to other mums about potty training – and how I used to be just like you. I don't remember everything that happened after we got back to the flat, but I do remember thinking that having sex with a gorgeous man like Alex was going to prove I was still an attractive woman – despite the baby-fat and the stretch-marks.'

'And do you still think that now you're sober?'

'No! Absolutely not. I love Rob and Jonah and Molly. I'd never want to do anything that could damage my family.'

'Then stop beating yourself up. You were exhausted, you had too much to drink, and tried to snog the nearest attractive male. Never going to happen again. End of story.'

'I don't think Rob would see it like that.'

'So don't tell him.'

'I guess there's not much point – it would only hurt him.' Beth's eyes brimmed with tears, but she blinked them away. 'I should phone him …'

'Yes, you should. He said to Alex that he'd drive over this morning and pick you up. Give him a call.'

'I will. Would it be all right if I took a shower?'

'Of course. I'll lend you some clean clothes.'

'Thanks, Anna. You're a good friend.'

Not that much of a good friend, considering how rarely I'd seen her lately.

Beth said, 'Is Izzy still here? I made such a show of myself in front of her last night. I'd like to apologise.'

'Izzy's gone home,' I said. 'But she's way too embarrassed by her own behaviour to care about yours.'

'What about Alex? I wonder if he's awake. I don't know what I'm going to say to him, but I have to say something.'

'Don't worry about him. He's decided that you were too drunk to know what you were doing.'

'He said that?'

'Not exactly. He went out before I got up. But he wrote it in a letter.'

'He wrote you a letter? But you live in the same flat!'

My heart constricted. I almost told Beth about the argument I'd had with Alex, but caught myself in time. She had enough stress in her life already.

'I have to write a reply.'

Leaving Beth to call Rob and to have her shower, I found some notepaper, sat myself down at Alex's desk, picked up my pen, and wrote:

Cher Alex,

I am sorry. Last night, I said some terrible things to you. I wish I could write that I was drunk or overtired, and didn't mean what I was saying, but I won't lie to you. All I can do is to tell you that I know now I was very wrong to accuse you of using Beth and Izzy, and to ask you to forgive me.

I don't want to lose you, Alex. I don't want the letter you put under my door this morning to be the last one you write to me. I don't want you to move out of my flat. Above all, I don't want our friendship to end. You mean so much to me. I hope that you will always be in my life.

Ton amie,
Anna

I put the letter in an envelope, wrote Alex's name on the front, and left it propped up against his laptop where he couldn't fail to see it.

I found Beth standing by the living-room window, staring out into the street. 'Rob's on his way,' she said.

'Would you like some breakfast while you're waiting for him?' I said.

She grimaced. 'The only thing I could swallow right now is a painkiller. I've the most ghastly headache.'

I fetched her an aspirin and a glass of water, and joined her by the window.

'There he is,' Beth said.

Following the direction of her gaze, I saw a man in a leather jacket walking towards us on the opposite side of the road. For a moment, I thought it was Alex, and my heart leapt. Disappointment flooded over me when I realised it wasn't him, but a passer-by, and Beth was talking about her husband, whose car was drawing up at the kerb.

'I'll go down to him,' Beth said.

'He and the children are very welcome to come in,' I said.

'I know, but I'd rather go straight home. The way my head is pounding, I need to lie down.'

'OK, hun.'

I walked with her to the front door.

'Rob does love me,' Beth said. 'Deep down, I do know that.'

'I never doubted it.'

'The thing is, when you're parents, it's easy to forget that you're also still a couple.'

'Maybe you should remind him by being *extra nice* to him.'

'Now that,' Beth said, 'is a very good idea. I definitely shall – the next night I don't fall asleep in front of the television.'

We hugged, and Beth walked down the stairs and out of the building. I went back to the window. As Beth approached the car, Rob got out, a huge smile on his face. Beth went to him, and he folded her in his arms and kissed her very thoroughly. It was some time before they broke apart. Rob got back into the driver's seat. Beth looked up at my flat and waved to me, before she too got into the car, and Rob drove off.

Beth and Rob were going to be fine. I only hoped I'd be able to say the same about me and Alex.

I looked up and down the street. Still no sign of him.

By now it was gone midday, and I was still in my pyjamas. I showered and dressed. I thought about making myself some lunch, but then decided I wasn't hungry. My phone rang, and I snatched it up, thinking it might be Alex, but it was my sister, Vicky, wanting help with her French homework. Once I'd told her what she needed to know, she passed the phone to my mother, who was eager to tell me about the latest scandalous escapade of one of my cousins. I tried to feign an interest that I didn't feel, but I think my mother was disappointed in my uncharacteristic lack of enthusiasm for family gossip. After she'd rung off, I switched on the TV, flicking from channel to channel, but couldn't find any programme that was the least bit entertaining.

The front door bell rang. I went into the hall, and picked up the intercom.

A disembodied voice said, 'Hey, Anna.'

Nick.

I buzzed him into the building and opened my front door. He stepped into the communal area on the ground floor, and started walking up the stairs.

'What are you doing here?' I said to him, as he reached me.

He raised one eyebrow, and brandished his laptop. 'We agreed that I'd come over today so we could look at online travel sites. Have you forgotten?'

'Oh, no, I remember ... I just wasn't expecting you so early.' I'd completely forgotten about our plans to book a holiday, and I wasn't in the mood to start trawling through the internet, but I made myself smile.

'I've already bookmarked a few places I think you'll like,' Nick said.

'Fantastic. I can't wait to see them. You go through to the living room – I'll make us some coffee.'

As soon as I was alone in the kitchen, I took hold of my

mobile and scrolled through my address book to Alex's number. My hand hesitated over the call button. What if we had another argument? Worse, what if he wouldn't speak to me? What if he saw my caller ID on his phone and didn't answer?

'Anna?' Nick called. 'Come and have a look at this hotel.'

'I'm coming.' I needed Alex to read my letter before I spoke to him again. I put my phone back in my jeans.

I sat with Nick at my dining table, staring at his computer screen, while he brought up hotel websites and checked availability of flights. However much I tried to focus on photos of turquoise infinity pools and five-star restaurants, phrases from Alex's letter kept invading my mind.

What I can't understand is why you refused to listen to me ... Our friendship has run its course ...

Nick broke in on my thoughts. 'So am I right in thinking we've narrowed it down to one of these four hotels?'

I forced my attention back to the images on the screen. Four luxury spa hotels. Two in Greece. One in Spain. One in Sharm el Sheikh.

'What do you think, Anna?' Nick said.

This is the last letter I ever will write to you.

'They all look wonderful,' I said. 'I don't know how we can possibly choose.'

'Well, the one in Spain does have a golf course ...'

'Not that one then.'

'If you took up golf, you might enjoy it. This holiday could be a good time to learn.'

'You're not serious?'

Nick grinned. 'You can't blame me for trying. But if you really can't decide between the other three, what about this –' He brought up another website. 'It's a bit further to go, but I think it'd be worth it.'

A slide show filled the laptop screen. I saw a deserted beach with pristine white sand, a man in a wetsuit swimming with dolphins, a young couple sitting on a balcony, drinking cocktails and gazing out at the sunset ...

'It's amazing,' I said. 'Where is it?'

'It's in Mexico,' Nick said. 'It's a new all-inclusive resort.' He paused, and then he said, 'I take it you prefer this to the other hotels we looked at?'

'Yes.'

Nick's blue eyes searched my face. 'You don't sound very enthusiastic.'

'Oh, I am. I just didn't think we'd be going anywhere so exotic.' And all I wanted right now was for Alex to come home.

Nick smiled. 'The best time to visit that part of the world is in June ...' He clicked through the rest of the slide-show, and brought up a page about the hotel.

'Oh. My. Lord,' I said. 'Have you seen those prices? Much as I would love a holiday in paradise, I simply can't afford it.'

'But I can.' Nick put his hand over mine. 'I earn a lot more than you. I'll pay for both of us.'

'I can't let you do that –'

I heard the front door open and close and footsteps in the hall.

'Sounds like Alex has just come in,' Nick said. 'Been out all night again, has he?'

'Not that I'm aware,' I said. 'Actually, I need to talk to him –'

'Now?'

'Yes. I'll be right back –'

I hurried out into the hall. Alex's door was closed. Taking a deep breath, I opened it and went into his bedroom. He was standing by his desk, reading my letter. When he'd finished, he let it fall from his hands, and looked at me.

'*Je suis désolée,*' I said. 'Can you forgive me?'

In two strides he was across the room, and pulling me into his arms. 'Do you really need to ask?'

'I'm so sorry.' I slid my arms around his waist, and rested my head on his chest. 'I said such mean things to you – When I read your letter, I thought I'd destroyed our friendship – and I couldn't bear it.'

107

'I was angry when I wrote that letter. So angry that I spent the entire morning walking around the streets on my own just to clear my head. Once I'd calmed down, I realised I couldn't just give up on you – on us.' He held me a little tighter. 'You're important to me, Anna, and you always will be.'

I could feel his heart beating, and the heat of his body through his shirt.

I said, 'I don't know why I got so mad at you last night, I really don't.'

'It was just a stupid argument.'

'I should have listened to you.'

'Forget it.'

Nick's voice sounded from the living room, 'Anna, are you going to be much longer?'

Alex's body tensed, and he let go of me. We took a step away from each other.

'Nick's here,' I said, somewhat unnecessarily. 'We're planning our first holiday together.'

Nick called out, 'Hurry up, Anna, if we're going to get the trip we want, we need to make a reservation.'

'I should go,' I said.

Alex nodded.

I headed out of the room. In the doorway, I turned and looked back at him.

'I will always be your friend,' I said.

'*Je sais,*' he said. 'I know.'

Fourteen

Alex put his head around the living room door.

'I'm going for a run,' he said. 'Do either of you want to come with me?'

Nick dragged his attention away from the television. 'Not me. This is a very important match. And I don't have any running gear with me.' Rather stiffly, he added, 'Thanks, all the same.'

I glanced at the window. Outside, the sky was bright and clear, and the first blossom had appeared on the cherry tree that grew in the front garden of the house opposite. I wouldn't have minded a run with Alex (assuming he'd match his pace to mine), but I suspected that Nick wouldn't appreciate my deserting him, even though he was watching the rugby.

'I'm not much of an athlete,' I said to Alex.

Alex laughed. 'No, I remember that about you. See you later.'

When he'd gone, Nick asked, 'What did you say to Alexandre that was so funny?'

I looked up from the book I was reading, the signed novel that Alex had given me. 'Didn't you hear me?'

'You were speaking in French again.'

'Was I? Sorry. I just reminded him that I'm a slow runner.' Note to self: Do not speak French to Alex in front of Nick.

'Oh.' Distracted by the action on the television screen – there was a lot of cheering and whistle-blowing – Nick made no further comment. Much to my relief. I'd had enough drama that weekend, and I certainly didn't want another argument with my boyfriend about Alex.

My mobile rang, and Beth's name and number appeared on the screen. I hit the answer button.

Beth said. 'Are you alone?'

'Just a sec.' I went into my bedroom. 'Nick's in the flat, but he can't hear me. How are you? Feeling better, I hope.'

'I'm a whole lot better than I was yesterday. I honestly don't remember ever having such a terrible hangover. All I could do was lie on the sofa with a cold flannel on my forehead. Rob had to put the kids to bed – for the second night in a row – and cook the dinner.'

There was a pause, and then Beth said, 'Rob and I had a serious talk last night.'

'You didn't tell him about your moment of madness with Alex?'

'No. I told Rob that I'd got stupidly drunk, partly because it was the first time I'd had a drink since I gave up breastfeeding and my body isn't used to alcohol, and partly because I was so tired. And then, everything just came tumbling out, how miserable I've been, how I worried he no longer found me attractive. It turns out Rob had no idea I'd been feeling so wretched.'

'What did he say?'

'The first thing he said was that I'm the most beautiful and sexiest woman he's ever met – which may not be true, but it was nice to hear.'

'Aw. That is so sweet.'

'Then he said that having looked after Jonah and Molly by himself for a couple of days, he'd realised just how exhausting they can be, and that he'd try to be a bit more of a hands-on dad – at least at weekends.'

'I thought being hands-on was compulsory for modern fathers?'

'Not when they work ten-hour days it isn't,' Beth said. 'But he's made a good start by taking the kids to the park this afternoon. Which means I've been able to call you and actually talk in complete sentences for once.'

'It does sound eerily quiet your end.'

'The other lovely thing Rob did,' Beth said, 'was to call his mum and ask her to babysit next weekend, so we could have a night out.'

'A date night!'

'What's even better, Rob told his mum that I'd been feeling tired and run-down – and she immediately offered to have the kids one afternoon a week. Seems she's been longing to get more involved with her grandchildren, but didn't want me to think she was an interfering mother-in-law. Jonah and Molly will be well looked after by their grandma – and I'll have time to do things like go to the hairdressers' – or maybe meet you for lunch.'

'Now that,' I said, 'is an excellent idea.'

'I don't want to keep going over what happened on Friday night,' Beth said, 'but I do think it was a wake-up call. It made me realise how much I love being a wife and mother, and how stupid I was to let everything get on top of me. All I had to do was talk to Rob, tell him what was wrong, and together we can put it right. Knowing he understands makes all the difference.'

'That's so good to hear, hun.'

There was a short silence and then Beth said, 'Thanks for looking after me this weekend. And for helping me to get my drunken misdemeanours into perspective.'

'Don't mention it,' I said. 'Seriously, we're not going to mention anything that happened on Friday night ever again.'

'Fine with me,' Beth said.

We chatted a while longer, and then Beth went off to do some baking before her family returned from the park ('Such a treat, Anna, I've not had time to make cup-cakes since before Molly was born'), and I went back to my boyfriend.

Seeing that the TV was showing adverts, I said, 'Is the match finished?'

'Yes – and England won.' Nick was examining my book. 'Is this any good?'

111

'It's terrific. Best book I've read this year.'

'How come you have a signed copy?'

'Alex gave it to me.'

None too gently, Nick put the book down on the coffee table. 'I didn't realise that you and Alexandre were in the habit of giving each other presents.'

'We're not. He happened to be photographing the author, and very kindly got her to sign her latest novel for me.'

'Why would he do that?'

'He knows she's my favourite writer,' I said. 'Shall we watch a DVD?'

'Actually, there's an old western just starting on BBC One that I wouldn't mind seeing,' Nick said, pointing the remote at the television.

I curled up next to him on the sofa. I'd have preferred a rom com, but I'd no objections to spending the next couple of hours in the company of a handsome cowboy. I heard Alex come in, and the sound of the shower, and then I heard him go into his bedroom.

Sunday afternoon became Sunday evening. I threw some easy-cook pasta shells into a pan of boiling water and heated up a jar of pour-over sauce (fancy cakes are Beth's culinary speciality, pour-over sauce is mine), and after Nick and I'd eaten, we watched the first episode of a new American detective series. Around nine, Nick decided that he wouldn't stay over ('I've got a conference call with our Frankfurt office first thing tomorrow, Anna, and I need to go over some figures tonight'), and went home. I was eager to get back to my book, so I didn't suggest that I go with him. Once he'd gone, it also occurred to me that I'd hardly seen Alex all day. My book could wait. I went and knocked on Alex's door.

'Nick's gone back to his, and there's half a bottle of wine left over from dinner,' I said. 'Would you like to come and help me drink it?'

There was a muffled reply, and then Alex opened the door a crack. 'I just need to put some clothes on.' He shut the door,

Behind that door, he wasn't wearing any clothes. I became aware of an intensely pleasurable sensation in the depths of my stomach. Stop it, Anna, stop it right now. I went back into the living room, and poured two glasses of wine. Alex came in almost immediately, and sat down on the sofa. He'd put on jeans and a sweatshirt, but the image of him naked kept floating into my mind.

'Nick bought this,' I said, holding out a glass. 'So it must be good. He knows about wine.'

Alex reached for the glass, but before he could take it, his phone rang. He fished it out of the back pocket of his jeans and checked the screen.

'It's my sister,' he said. '*Bonsoir,* Hélène ... *Non* ... No, it's not too late to talk. We're an hour behind you here in London, don't forget ... No, I've not heard from anyone in Paris for a couple of days ... No ... No, I didn't know that ...'

Alex's voice trailed off and to my concern, I saw that his face had turned very pale.

After listening to his sister for some time, he said, 'You were right to call me ... I'll be fine ... I'm with Anna ... Listen, I'm going to go now, I'll call you back tomorrow.' He rang off, and sat very still, staring at his phone.

'Alex?' I said. 'What's wrong?'

'Cécile is getting married. I shouldn't care. But I do.'

'Oh, Alex.' I went and sat next to him on the sofa.

'Hélène just heard it tonight from a mutual friend. She thought it was best to tell me straight away, rather than for me to hear it from someone else.'

'I'm sure she's right about that. Listen, Alex, this is bound to hit you hard but –'

'I can't talk about Cécile right now ... Just ... give me a minute ...' He picked up his wine and drained it. '*Merde*!'

He'd grasped the empty wineglass so tightly that it'd broken. As soon as he opened his hand to let go of the glass, blood welled up in his palm. His eyes widened with shock.

'Bathroom.' I said. 'Now.'

Seizing him by the wrist, I frog-marched him into the bathroom, and made him hold his hand under the cold tap to wash out any splinters of glass. Then I poured half a bottle of antiseptic over the cut.

'It's deep,' I said. 'It may need stiches.'

'It's nothing,' he said. 'Do you have any plasters?'

Men! I passed him a wad of cotton wool to press against the cut while I rooted through the meagre first aid supplies in my bathroom cabinet. Fortunately, I found some gauze and a bandage. He sat on the side of the bath so that I could bind up his hand. While I was doing this I was completely calm, but once I'd finished, my legs felt shaky, and I had to sit down next to him.

'Jeez, Alex,' I said.

'Yeah. Sorry about the glass. I'll replace it.'

'Forget the glass. It's you I care about. I hate to see you hurt.'

'Hearing that Cécile is getting married to someone else … I lost it for a moment, but I'm over it now.'

I wished he was over her. I felt so protective of him. This lovely guy, who was still in love with the girl who'd betrayed him and broken his heart.

Alex examined his bandaged hand and wriggled his fingers. 'My hand is throbbing like hell, but I don't seem to have damaged anything vital.'

'I still think you should have gone to A&E. Do you want some aspirin?'

He smiled. 'I'd rather have another glass of wine.'

'How very French.'

He stood up, and with his good hand helped me to my feet. His dark eyes met mine.

He said, 'That photograph of you that I want to take – Would you be able to get an afternoon off work next week to come into the studio?'

I nodded. 'As long as I have a couple of days' notice.' Nick wasn't going to like this, though.

114

'*Bon.* I'll let you know exactly where and when.'

Note to self: Do not tell Nick that you're posing for Alex.

'I'll look forward to it.'

Fifteen

From the outside, the photographic studios looked like the run-down Victorian warehouse they'd been in a previous existence, but once I stepped through the front door, pulling my suitcase behind me, I found myself in a modern reception area, with cream leather sofas, steel and glass coffee tables, and black and white photos on grey-painted brick walls. The receptionist, seated behind a glass desk, greeted me with a dazzling smile.

'Welcome to Light Box. How may I help you?'

'Hi,' I said. 'I'm looking for Alexandre Tourville. He's on *The Edge* shoot.'

'Oh, yes, Alex is here today.' The receptionist smiled even more broadly. 'May I ask your name?'

I wondered if smiling was part of her job description, or if it was sharing her workplace with a certain handsome photographer that made her so cheerful.

'I'm Anna Mitchel.'

'Super.' Another smile. 'Alex is in Studio One – just along the corridor.'

I left her still beaming, trotted along the narrow corridor to Studio One, and went inside.

I was in a large, airy, white-painted room. Directly in front of me was a seating area with a couple of armchairs, and beyond that a work bench with a mirror surrounded by light bulbs. Through an archway, I saw a small kitchen, where a girl of about twenty with a mass of blonde curls was washing up plates and coffee mugs. Various items of furniture – a rocking chair, a brass bed – and painted canvas backdrops lined one wall. At the far end of the room, amidst a forest of bright lights

117

made all the brighter by silver reflectors, Alex was photographing a group of young men and women posed in front of a white backdrop. As I watched, fascinated to see him at work, he said something that made them all laugh. A bespectacled, grey-haired make-up artist, the elder of two women hovering at the side of the shooting space, darted in to retouch smudged lipstick.

At that moment, the blonde girl came out of the kitchen. 'Hello there. I'm Louise, Alex's assistant. You must be his friend Anna.'

'Yes, I'm Anna,' I said.

'Good to meet you. If you take a seat in the make-up area, I'll let Alex know you're here.'

While I sat perched on a swivel chair in front of the mirror, Louise went up to Alex and alerted him to my presence. He smiled and waved at me, before returning his attention to his job.

Louise came back, bringing the grey-haired woman with her.

'This is Maggie, who's going to do your make-up,' she said.

Maggie and I exchanged the usual pleasantries, and then I had the strange experience (strange for me, at any rate) of having someone else make up my face. Louise looked on, telling me that today was only the third time she'd worked as Alex's assistant, and that she hoped *desperately* that he'd ask for her again.

'He's so good at what he does,' she said. 'If I get the chance to go on working with him, I'm sure I'll learn more about being a photographer than I ever learnt in college.'

Maggie said, 'He's a talented young man – not to mention he's also very easy on the eye. If I were thirty years younger …'

Louise grinned. 'He's gorgeous, isn't he? But don't tell my boyfriend I said that.'

They smiled conspiratorially. Louise, muttering something about memory cards, re-joined Alex on set, while Maggie continued to work on me.

'There,' she said, eventually. 'You're done.'

I surveyed myself in the mirror. Somehow, using much less make-up than I'd slap on for a day at the office, Maggie had made my eyes look bigger my lips fuller, and had found contours in my face that I didn't know I had. I'd been surprised when Alex had insisted that I turn up at the studio without my usual lashings of mascara, but now I understood why.

'Oh, my goodness,' I said. 'I look incredible. Thank you.'

Maggie laughed. 'You're a pretty girl, Anna. I really didn't do that much – Ah, it looks like Alex is almost finished ...'

I saw that Alex was no longer taking photographs, but talking to the other woman who'd been watching the shoot (Maggie told me she was *The Edge's* art director), breaking off to say goodbye to his models as they donned coats and trooped out of the studio. The art director soon followed, nodding at Maggie, and looking at me with unashamed curiosity as she headed towards the door. While Louise switched off lights and folded tripods, Alex sauntered over to the make-up area.

'Anna's all ready for you,' Maggie said to him.

He tilted up my chin and examined my face. 'She looks great. Very natural – just how I wanted her. Thanks, Maggie, you're a star.'

'You're welcome,' Maggie said. 'Well, I'll be getting along. I've enjoyed working with you, Alex.'

'Likewise,' Alex said.

Louise appeared at Alex's side. 'I'll be off, too – unless you'd like me to stay on for a bit, and help you set up for your session with Anna.'

'Thanks, Lou,' Alex said, 'but I can take it from here.' He added, 'You did really well today. I hope we'll be working together again very soon.'

When Alex had declined her offer to stay on longer at the studio, Louise had been unable to hide her disappointment, but now her face lit up with delight.

'Thank you,' she said. 'Thank you so much.'

She and Maggie left together, and Alex and I were alone.

'Anna,' he said. '*Tu es très belle aujourd'hui.*'

'*Merci,* Monsieur.'

'I've only got the studio for another hour. Shall we get started straight away?'

I nodded. '*D'accord.*'

'I want to begin with some photos of you in your white shirt. You can change behind that curtain, while I set up the first shot.'

Retrieving my suitcase, I went behind the curtain that screened off a corner of the studio, where I found a clothes rail, a chair, and a full-length mirror. I hung up the garments that Alex had picked out from my wardrobe the previous evening, wriggled out of my jeans and jumper, put on my over-sized shirt, which hung to my knees, and ran a comb through my hair. By time I emerged from behind the curtain, Alex had moved the brass bed onto the set, and replaced the white backdrop with one painted and textured to resemble a crumbling plaster wall. The scene was lit with a soft, diffused light.

'This set looks like the background to a painting.'

'That's the intention,' Alex said. 'I've got this image in my head – a girl waking from a deep sleep and – well, you'll see. If you could lie on the bed, on top of the sheet.'

I walked over to the bed and lay down on my side, facing Alex. He checked the lights, and then picked up his camera and pressed the shutter.

'Relax, Anna,' he said, still clicking away. 'Look directly at the camera – now shut your eyes – straighten your right leg – open your eyes – hold still – undo another button on your shirt – looking good, *mon amie.*'

At first I found it hard to hold myself in the positions Alex wanted, and at the same time look natural and relaxed, but he was very patient with me. Once I got into the way of following his instructions, I found that I actually liked being photographed – and being assured that I was beautiful, and that the camera adored me. I was sorry when he told me to take a break.

I sat up. 'Am I doing all right?'

'You're doing great,' Alex said, 'but the shirt isn't working for me. Can you undo a couple more buttons and let it hang off one shoulder?'

'Like this?'

He tilted his head to one side. 'It still doesn't look right. It's too modern, too twenty-first century. I want these photos to be timeless.'

'Shall I get changed into something else?'

Alex regarded me thoughtfully. 'What would work best for the effect I'm trying to create, is for you not to wear anything at all. Would you be comfortable with that?'

'You mean – in the photographs – I'd be n-naked?' This was so unexpected that I was completely taken aback. 'I-I don't know, Alex. I'm not exactly built like a glamour model.'

A flicker of amusement passed over Alex's face. 'I'm not a glamour photographer. I wouldn't expect you to show any more flesh in my photos than you would on the beach.'

'So the pictures would be – tasteful?' I was pretty sure I was blushing – I only hoped my naturalistic make-up was heavy enough to disguise my lack of sophistication.

'*Bien sûr*,' Alex said. 'But taking some nude shots was just an idea. I completely understand if you'd rather not.'

I thought of the many paintings, and line drawings of nude women – and men – that hung in art galleries all over the world. It seemed to me that Alex, a professional photographer, was just as much an artist as a man (or woman) who worked in oils or watercolour. I reminded myself that photographing girls in various stages of undress was an everyday part of his work. There was a striking photo on his website of a doe-eyed, copper-haired girl, wearing no more than a scattering of russet autumn leaves, that had won a prize.

I heard myself say, 'It's fine. I don't mind.'

'Great,' Alex said. 'Go and strip off in the corner. Use your shirt as a dressing gown.'

Again, I concealed myself behind the curtain. With shaking hands, I took off my shirt and underwear. I stared at myself in

121

the full-length mirror, and thought, am I really going to do this? One part of me felt that getting my kit off was just plain embarrassing, but another part of me, the part that admired Alex's artistry, was flattered that he wanted to photograph my body. Come on, Anna, I thought, it's no big deal. It's not like it's the first time you've ever been naked in front of a guy. I put the shirt back on, took a deep breath, squared my shoulders, and pushed the curtain aside.

Alex said, 'I've switched on the "Do Not Enter" sign above the studio door, so you needn't worry about any of the Light Box people barging in on us.'

I smiled weakly. The possibility that a Light Box employee might come wandering into the studio while I was lying there butt-naked hadn't occurred to me.

Now what did I do? Was there an etiquette for nude modelling? 'Shall I get back on the bed? D-do you want me to take off the shirt now?'

'*S'il vous plait.* I'll turn around while you cover yourself with the sheet.'

He swung around on his heel. I dropped my improvised dressing gown to the floor, flew over to the bed, and dived under the cotton sheet, pulling it up to my chin.

'I – I'm decent now,' I said.

Alex came and stood by the bed. 'Lie on your front. Turn your head towards me.'

I rolled onto my stomach.

'I'd like to arrange the sheet so that it's only covering your hips,' he said. 'Are you OK with that?'

'Ye-es,' I said.

Alex leant over me, and I caught the scent of his aftershave. He took hold of the sheet and raised it up in the air, letting it fall so that one corner was draped in soft folds across my rear, leaving my back and legs bare.

He said, 'Rest your head on your right arm – let your left arm hang over the mattress – bend your left leg towards me – that's it – *merveilleux* – close your eyes –'

His voice caressed me, a mixture of English and French, telling me I was wonderful. The awkwardness and tension I'd felt earlier faded away. I thought, I can do this.

He said, 'Keep your eyes closed – I just need to fetch a prop.'

His footsteps retreated across the studio and returned. I felt his hand brush against my shoulder as he put something down on the bed. A pleasurable shiver ran along my spine. I heard the whir of his camera.

'Will you try something for me, Anna?' he said. 'Imagine that you're in your own bed, and it's the morning after you've slept with a man for the first time. Think about your first night with Nick, if you like.'

I imagined how a girl might feel after a night with Alex. A warm glow spread through my entire body.

Alex said, 'Now, open your eyes.'

I did as he asked.

'Ooh.' By my head, there was a red rose.

'*C'est parfait!*' Alex walked round the bed, photographing me from different angles. 'The expression on your face when you saw the rose was exactly what I hoped for.' His mouth lifted in a smile. 'Your lover has gone, but he has left a rose on your pillow. *Il est romantique, ne c'est pas?*'

'It's very romantic.'

Alex took a few more shots and then he lowered his camera.

I hope he likes what he sees, I thought,

'Anna –'

'Alex?'

'We're out of time. We'd better call it a day.'

I sat up, instinctively folding my arms over my breasts. 'You can't have been photographing me for a whole hour!'

'Almost. I'll give you some privacy while you go and get dressed.' He turned around and walked to the other end of studio.

The sensuous languor that had stolen over me during the shoot, the *frisson* of pleasure I'd experienced as Alex's dark eyes rested on my naked body, was replaced with an urgent need to be wearing clothes. I clambered off the bed, snatched my shirt up off the floor, and scurried back behind the curtain. It seemed to take forever to hook up my bra and squeeze into my skinny jeans, but once I was fully dressed, I felt a whole lot calmer. I re-packed my suitcase, and joined Alex, who was sitting at the workbench, studying his laptop.

He said, 'The photos are great, Anna.'

'You've downloaded them already? Let me see!'

'Not before I've had a chance to edit them.' He closed his laptop. 'You make a terrific model.'

I strongly suspected that professional models did not indulge in unprofessional fantasies about their photographer, but decided this was not a subject I was going to bring up with Alex.

'You made it easy for me,' I said.

'I hope I did. It's important for a photographer and his model to have a good rapport. His or *her* model, I should say. Particularly as I learnt most of what I know about photography from a woman.'

'Caroline?'

'Yes. I like to think I can pass on the skills she taught me to my own assistants.' As always, when he talked about photography, Alex's eyes shone. 'Lou, for instance, has the makings of a good photographer. She has much to learn, but she is an eager student, and I never have to tell her something more than once. It will be my pleasure to help her, the way Caroline helped me.'

I said, 'I wish I felt about my job the way you do about yours. Not that I don't like working at Nova Graphics – but it isn't my *passion*. Do you know what I mean?'

'Yes, I do. There are times when I find it hard to believe that people actually pay me money to take photographs. I'm very fortunate.' He got to his feet, and picked up his laptop and camera case. 'We should make a move.'

'Sure.' I took a last look around the studio. 'Where's the

rose?'

'I threw it away.'

'That rose was a gift from my lover! A red rose – the symbol of true love. And you *threw it away?*'

Alex laughed. *'Je suis désolé.'*

'I don't know why you're laughing, Alexandre Tourville.' I smiled at him, and he smiled back.

'Let's get home, Anna. I'm going out later, but I'd like to make a start on editing your photos tonight.'

As soon as we were back at my flat, Alex vanished inside his bedroom, dismissing my suggestion that I watch him edit the photos with a firm shake of his head. I went into the living room, and managed to read Verity Holmes' novel for a whole twenty minutes before going and knocking on his door.

'Would you like a coffee?' I said.

'Non, merci.'

'Some wine?'

'Go away, Anna.'

With a sigh, I returned to my book.

It must have been nearly two hours later when Alex came into the living room and set down his laptop on the dining table.

'Now, you may see,' he said. 'This is not the only good photo of you that I shot this afternoon, but it is, I think, the best.' He pulled out a chair and gestured for me to sit.

I looked at the screen and saw that it was filled with a black and white photograph of me reclining languidly on the brass bed. I was obviously naked, the white sheet barely covering my hips, the swell of my breasts clearly visible above the arm that I'd flung carelessly across my body. A smile played about my mouth, as I looked dreamily at the rose. The scene was bathed in a pale light, suggestive of the early morning.

My voice came out as a whisper, 'The photograph … It's beautiful … sensual … exquisite. Oh, Alex.'

'*You* are beautiful.'

'In this photo, I am.'

'Let me show you some of the others.' Alex leant over my shoulder, and brought up more of the photos that he'd taken that afternoon. I studied each of them, the full-lengths and the close-ups, the photos of me naked and the others where I was wearing the shirt, and to my delight, I realised that I looked beautiful in every one of them.

'These photos are amazing,' I said. 'You've made me look wonderful.'

'I'm glad you like them. I hope Nick does too.'

Nick. Until that moment, I hadn't given a thought as to how he might feel about my stripping off for a photographer. Or how he might react if that photographer were Alex.

Nick could not find out about these photographs – I couldn't face another row.

'You're frowning,' Alex said. 'What's wrong?'

'It's just that – I don't think Nick would be very happy if he discovered that his girlfriend had been posing for photos without any clothes on. I didn't even tell him about the shoot.'

Alex raised his eyebrows. 'I didn't realise Nick was so uptight. Or is it just that he's English?'

'Don't joke, Alex, this is important. I think these photos are works of art, but Nick wouldn't see them that way. So please don't show them to him. Or anyone else.'

'I won't, if you don't want me to.'

'Thank you. *Merci.*'

Alex gave a very Gallic shrug. 'I wouldn't want a photograph I'd taken to cause problems between you and Nick.'

'When you were photographing me, I got so caught up in the moment, I didn't think it through.'

'Don't worry about it. I understand. I'll email you copies of the photos I've edited, and you can print off any that you want.' He grinned. 'You can always hide them somewhere your jealous boyfriend won't find them.'

'That is *so* not funny.' I couldn't help smiling.

'It so is.' Alex stretched, and looked at his watch. 'I have to go out. An American friend of mine, a photo-journalist, is in

London for a couple of days, and I've said I'll meet him for a drink. Would you like to come too? He's an interesting man.'

I hesitated. The thought of spending the rest of the evening in the company of Alex and his photo-journalist friend was very tempting, but I was expecting Nick to come round after he'd finished work. Briefly, I considered texting him and telling him not to come.

I can't tell Nick I'd rather go for a drink with Alex and a total stranger than spend time with him, I thought.

'I'd love to meet your interesting American, but I can't tonight. My jealous boyfriend is working late, but he's coming on here afterwards.'

'I'll say goodnight, then. You'll probably be asleep by the time I get back.'

'*Bonne nuit*,' I said. 'Just so you know, *mon ami,* I enjoyed modelling for you today.'

'I enjoyed photographing you,' Alex said.

An hour or so after Alex had gone out, leaving me alone, I was lying on the sofa reading the last chapter of Verity Holmes' novel, when I had a phone call from Nick. Whatever it was that he and his hand-picked team were working on (he did tell me, but I'd no idea what he was talking about) was still not completed to his satisfaction. He couldn't see himself getting away from his desk much before midnight.

'It's best I don't come over to your place tonight,' Nick said. 'I have to be back in the office very early in the morning. The Frankfurt team are flying in tomorrow, and I need to set up for my presentation.'

If he'd phoned an hour earlier, I could have gone out with Alex.

'I hope you don't mind,' Nick said, but I did.

Through gritted teeth, I said, 'It's fine. Don't worry about it. I know this … assignment … you're doing is important.'

'It's a huge project. If it goes well, it could mean a promotion.'

127

'That's good,' I said. 'I mean, that's great.'

'I'll see you on Saturday.'

'Yes,' I said. As an afterthought, I added, 'Good luck with your presentation.'

'Thanks –' He broke off to listen to something another person was saying. 'OK, I'll be right with you – Anna, I'm going to have to say goodnight.'

'Night,' I said, but he'd already ended the call.

I could have been with Alex right now.

I picked up my book and opened it.

If I'd prefer a night out with a friend to a night in with my boyfriend, what did that say about my and Nick's relationship? I tried to read the last few pages of my book, but the words swam before my eyes.

What did I feel for Nick?

My hand shook, and the book slid from my grasp. On trembling legs, I stood up, went over to the window, and stared unseeing out into the street.

Did I love him?

I cast my mind back over the last year – almost a year and a half – that Nick and I'd been together to the day we'd met, remembering how delighted I'd been to discover that the tall, good-looking man seated next to me at my old friend Polly's wedding was single. Having chatted and danced with him for most of the reception, I'd flushed with pleasure when he asked me to have dinner with him the following week. I'd been on some truly awful dates since I'd last been in a steady relationship, and it'd been wonderful to be wined and dined by an intelligent, well-mannered man like Nicholas Cooper. Soon we were seeing each other two or three times a week, and after a month or so, when he asked if he could stay the night, I'd no hesitation in saying yes. It was a couple of months later that he'd told me he loved me. I'd been so happy that night, contentedly drifting off to sleep in my boyfriend's arms …

I tried to recall the last time being with Nick had made me feel completely content. I honestly couldn't remember.

Sixteen

On Saturday evening, Nick arrived at my place with an Indian take-away, which we ate sitting opposite each other at my dining table, while he talked about his presentation to his German colleagues.

'It went even better than I expected,' he said. 'Nothing's been confirmed, but my chances of promotion are looking pretty good at the moment.'

'I'm so pleased for you.' I was, but no more pleased than I would be for any one of my friends who'd told me they'd got a promotion at work.

'It'll also mean a significant increase in my salary, of course,' Nick said.

'I'm sure it's well-deserved.' Was it love I felt for him? Or was it that I was just used to being half of a couple?

'More money for us to spend on trips abroad like our holiday in Mexico.'

'Mmm.' If I don't love him, I wondered, how can I spend two weeks with him in a luxury resort?

'Do you want that samosa?' Nick said.

'No, you have it.' I'd only eaten half my chicken tikka, but I no longer had any appetite.

Nick said, 'I know some people claim that having a well-paying job isn't important to them, but I happen to believe it is.'

He sounded so pompous. How had I never noticed before? Maybe I was blinded by love. And maybe now I wasn't.

Nick said, 'A man who doesn't have a career structure or a guaranteed income can't possibly plan for the future the way he should. Take your friend Alexandre, for instance: working freelance, he'll never be financially secure.'

'Alex does OK. More importantly, he's doing something he feels passionate about. Photography is more than a job to him – it's part of who he is.'

'Well, perhaps it's different for creative types, but I couldn't live the way he does.'

'No, I don't suppose you could,' I said. 'More biryani?'

Nick proceeded to spend the rest of the meal re-enacting his presentation. I pushed my food around my plate.

Later, while I cleared the table, Nick, without asking what I wanted to do for the rest of the evening, switched on the TV, flicking through the channels until he found the football. Smothering my irritation, I went and stacked the dishwasher, made coffee, and counted slowly to ten before re-joining him on the sofa. Unexpectedly, he put his hand on my thigh.

'The match'll be over in twenty minutes,' he said, never taking his eyes off the screen. 'Then we'll go to bed.'

Was he planning on us having sex tonight? For the first time in my life, I was tempted to tell a man I was sleeping with that I had a headache.

I lay on my back staring up at the shadows on the ceiling. Nick, lying beside me, was snoring. I elbowed him in the ribs, and he stopped. I turned onto my side. It was just light enough for me to make out his features. He looked younger with his face relaxed in sleep. Did I love him? An hour or so earlier, when he'd got into bed and reached for me, I hadn't feigned tiredness or told him I wasn't in the mood, but pulled him to me and held him desperately tight while he banged away on top of me. It wasn't the worst sex I'd ever had, but when he'd rolled off me and gone straight to sleep, all I'd felt was relief.

The sound of the front door opening and shutting told me that Alex had just come in. He'd been going out that night with a bunch of guys from *The Edge*'s art department (for someone who'd only been living in London a couple of months, he'd certainly established an impressive social life), but as far as I could tell from the footsteps in the hall, he'd come home alone. Suddenly, I wanted desperately to talk to him, to talk through my feelings towards Nick, and to ask his advice. I sat up and swung my legs over the side of the bed. Nick stirred and muttered, but didn't wake up. I sat very still, as the thought came to me that talking to Alex about Nick, when Nick so patently disliked him, would be incredibly disloyal to my boyfriend. There were enough things that I'd shared with Alex that Nick knew nothing about, without my adding to them. If I stayed with Nick, if I wanted to make our relationship work, I would have to start putting him before anyone else in my life, including Alex. *If* I stayed with Nick.

Seventeen

'Did you have a good weekend?'

I looked up from my computer screen to see Alfie hovering in front of my desk, his earphones dangling from his hand.

No, I did not have a good weekend, but I didn't want the whole of Nova Graphics to know that I was having serious doubts about my relationship with my long-term boyfriend.

'Yes, thanks.'

'What did you do? Go out with Nick?'

'I did see him, but we didn't go out. He's had a lot on at work recently, so we spent most of Saturday and Sunday relaxing in front of the TV. What about you?'

'Oh, I didn't do anything much, either,' Alfie said. 'Did you see Alexandre over the weekend?'

I raised my eyebrows. 'He lives in my flat so do I tend to see him occasionally.'

Alfie shifted his weight from one foot to the other. 'I've been wanting to ask you something about Alexandre. Well, not so much about Alexandre as about him and Izzy. She hasn't talked about him in days. Do you know why?'

I glanced towards the other end of the office where Izzy, a smile of satisfaction playing about her mouth, was engrossed in designing a new menu for a Greek restaurant. Since the debacle of our trip to the National Gallery, she seemed to have recovered completely from her infatuation – and her embarrassment. Only that morning, I'd been thinking how much I preferred working with her now that she'd stopped mooning over Alex and was back to her normal bubbly self.

I said, 'Izzy has decided that Alex isn't boyfriend material.'

'Really?' Alfie's face lit up. 'Do you think I might stand a chance with her?'

Izzy had never given me any indication that she viewed Alfie as anything more than a guy she happened to work with. There again, she'd never said that she *didn't* find him attractive.

Choosing my words with care, I said, 'Izzy's the only person who can answer that.'

Alfie sighed. 'I really want to ask her out on a date, but if she turns me down, it's going to make working with her very awkward.'

'Then why don't you keep it casual? Invite her to go for coffee or a drink after work – as a friend. Spend some time alone with her. See what comes of it. No pressure.'

Alfie pondered this for a while, and then he said, 'I may just do that. If I can find the right moment.' He turned to go, but then he turned back to me. 'Thanks for the advice, Anna. It's good to get a female perspective.'

I watched him walk over to his desk. Izzy looked up at him and smiled. He smiled back, before sitting down, and switching on his computer. I could easily imagine them as a couple.

Ignoring a sudden impulse to march over to Alfie and tell him to get this act together, I went to meet Beth for lunch.

'You did *what?*' Beth stared at me wide-eyed.

'I took off my clothes.'

'Have I got this right? Alex says he wants to photograph you naked, so you whip your kit off?'

'Shh.' I glanced around the coffee shop. The two men at the next table were obviously listening to our conversation with great interest. Lowering my voice, I said, 'Alex is a professional photographer. I decided that posing nude for him was no different to posing for any other artist.'

'Wasn't it hideously embarrassing?'

'To be honest, I did feel awkward at first, but once I relaxed, I liked it. I felt good about myself, and my body.'

'Anna Mitchel!'

'Have I shocked you?

'Yes. No. I don't know. Taking your clothes off for a photo shoot is pretty daring. Should I be shocked?'

'See for yourself.' I fished the photo that Alex liked best, the one of me with the rose, out of my bag. 'This is mine and Alex's favourite. It's a very sensual image –'

'When you say *sensual*, do you mean *erotic*?'

'I guess some people might describe it as mildly erotic, but only because of the story it tells and the way Alex lit the set. There's nothing *explicit* about it.' I passed the photo to Beth.

'Oh,' she gasped. 'You look *amazing*.'

'That was my reaction – even if I say it myself.'

'The way you were talking, I thought it would be X-rated, but this is beautiful.' She hesitated, and then she added, 'Isn't it weird though, being around Alex after that photo shoot, knowing that he's had an eyeful?'

'No. Not at all.'

Beth said, 'I'm not a prude, honestly I'm not, but I could never pose naked for a photographer. I'd be far too shy. Besides, Rob wouldn't like it. I'm surprised Nick didn't mind.'

'Nick doesn't know.'

Beth stared at me.

'The way he feels about my friendship with Alex, I didn't even tell him about the shoot. I'm certainly not going to show him the photos. I don't want another row.'

'But – I'm not judging you – but why did you let Alex take pictures of you, if you knew it would upset your boyfriend?'

'When I was in the studio, when Alex was photographing me, I wasn't thinking about Nick.'

Beth gave me a searching look, and laid the photo down on the table. 'Anna, I know I've asked you this before, but are you and Nick still solid?'

'We're – I-I'm not sure – I –' I broke off in confusion.

'What is it?'

I couldn't speak to Alex about Nick, but pouring out my

135

troubles to a female *confidante* felt very different. And I simply had to talk to someone.

I said, 'I do care about Nick, really I do, but I don't think I'm in love with him. I don't know if I want to be with him. Not any more.'

There was a long silence, then Beth said, 'I know you and Nick have had a few arguments lately, but he's a nice guy –'

'I'm not saying he isn't. He's kind and generous, but our relationship seems to have become nothing more than a habit. It isn't enough.'

'Are you saying that you're going to break up with him?'

'I don't know what I'm going to do. But I can't go on pretending nothing's wrong.'

Beth picked up the photo and looked at it again before handing to me. I stashed it in my bag.

She said, 'Has the way you feel about Nick changed because you've got feelings for Alex?'

'No,' I said. 'It has nothing to do with Alex. I do find him attractive – every woman with a pulse finds Alex attractive – but this really isn't about him. It's about me and Nick.'

A waiter came to our table and asked if we wanted more coffee, but my lunch hour was nearly over, so I told him we'd just have the bill. We paid, scrupulously dividing the amount between us, just as we had when we were flatmates, and left the coffee shop.

'What are your plans for the rest of the day?' I asked.

'I,' Beth said, 'am going to the gym. There's a beginners' yoga class that I want to try, and I'll probably do a work-out after that. Rob's mum is giving the kids their tea, so I've no need to hurry back. What about you?'

'I'll have to see what's waiting for me in my inbox.' I hugged her, and turned to go. 'Give my love to Rob, and Jonah, and Molly.'

Beth put her hand on my arm. 'Lots of relationships go through a rough patch – as I know only too well. Think very carefully before you give up on you and Nick.'

I nodded. 'See you soon, hun.'

'Yes, see you very soon.'

Beth went off to Camden station and I started walking back to Nova Graphics, my thoughts all of Nick and what I could do to salvage our relationship. Or if I even wanted to. I had a long afternoon at my desk to get through, but my head was all over the place.

Stop stressing, Anna, I thought. Compartmentalise. Leave your troubles at the office door and concentrate on your work.

Ten minutes later, I was sitting at my workstation and logged onto my computer. I clicked on the first of the huge number of emails that had accumulated during my absence. A garden centre wanted a quote for advertising flyers. I started to draft a reply. My mind drifted to the photo in my bag. I thought about Alex, and the way his dark eyes shone when he talked about photography.

Focus, Anna.

My mobile announced the arrival of a text:

Need 2 talk 2 u!! URGENT!! Call me asap!! Love you xx Vicky xx

I doubted very much that my sister's need to talk was in any way urgent, but I was getting nowhere with the garden centre, so I called her back.

'Anna!' Vicky squealed. 'I'm on the Prom Committee!'

'I'm guessing that's a good thing,' I said. 'Well done. Congratulations.'

'It's a popularity thing,' Vicky said.

'Ah.'

'The senior prom is the most important event in the school calendar.'

'Wouldn't that be your A-Levels?'

'My what?'

'Victoria! Doing well in your exams is much more important than organising a dance.'

'Have you been talking to Mum and Dad?'

'No. But whatever they've said to you, I'm sure they're

right.'

'Honestly, Anna, being on the Prom Committee isn't going to interfere with my studies, but it *is* a really big deal. I *have* to do it right. And I need your help.'

'With what exactly?'

'I've told the rest of the Committee that I'll sort out the posters, the flyers, and the tickets, so I thought you could get those designed at your office. And if you could recommend a cheap printers, because we don't have much money –'

'Whoa ... I can't just waltz up to one of Nova Graphics creatives and tell them to design a poster for my sister's prom. They have *work* to do. For which they get paid.'

There was a heavy silence, and then Vicky said, '*Please*, Anna. I *can't* mess this up.'

I sighed. 'Does your prom have a theme?'

'A theme? Not really. It's, you know, a senior prom.'

'So we're talking girls in evening gowns and boys in tuxes? Stretch limos?'

'Oh, *yes!*' Vicky said. 'And a prom king and queen.' In a timid voice, she added, 'So will you help me with the posters and the other stuff?'

I looked towards the creatives' end of the office. Izzy and Alfie were working at their adjacent desks. Spinning around in her swivel chair, she tapped him on the arm to get his attention. Once he'd removed his earphones, she asked him a question, and he leant across to point at something on her screen. An idea began to take shape in my head.

'Anna?' Vicky said. '*Please. I'm desperate.*'

'I'll see what I can do.'

Vicky actually screamed. 'Thank you, thank you, thank you. You are the best sister *ever*.'

'Email me all the details,' I said. 'Date, time, venue.' I couldn't resist adding, 'Asap.'

'I'll do it now. Love you.'

'Bye, Vicky. Love you too.' I ended the call.

To my surprise, because my sister was the least organised

girl I knew, her email arrived almost immediately. She'd included all the information I'd asked for, and had even attached the minutes for the most recent meeting of the Prom Committee.

Meet my little sister – the event manager. I hoped she would put as much effort into her exam revision.

I got up from my desk, fetched two coffees from the machine, and walked over to Izzy and Alfie.

'Hey, guys,' I said, putting a coffee on each of their desks. 'I come bearing gifts. Or maybe that should be bribes? Anyway, I need to ask you both a massive favour.'

'Ask away,' Izzy said.

'There's not much I wouldn't do for someone who brings me a mochaccino,' Alfie said.

'My sister Vicky,' I said, 'is leaving school this year, and apparently, the crowning achievement of her academic career is for her to organise a successful senior prom – on a non-existent budget. I was wondering if either or both of you would have the spare time to design the posters – and the flyers – and the tickets?'

'Ooh, I'd love to,' Izzy said, immediately. 'I adored my school prom. My date picked me up in a white limousine, and gave me a corsage the exact shade of pink as my gown. We danced every dance ...' She smiled dreamily. 'It was *wonderful*.'

'What about you, Alfie?' I said. 'It's a lot of work for one person, but I thought maybe you and Izzy could work on it together?'

'Sure,' Alfie said. 'Happy to be of assistance. Have your sister and her friends thought about setting up a Facebook group for their prom?'

'Not as far as I know.'

'I could help with ideas for that as well, if you like. I set up a group for my school prom, and the girls all posted photos of their outfits so no one turned up on the night wearing the same dress as their BFF.'

139

'That's brilliant!' Izzy said.

'You and I should have a proper thought-showering session about this project,' Alfie said to Izzy. 'Have you had lunch yet? Shall we go and grab a sandwich and talk through some ideas?'

Izzy nodded eagerly. 'Absolutely. I'm starving.'

'Thank you both so much,' I said. 'I really appreciate this. I'll forward you Vicky's email with all the details.'

I went back to my desk and sent the email. After a few minutes, Izzy and Alfie stood up, and started making their way toward the door. As they passed my desk, Alfie caught my eye. Hanging back so that she couldn't see his face, he mouthed 'thank you' at me, before following Izzy out of the office.

Eighteen

I stood on the pavement outside Leicester Square station. The thought of spending another evening with Nick – me wondering if I should end our relationship, him cheerfully oblivious – made my stomach churn.

I couldn't go on like this. I had to make a decision.

I scanned the crowds milling about the pedestrianized square. No sign of him as yet. I checked the time on my phone. He wasn't due to arrive for another five minutes. I felt the beginning of a headache in my temples.

'There you are, Anna.'

I spun around and almost collided with him. He bent down and kissed my cheek. 'I'm not late, am I?' he said.

'Oh, no,' I said. 'I was early.'

'You were eager to see me?'

I managed a weak smile.

'You look very lovely tonight.' He put his arms around me and kissed me on the lips. 'Is that a new dress?'

'N-no. No, it isn't.' I looked up into Nick's face, noticing that he had a small cut on his chin from shaving. His blue eyes met mine. And I felt ... I felt *nothing*. That moment when he was gazing into my eyes, that was when I knew for sure. I couldn't be with him. He and I were over.

'I booked us a table for eight o'clock,' Nick said. 'It's a mild night, so I had an idea that we might do a bit of sightseeing before we eat.'

I stared at him. Sightseeing? He wanted to go sightseeing now?

'Unless,' Nick said, 'you'd rather go straight to the restaurant and have a drink?'

I shook my head.

He started walking.

'Nick, wait.' I ran to catch up with him. 'Where are we going?'

'You'll see.' He took my hand and quickened his pace. I walked beside him, knowing I was going to hurt him terribly, wracked with guilt, as he led me out of Leicester Square, over Charing Cross Road, and along Long Acre. When we came to Covent Garden, we cut across the piazza, and turned left onto the Strand.

I didn't want to be with him. My thoughts skittered around my head. I had to break up with him.

'I thought you could show me your favourite view,' Nick said, letting go of me.

We'd reached Waterloo Bridge.

Tell him. Tell him now, I thought.

'Where's the best place to stand?' Nick said. 'In the centre, I guess.'

Before I could put out a hand to stop him, he marched purposefully onto the bridge. Wordlessly, I followed him. When he reached the middle, he stood still and rested his elbows on the parapet, looking upstream. I did the same. It was dusk, and the lights of the buildings along the riverfront – the bright circle that was the London Eye, the yellow glow of the Houses of Parliament – were reflected in the dark waters of the Thames. I waited for Nick to make some comment about the view, but he seemed content to contemplate the scene in silence. I stood next to him, my heat thudding in my chest, unable to summon the words to tell him that I'd fallen out of love.

I can't break up with him while I'm looking at my favourite view, I thought. I'll tell him as soon we've left the bridge.

After what seemed a very long time, Nick turned to me and said, 'Anna, I'm thirty-two years old. I earn a good salary, and I'm confident that the considerable success I've enjoyed in my career will continue. I've been thinking about my future. Our future. Together.'

'Our f-future?' I stammered.

'I love you, Anna.'

To my consternation, he stepped away from the parapet, and knelt down on one knee on the pavement.

My head reeled. *Oh, no. Please,* please *let this not be what I think it is.*

'Anna Mitchel,' Nick said, 'will you marry me? Will you be my wife?' Reaching into the inside pocket of his jacket, he brought out a blue velvet box. He opened it, so that I could see the ring with its cluster of diamonds that glittered inside.

This could not be happening.

'Nick, please get up.'

'Not until you give me your answer,' Nick said, with a confident smile. 'Will you marry me, Anna?'

I was standing on Waterloo Bridge. A man I didn't love had asked me to marry him. This was too awful.

'No,' I said. 'Oh, Nick, I'm *so* sorry, but I don't want to marry you.'

Nick's smile faltered, but only for a moment. He shook his head. 'You don't mean that.'

'I do – I'm sorry.'

'But – we're good together –'

'I- I'm not in love with you, Nick. I don't want to spend my life with you. *Please* get up off the pavement.'

The smile faded from Nick's face. He closed the ring box, returned it to his jacket, and got slowly to his feet.

'You don't love me?' His face had gone white.

'I don't love you,' I echoed.

Nick visibly flinched. 'I thought you were the woman who was going to bear my children.'

'Oh, Nick, don't –'

'Did you ever love me?'

'I did – but I haven't loved you for – for a while – I should have told you – I tried – I've been so confused –'

'Is there someone else?' Nick's eyes hardened. 'Is it Alexandre? Have you slept with him?'

'*What?* No. *No*!'

'Don't lie to me, Anna. I'd rather know the truth.'

'There's no one else. Surely you know me better than to think I'd cheat on you.'

'I feel like I don't know you at all.' He raked his hand through his hair. 'I think it's best if I go. I need to be on my own for a bit.'

'If that's what you want –'

'It's not what *I* want. Apparently, I can't have what I want.'

Before I could form a reply, he swung away from me and walked stiffly back across the bridge towards the Strand. I watched him until his tall frame was lost among the crowds. He didn't look back. I'd never again be able to walk over Waterloo Bridge without thinking of this moment.

I went to the parapet and looked out over the river, but the panoramic picture-postcard view was spoilt for me now. The scene blurred as my eyes brimmed with tears. I wiped them away with the back of my hand. Suddenly, I felt very tired, and wanted desperately to be at home. I headed off the bridge in the opposite direction to Nick, towards the South Bank and the tunnels that led to Waterloo Station.

By the time I reached my flat, I felt so weary that I could barely put one foot in front of the other. I vaguely remembered Alex mentioning that he was out tonight at some media event, but I knocked on his bedroom door anyway. When he didn't answer I looked inside, but his room was empty.

I hoped he came home soon. I really could have done with his company. It struck me that in the past, every time I'd broken up with a boyfriend or been dumped, the first thing I'd done had been to write a letter to Alex.

I went into the living room, kicked off my shoes, and sank down on the sofa. Shutting my eyes, I rubbed my temples with my fingers. And then, numb with tiredness, I fell asleep.

I awoke to find myself lying sideways on the sofa, and Alex bending over me, his hand on my arm.

'Anna,' he said, softly. 'Wake up.'

'I am awake. Just about.' I pushed myself upright, wincing at the stiffness in my neck and shoulders. 'What time is it?'

'Two-thirty in the morning. I've just got in. I wasn't sure whether to wake you, but you didn't look very comfortable –' He frowned. 'Why are you on your own? Where's Nick?'

'Nick and I broke up,' I said.

'*Mais pourquoi*? What happened? Did you have a fight?'

'No. Nothing like that. I realised that I'm not in love with him –' Unable to continue talking for the tightness in my throat, I burst into tears.

'Oh, Anna. *Ne pleure pas, ma chérie.*' Alex sat down next to me, and gathered me in his arms. I sobbed against his shirt, and he held me close and stroked my hair, until I was able to get myself under control.

'I don't know why I'm crying,' I said, raising my head from Alex's chest. 'It was me who ended the relationship.'

'You and Nick were together for – what? A year and a half? When you've been with someone that long, you're bound to feel sadness when you part. Even when it is your choice.'

'I am sad – for Nick. I've hurt him very badly. I was trying to find the words to tell him that we were over, and he was going on about his career, and then – it was *dreadful* – and then he asked me to marry him, and I refused him.'

'Nick proposed! *Mon Dieu.*'

'He went down on one knee. He had a ring. We were on Waterloo Bridge.'

'Your favourite London landmark.'

'Not any more.' I sat up, and tucked my hair behind my ears.

Alex put his hand over mine. 'What did Nick do after you turned him down?'

'He walked off. Out of my life. I may never see him again. There's actually no reason why I should – we've very few mutual friends. There are some things of his here in my flat that he might want, but I can send them to him – Oh …'

'What is it?'

'Our holiday. Nick spent a fortune for us to go to Mexico. If he can't cancel the trip, I'll have to pay him back my half of what it cost. It's only fair.'

Alex shrugged. 'If you say so. But if the holiday was a gift, surely Nick wouldn't expect you to pay for it, however expensive it was?'

'No, he wouldn't, but I want to do the right thing.'

'Well, you don't have to decide anything tonight.'

'Just as well, I'm too tired to think straight.' I yawned. 'We should go to bed.'

'I'm very flattered, but don't you think it's a bit soon for you to take another lover?'

'Ha, ha. You crack me up, you really do.'

Alex held out a hand to haul me to my feet.

Outside my bedroom door, he said, 'If you're up before me tomorrow, and you're feeling fragile and don't want to be on your own, come and wake me.'

'I will. *Merci.*'

'Maybe we could go out? I saw a sign outside the pub down the road advertising Sunday lunches. All these weeks I've been in London, I've still not had a traditional English roast.'

'We should certainly rectify that.'

He kissed each side of my face. 'Goodnight, Anna. *Á demain.*'

'*Bonne nuit.* See you tomorrow.'

He went off to his room. I went into mine, and started getting ready for bed.

Nineteen

I slept late the following morning, and would have slept on even longer if it hadn't been for the ringing of my mobile phone. By the time I'd picked it up off my nightstand, it had stopped ringing. I groaned when I saw that I had a missed call from Nick. Then my phone announced the arrival of a text:

I have to talk to you. Call me when you get this. N.

Knowing that I'd have to speak to him at some point, if only to find out how much I owed him for the holiday, I called his number, but his phone went straight to voicemail. I left a message to say that I was returning his call, and phoned Beth.

'Anna,' she said, 'I was just thinking about you. How are things with Nick?'

'We broke up.' I wondered how many more times I was going to have to utter those words before every one of my acquaintance was aware that Anna Mitchel and Nicholas Cooper were no longer a couple. I described to Beth what had taken place between me and Nick the previous night, and how I'd come home and cried all over Alex.

She listened without interruption, and when I'd finished, she said, 'I'm not surprised you were upset. You and Nick were together a long time. You'd have to be heartless not to feel bad for him after you'd turned down his proposal.'

'That's more or less what Alex said to me last night.'

Beth was silent for a moment, and then she said, 'I have to ask … is there really nothing going on with you and Alex?'

'No,' I said, 'there really isn't.'

We chatted for a few more minutes, before Beth went off to

do a jigsaw with Jonah, and I again tried to call Nick. Again, I got his voicemail, so I left him another message, before calling my parents' landline.

'Hi, Dad, it's me,' I said, when my father answered.

'Hello, you,' my father said. 'I trust this fine spring morning finds my eldest daughter healthy, happy, and solvent.'

'Yes, I'm fine. But the reason I'm calling is that I wanted to tell you – you and Mum – I've broken up with Nick.'

'Oh, sweetheart –'

'It's OK, Dad. I'm OK. It was me who finished with him.'

'I don't need to invest in a horsewhip and hunt him down?'

'No horsewhips,' I said. 'No pistols at dawn.'

I could hear my mother in the background, saying, 'Is that Anna on the phone? Is she all right? What's wrong?'

My father said, 'Anna's perfectly all right. All that's happened is she's given Nick his marching orders.'

'They've split up? Then obviously she's not *all right*. Give me the phone – Anna? Are you still there?'

'Yes, I'm still here, and I'm really fine, but I'm no longer dating Nick.'

'Oh, darling, I'm so sorry to hear that, but if he wasn't the right man for you, better you found out now rather than after you had a joint mortgage and a dog, like your cousin Maria.'

'I didn't know Maria had a dog.'

'She doesn't any more. That was rather my point. Of course, Maria's boyfriend played away – Nick hasn't been playing away, has he? He always seemed so reliable. What we used to call a good provider.'

'Nick's done nothing wrong. I wish him well, really I do. I just don't want to be with him.'

'Was he very upset?'

The image of Nick walking away from me on the bridge floated unbidden into my head.

'Yes,' I said.

'He will get over you, you know,' my mother said, 'however much he might not believe it at the moment.'

'Yes. I know. But right now he's hurting – and I'm sorry.'

My mother said. 'I don't like to think of you sitting there all alone in your flat feeling sorry for Nick. Would you like some company? Shall I ask your father to drive over and bring you back here for the day? He won't mind.'

'Thanks, Mum,' I said, 'but I'm not on my own. Alex is here. We're going out for a pub lunch.'

'The little French boy?' my mother said. 'Oh, yes, you said he was staying with you for a few weeks.'

'He's staying 'til July.' Not that I'd describe him as little.

'He was such a sweet, polite child. Although I do remember being amazed at the amount he ate …'

'I could come over next weekend,' I said. 'I could bring my washing like I did when I was a student.'

'Don't push your luck,' my mother said. 'But it would be good to see you. I've said I'll take Vicky to buy her prom dress next Saturday – why don't come with us? We could make a day of it. It's ages since we all went shopping.'

'A mother-daughter day out does sound fun.'

'That's settled then.'

We arranged a time and place to meet up, and with many exhortations to take care of myself, my mother rang off, leaving me feeling very grateful that I had such supportive parents. That got me thinking about Nick's relatives. His mother and father were still away on their cruise, but I could imagine the gloating expression on Mrs Cooper's face when she arrived home to the news that I was no longer in a relationship with her son. She'd probably do a victory dance on her dining table. No doubt the rest of Nick's family would now dislike me as much as she did. I was sorry about that, because I'd felt that Georgina and I were on the verge of becoming friends. Not that there was anything I could do about it. When a couple broke up, there was always fall-out.

My thoughts were interrupted by a rap on my door.

Alex said, 'Anna? Are you up? Do you still want to go to the pub?'

I really should try and call Nick again before I go out. Then I thought, Nick is now my ex-boyfriend. I don't have to fit my life around him any more. 'I'll be right with you.'

At lunchtime on a Sunday, the bar of the Red Lion was packed, so while Alex queued for drinks and ordered our lunch, I went and sat at one of the wooden tables in a sheltered corner of the marginally less crowded garden. He appeared sooner than I expected, carrying two glasses of red wine.

'It's so warm today,' he said, shrugging off his leather jacket and rolling up his shirt-sleeves.

I raised my glass. '*Santé.*'

'Cheers.' Alex clinked his glass against mine.

I swallowed a mouthful of wine and looked up at the sky, enjoying the warmth of the sun on my face, hearing the murmur of conversation from the people at the other tables in the garden, and the occasion burst of laughter.

Alex reached into his jacket pocket and produced the smallest of his several cameras. 'May I?'

'*Bien sûr.*'

'Tilt your face up again.'

I did as he asked, and heard a faint click and whir.

'I try not to annoy my friends by recording their every move with my camera,' he said, 'but sometimes I cannot resist.'

'I don't mind,' I said. 'Can I take a photo of you on my phone?'

'I guess that would only be fair, as I have so many photos of you now. How do you want me? Smiling or serious?'

'Both.' I held up my phone. Alex obliged with a broad smile. Then he drew his brows together in a frown and stared moodily into the distance.

'You do brooding very well,' I said.

'Can I see?'

I passed him my mobile.

'That's not a bad composition,' he said, 'but there is a slight camera-shake. Try holding your breath when you take a photo;

that'll help you keep your hand steady.'

'I'll remember that. Now we need a selfie of both of us.'

Alex rolled his eyes, but handed me back my phone, and came round to my side of the table. I stretched out my arm and took a picture of us sitting next to each other. Looking at the result, I could only grimace.

'No good?' Alex said.

'I seem to have missed our heads,' I said, 'but it's a great shot of your shirt.'

'Shall I have a try?'

'Well, you are the professional.'

'And my arms are longer than yours, which makes taking a selfie a little easier. I think we need to be sitting closer together –'

He shifted along the bench, put one arm around me, and held out his camera with the other. His face was very close to mine, and I felt his stubble brush my cheek. Suddenly, I was acutely conscious of his strong hand resting on my shoulder, and the press of his jean-clad thigh against my leg.

'Years of training to be a photographer, and I'm taking selfies in a pub garden,' he said. 'Caroline would be horrified. There – it's done.' He removed his arm from my shoulder, and showed me the photos he'd taken. 'Not quite up to my usual standard.'

The photos might have been snapshots rather than works of art, but I couldn't see anything wrong with them.

'Well, I like them,' I said. 'Maybe not as much as the ones you took of me in the studio, but I'm pleased to have a picture of us together.'

'*Moi aussi.*' Alex's mouth lifted in a lazy half-smile. His dark hair, which he hadn't had cut since he came to England, fell forward, and he shook it out of his eyes. I had an unexpected longing to run my fingers through his hair. Low in my stomach, I felt the sinuous uncoiling of desire.

I thought that if I kissed Alex right now, he would taste of wine and sunlight. Instantly, guilt swept through me, but then I realised that being aware of Alex's attractions was nothing to feel guilty about. I no longer had a boyfriend. I was a single woman. And Alex was a single man.

My mobile rang, making me jump. I glanced at the screen, and saw that it was Nick.

'Aren't you going to answer that?' Alex said.

'No.' I switched off my phone. 'It was my *ex*-boyfriend. I'll call him later.'

'It's OK with me if you want to call him now – Ah, here's our food.'

The arrival of a waitress bearing two plates of roast beef with all the trimmings and two more glasses of red wine prevented any further discussion about Nick and whether I should call him. Alex returned to his seat opposite me, and set about devouring his lunch, pronouncing Yorkshire pudding covered in gravy to be much to his liking, and talking about the exotic dishes he'd eaten when working in Japan. I ate my meal, and listened to his travellers' tales, and dared to imagine how it would feel to lean across the table and kiss him on the mouth. What with the sunlight, the laughter, and Alex's dark eyes, I simply couldn't help myself. After we'd eaten, we strolled back home arm in arm, Alex shortening his stride to mine, while I stole covert glances at his handsome profile. We'd reached my gate, when he came to an abrupt halt.

I said, 'What's the matter? Oh –' My heart sank. Nick was standing at the top of the short flight of steps that led to the flats' communal front door. Even as I watched, he rang my doorbell, and bent his ear to the intercom. When he didn't get an answer, he craned his head backwards to look up at my windows.

Alex said, 'Would you like me to make myself scarce? I can go back to the pub –'

'No,' I said. 'There's no reason for you to go anywhere.'

At the sound of our voices, Nick turned around. His gaze went from me to Alex and his mouth became a thin tight line.

'Hello, Nick,' Alex said.

Nick gave a curt nod of his head. 'Alexandre.'

I said, 'Why have you come here?'

'I want to talk to you,' Nick said. 'As you're avoiding my phone calls, I had no choice but to arrive at your flat unannounced.'

'I haven't been avoiding your calls,' I said. 'I left you messages.'

'I'm not here to argue with you, Anna,' Nick said. 'Could we go inside?'

I said, 'Yes. Yes, of course.' Letting go of Alex's arm, I climbed the front steps. Alex followed, and the three of us stood there in silence while I rummaged in my bag for my keys. After what seemed an interminable length of time, I unlocked the door, and we all trooped in and up the stairs. On the landing there was another excruciatingly awkward pause while I let us into my flat. Alex made a tactful withdrawal into his bedroom, leaving me alone with Nick.

He cleared his throat. 'Are we going to talk here?'

'Oh, no, sorry –'

Nick took a step towards my bedroom, but I leapt past him and flung open the door to the living room. I didn't want to talk to him. I *certainly* didn't want to talk to him in the room where just a week ago, we'd had sex. I reminded myself that however hideous this meeting was for me, it was probably a whole lot harder for him.

I heard myself say, 'Have a seat. Would you like a coffee?'

'No,' Nick said, 'but thank you.'

Why was he here? Surely it wasn't just to pick up his CDs? 'You want to talk to me …'

'Yes, Anna, I do. Since yesterday – I've done a lot of thinking – I think we should start again.'

I gaped at him. I'd told him I didn't love him. I'd refused his proposal of marriage. Why would he think there was a way back from that?

'I see now that asking you to marry me was a mistake,' Nick said. 'For you, it was a complete surprise.'

'Y-yes, it was. It was a huge shock.'

Nick nodded gravely. 'As I suspected. You need more time to get used to the notion of marriage.'

'No, I don't –'

'Anna – please – just listen to me.'

I subsided into silence.

'What I think we should do,' Nick said, 'is carry on as we were. I won't put any pressure on you, I won't ask you again until I'm sure you're ready, but I'm confident that you'll soon see that at this stage of our lives, marriage makes perfect sense.'

'I won't –'

'I know I messed up yesterday. Just give me a second chance, that's all I'm asking.'

As gently as I could I said, 'I'm not going to change my mind, Nick. I'd already decided to end our relationship before you proposed.'

Nick shook his head as if to deny my words. He stood up, and before I could protest, he took hold of my wrists, pulled me to my feet, and kissed me, his mouth open and wet on my firmly closed lips.

When he broke off and I was able to speak, my voice came out as a shriek. 'Nick – *Don't* –' He immediately let me go. I stepped away from him, wiping my mouth with my hand, just as the living-room door crashed open to reveal Alex standing on the threshold.

'Is everything all right in here?' He frowned at Nick, who glared back. The tension between the two of them was palpable.

'*Oui,*' I said, quickly. '*Tout va bien.*'

'*Es-tu sûre?*'

'*Oui.*'

'*D'accord.*' Alex said. In English, he added, 'My apologies, Nicholas, for bursting in on your private conversation. It seems there has been a misunderstanding.'

Nick gave a bitter laugh.

Alex shot him a look, but all he said was, '*Cri* ... call, if you need me, Anna.' He left the room.

I said, 'Nick, this conversation is going nowhere –'

'Oh, I'm not staying,' Nick said, 'I came here today because I thought I could make you see sense, but I'm obviously wasting my time.'

'I'm so sorry,' I said. 'I never meant to hurt you.'

Nick's eyes were unforgiving and hard as blue steel. 'You would have had a good life with me, but you threw me over for your Frenchman.'

'No – I –' To my confusion, heat flooded my face. 'Alex and I – we're *friends*.'

'I was so very wrong about you.' Nick stalked across the living room and out into the hallway. The whole flat juddered as he slammed the front door.

I sank down onto the sofa. Whatever Nick thought, things had gone stale between me and him long before Alex came to London. I should never have let the relationship drag on as long as it did. Having 'my Frenchman' around had only helped me realise that.

A creaking floorboard made me look up. Alex stood in front of me, holding two large mugs.

'Your talk with Nick did not go well, I think,' he said, 'but according to my English mother, "There are few of life's tribulations that are not eased by a pot of tea".' He passed me one of the mugs, and sat down in an armchair.

'*Merci*.' Nick's anger had left me shaken, but I managed a small smile. I slowly sipped the tea, and I did actually begin to feel much calmer and more like myself.

After a while, Alex said, 'What did Nick do that made you shout at him?'

'He'd got it into his head that he could bring me round to the idea of having his ring on my finger, and to prove it, he kissed me – and I over-reacted.'

'His kissing technique is that bad?'

'Don't joke about Nick. I feel bad enough for him already.'

'*Pardonnez-moi*. I shouldn't have said that.'

'No you shouldn't, but you're forgiven. And thank you for

looking out for me. It's good to know you've got my back.'

'That is what friends do, *ne c'est pas*?'

'You are a very good friend to me, Alex.'

'I try to be. I'll even fetch you another mug of tea.' He picked up my now empty mug and went off to the kitchen.

I stared after him, this ridiculously good-looking, straight, single man who shared my home. Given the way I'd been feeling in the pub garden, I couldn't help wondering what might have happened between me and him, if Nick hadn't been waiting for us when we'd arrived back at my flat. Instead of being kissed by my ex-boyfriend, I might have found out what it was like to be kissed by Alexandre Tourville. Except that in all the time he'd been living with me in London, Alex had given me no sign that he thought of me as anything other than a friend.

And I'd been writing to him for fifteen years, signing my letters, *Ton amie,* Anna.

Twenty

Beth stared wide-eyed at me across the restaurant table. 'So what you're saying is that nothing has happened between you and Alex – but you've realised that you like him in that way.'

Alex. Nothing had happened between us, but the feelings I'd had towards him in the garden of the Red Lion hadn't gone away. Rushing past him in the mornings on the way to work, I was aware of a delicious fluttering in my stomach. The previous night, sitting next to him on the sofa reading, while he did some editing on his laptop, I'd caught myself watching his strong hands as they moved over the keyboard, and imagining how it would feel to have those hands moving over my body. I'd been quite unable to concentrate on my book.

'I do *like* him,' I said, 'I like him *a lot,* but I can't see anything coming of it.'

'Why not, now that Nick's out of the picture? Or is it too soon?'

'No, it isn't that.'

Only four days had passed since Nick had stormed out of my flat, but that had been quite long enough for me to pick up the reins of my life as a singleton. I hadn't gone into Nova Graphics on Monday morning and announced in the weekly staff meeting that I'd broken up with my boyfriend, but I had told Izzy and a couple of other people, and word had spread. I'd already received an invitation from one of my co-workers to a supper party that I doubted I'd have been invited to if I'd still been half of a couple, ('Do come, Anna, I know my brother would love to meet you.'). Outside of work, I'd phoned just a few close female friends to tell them that Nick and I were over, but I'd received enough calls and texts (Heard about u & Nick. Soz ☹. Girls' night out next week? xx) to know the gossip had reached beyond my inner circle. Polly, my old school-friend, at whose wedding Nick and I had met, called to let me know that she was determined to stay friends with both of us, and that she hoped that one day Nick and I would also be able to meet as friends. I said I hoped so too, while thinking it extremely improbable. It struck me after that call that Polly was the only one of the people I'd told of our break-up who would be likely to have any contact with my ex in the future.

From Nick, I'd heard nothing more. I'd looked up the cost of our proposed holiday on the internet and sent him a cheque for what I hoped was the right amount, along with a brief typed note, but it had been sent back by return, torn in half, with no note. I'd also sent him a parcel containing those few possessions of his he'd left at my flat (two white office shirts, a tie, a couple of classical music CDs, a rather good fountain pen). It was, I reflected, a very small package, considering the amount of time we'd been together, and indicative of how little his and my lives had become entwined. I'd had other failed relationships where the eradication of all traces of the guys from my flat had taken weeks, and the retrieval of my clothes and shoes from their homes had never achieved closure. I couldn't think of anything I'd left at Nick's place, apart from a toothbrush.

'I don't need more time to get used to being single. I'm ready to date again.'

Beth leant forward, her elbows on the table, and rested her chin on her steepled fingers. 'So what's stopping you letting Alex know how you feel about him?'

Mon ami.

I said, 'Alex has never given me the slightest hint that he wants to be anything other than my friend.'

'You mean, if you came on strong to him, and he wasn't interested … I guess it would make sharing a flat with him a

158

little problematic.'

'It could ruin our friendship.'

'Well, if posing seductively on your kitchen workshop in your underwear is out, couldn't you just flirt with him a bit? See if that sparks his interest.'

'Define "flirt a bit".'

'Honestly, Anna, I know you've been in a long-term relationship, but you can't have forgotten how to flirt. You were always so good at it. Admire the guy's biceps, and ask him how often he goes to the gym. Toss your hair. Giggle when he tells a joke and tell him he's so *funny*.'

I rolled my eyes. 'Because that would *definitely* appeal to a sophisticated twenty-eight-year-old Frenchman.'

'OK, forget the flirting,' Beth said. 'Do you want more coffee?'

'I'll get it.' The sandwich bar in which Beth and I had chosen to meet for lunch was one of those establishments that allowed its customers an indefinite number of caffeine refills. We'd decided it was going to become our regular lunchtime rendezvous.

When I got back to our table with two brimming cream-topped glasses of café latte, Beth was looking thoughtful.

'What you need,' she said, 'is for someone else to tell Alex that you fancy him, and that he ought to ask you out on a date.'

'For goodness' sake – we're not in high school.'

'Seriously, why don't I get Rob to drop a few hints the next time they play squash?'

'Seriously, no,' I said. 'Alex's friendship is important to me. I don't want to risk losing it.' I thought I'd lost it once, and I couldn't bear it.

'Alex could be feeling exactly the same way about you.'

'I'll hold that thought.' I checked my watch. 'Oh, no. I'm going to be late back at work.'

'You go,' Beth said, immediately. 'I'll get the bill.'

'You're a star – I'll pay you back next week.'

'That's OK – but you have to call me if anything happens

between you and Alex.'

If only.

Despite my high heels, I ran all the way back to Nova Graphics. How could I have let myself get so caught up in talking about Alex that I lost all track of time? I was getting as bad as Izzy.

Twenty-one

Vicky said, 'I'm going to try my prom dress on again. Which bag is it in?' With total disregard for the survival of their contents, she began rummaging amongst the numerous carrier bags on my living room floor.

'Mind out, Vicky,' I said, 'My photo frames are in that one.'

'Do you really need to put that dress on now?' my mother said.

'Here it is.' Vicky flourished the fabulous dress that was the *pièce de résistance* of our mother-and-daughters shopping trip. A gorgeous shade of coral, it had thin straps that crossed over at the back, and was tightly fitted to the waist before flaring out over the hips to fall softly to the floor.

'Aren't you glad I talked you out of the yellow organza?' I said.

'I *so* am. What was I *thinking*?' She started to pull her T-shirt over her head.

'No, don't strip off in here,' I said. 'Alex'll be home soon. Go and get changed in my bedroom.'

'Oh, yeah. You said he'd probably appear at some point. I forgot.' Holding her dress reverently before her, Vicky fairly skipped out of the room.

'*I'm* glad you talked her out of that yellow concoction,' my mother said. 'She never listens to anything I say about clothes. But who goes to their mother for fashion advice when they're a teenager?'

'I never did. Though maybe I should have. The leather dress I wore to Beth's Sweet Sixteen party – I can't believe you

161

actually let me leave the house in that.'

'Some arguments just aren't worth having.' My mother smiled at me fondly. 'Vicky showed me the posters you had designed. Thank you for doing that. This prom means so much to her.'

'Oh, that's OK. My taste in clothes may be more refined these days, but I can still remember what it's like to be eighteen and about to leave school.'

'Well, it was very generous of your friends to give up their free time.'

The posters that Izzy and Alfie had created for Vicky's prom were terrific, and I was very grateful, as I'd said to Izzy when she'd shown them to me. She'd told me that she hadn't minded in the least. Spending time with Alfie outside office hours had been fun. He'd been very complimentary about her designs, and after they'd finished the artwork, they'd gone for a curry. When I had a chance to thank Alfie, he'd told me that the pleasure was all his, and Izzy was coming over to his place the following weekend to work with him on the flyers and the tickets. I'd raised one questioning eyebrow, but he'd merely smiled and told me that he'd keep me updated.

'Vicky's prom may turn out to be one of best projects Alfie and Izzy ever work on,' I said.

My mother gave me a puzzled look, but was distracted by Vicky making her entrance in her new-bought finery. She'd caught her hair up in a messy ponytail, with curls escaping around her face, and although she wasn't wearing much make-up, she looked absolutely stunning.

'Oh, Victoria,' my mother said. 'I like that dress even more now than I did in the shop.'

'You look great, Vics,' I said. 'Really glamorous. No one would think you were a schoolgirl.'

Vicky beamed. 'I'm going to put the shoes on as well.'

My mother and I were still admiring Vicky's dress, the vertiginously high gold shoes (she was as tall as me, but had never shared my adolescent angst about her height) and the gold

162

clutch that completed her outfit, when Alex walked in. I became aware of a familiar fluttering in my stomach.

'I see you've had a successful shopping expedition,' Alex said, his gaze taking in the carrier bags strewn all over the carpet.

'We did,' I said, adding, 'Mum, you remember Alexandre?'

'I do remember you, Alex, of course I do,' my mother said, 'but I have to say that I wouldn't have recognised you. You've changed a great deal since you stayed with us.'

'While you, madame,' Alex said, 'haven't changed at all. I have many happy memories of the time I spent with Anna's family. It's very good to see you again.'

'Oh, please call me Cheryl,' my mother said, her smile broadening.

'And this is Vicky,' I said, 'who is currently modelling the gown she'll be wearing to her senior prom.'

'*Enchanté, mademoiselle.*' Alex said. 'I remember Anna's sister as a very small girl – but now you are all grown up.'

'*Bonjour*, Alexandre,' Vicky said. 'As I was only three the last time I met you, I'm afraid I don't remember you at all, but I've heard a lot about you. Anna says that you're a brilliant photographer. She talked about you all through lunch.'

As far as I recalled, while I may have mentioned Alex once or twice, it had been Vicky who had dominated our lunchtime conversation with endless wittering about the boy whose (apparently) sole ambition in life was to escort her to the prom. My mother had remarked that she hoped Vicky wasn't distracting him from his schoolbooks.

'Anna is very flattering about my work.'

Vicky glanced at me, and then she said, 'Alex, do you think you might be able to take photos at my prom? Anna says you do fashion shoots, and portraits –'

'Vicky!' I said. 'You can't expect a photographer like Alex to take pictures of teenage couples at a school dance.'

'Why not?'

'Well, for one thing, you can't afford him.'

'We can't *pay* anyone,' Vicky said. 'That's the problem. We've completely used up our budget. A boy in my class who's doing A-Level Photography has said he'll step in if we can't get anybody else to do it for free, but it would be *so* much better if we could find a *real* photographer.'

'When is the prom?' Alex said.

'It's the last Saturday in June. After all the exams are finished.'

'I'll still be in England then—'

'So you'll take the photos?' Vicky said. '*Please* say you will.'

'Alex, you really don't have to,' I said.

'*S'il vous plait, monsieur*,' Vicky said.

'How can I resist, if you ask me in French?' Alex said. '*D'accord.* I will be your prom's official photographer, mademoiselle.'

'Thank you *so* much! The Committee are going to be ecstatic.' Vicky's eyes were shining. '*Merci très très beaucoup.*'

'Vicky, you are shameless,' I said. 'You shouldn't have given into her, Alex, but thank you.'

'Yes, it really is very good of you,' my mother said.

'It will be interesting for me to see how students in England celebrate their high school graduation,' Alex said. 'Vicky, I'll talk to you again before the event. For now, if you ladies will excuse me, I've some photos I need to upload or I'm going to miss my deadline. I'll see you later, Anna.'

'*Á bientôt*,' Vicky said, as Alex left the room.

'So that's Alexandre Tourville,' my mother said. 'Didn't he turn out well? Such a charming man.'

'He's *gorgeous*,' Vicky said. She put one hand on her heart, and fanned her face theatrically with the other. 'If I'd had a hot guy like him for a penfriend, I'd be as good at French as you are, Anna.'

'He is very good-looking,' I said. 'Not that I knew that before he came to England, so I can't say that it was his square jaw and chiselled cheekbones that made me write all those letters to him.'

'He's a lot better-looking than Nick.'

'Victoria!' My mother gave Vicky a long, meaningful stare. 'Remember what I said to you before we came out.'

'You don't mind talking about Nick, do you, Anna?' Vicky said. 'Mum said it might make you upset, but it was you that dumped him, so I don't see why.'

'I expect I can hear his name without being traumatised.'

'I totally get why you got rid of Nick, now I've met Alex. Does he have a girlfriend?'

'Alex? No, he doesn't.'

'You should so get with him.'

'That's *enough*, Victoria,' my mother said. 'If Anna wants your advice about whom she should date, I'm sure she'll ask you for it. And you need to go and get out of that dress – your father will be here to pick us up in five minutes.'

'Oh, but I'd like to show Dad my prom outfit.'

'And I'm sure he'd love to see you in it, but there won't be time. We're off out to the cinema tonight, and we're on a tight schedule – especially if you want us to drop you at your friend's on the way.'

Vicky pouted, but went off to get changed. My mother started sorting the bags that contained out various purchases into separate piles.

'How long is it that Alexandre has been staying here with you?' she said.

'Nearly two months,' I said, 'and before you ask, I didn't break up with Nick because of Alex.'

'Did I say that you did?'

'Well, no.'

'That would never have occurred to me, if you hadn't mentioned it. Although now I've seen the man you're sharing your flat with, I can't help wondering – Oh, was that the doorbell? I expect it's your dad.'

The arrival of my father put an end to my mother's

speculations. Determined not to miss the start of the film, for which he'd booked tickets, he paused only long enough to shake hands with Alex (who'd let him into the flat and introduced himself before I'd got there), offer his services as the bearer of shopping bags, and give me a hug, before shepherding his wife and younger daughter outside to the car.

'Come and see us anytime, Alex,' my mother called over her shoulder, as she preceded my father down the stairs. 'Come with Anna next time she visits.'

'Thank you, Cheryl,' Alex called back. 'I will.'

'Ooh, yes, Anna,' Vicky said, 'you should definitely bring Alex with you – *OK*, Dad, I'm coming.' She clattered after our parents.

When my family had gone, I said, 'Professionally designed posters and flyers, and now a top French photographer. I reckon my sister has every chance of being voted Prom Queen. Thank you, Alex, I really appreciate it, and even if Vicky doesn't realise quite how big a favour you're doing her, I know she appreciates it too.'

Alex shrugged. 'An evening taking photographs is never going to be a hardship for me.' His face creased into a smile. 'Besides, I have every intention of making you my assistant for the night.'

'Do I get to wear a prom dress?'

'Only if I *don't* have to wear a tux.'

'Agreed.'

We smiled at each other.

Alex said. 'Are you going out tonight?'

'No,' I said, 'I may have been single for a whole week, but I've not yet filled every date in my social diary.'

'Come out with me? We could go to a club, if you like.'

'I would like. But haven't you already got plans? You're not usually at a loose end on a Saturday evening.'

'I'm on the guest list for several media events, but I'm not in the mood for networking. I'd much rather have a night out with you.'

166

'Then I would very much like to go clubbing with you tonight.'

'*Bon*,' Alex hesitated, and then he said, 'Anna ... There's something I've been meaning to say to you.'

'Is there, Alex?' We were standing very close together, so close that I could feel the warmth radiating from his body. I breathed in the tantalisingly familiar, masculine scent of his aftershave. He bent his head and looked at me through hooded eyes. The thought sprang into my head that he was about to lean in and kiss me. Suddenly, my pulse was racing.

'Those photos I took of you in the studio ...'

My voice scarcely above a whisper, I said, 'The ones where I wasn't wearing any clothes?'

'Yes. I know that you were worried what Nick might think, but now that you've broken up with him, how would you feel about other people seeing them?'

Or maybe he isn't going to kiss me. 'Oh – I – I don't know – I guess – I wouldn't mind.'

'Are you sure? Because I'd really like to show some of them to my agent. I want to reassure him that I'm not just doing commercial shoots while I'm in London.'

'I'm fine with that.' I looked at Alexandre, my childhood penfriend, who'd turned into this tall, strong, beautiful man now standing so close to me in my narrow hallway, talking about his work and his agent, and it shocked me how much I wanted him to kiss me. How much I wanted him.

'Great,' Alex said. 'I'll email them over to him before we go out.' He glanced at his watch. 'Can you be ready to go into town by 9.00?'

My head was all over the place, but I gave myself a firm mental shake and managed to answer him coherently. 'Alex! What are you insinuating? It's only seven o'clock now. When have you ever known me to take two hours to get ready to leave the house?'

'You're right. That's one of the things I like about living with you. You've never made me late for work by hogging the bathroom in the morning.'

I laughed. 'I'll see you at nine o'clock precisely.'

'It's a date.'

It isn't a date, I thought, but I wish it was.

I went into my bedroom and surveyed myself critically in my full-length mirror. After a day spent negotiating the scrum of shoppers on Oxford Street, I wasn't exactly looking my best. I only hoped that two hours was in fact enough time for me to transform myself into an elegant, classy, and at the same time highly desirable woman. The sort of woman that a ridiculously handsome French photographer would find irresistible.

Twenty-two

I lie on Alex's bed in my spare room, naked, covered by a pink floral cotton sheet, my head resting on my arm, my fair hair fanned out behind me. Alex is standing beside me. He takes a photograph. Slowly, I push back the sheet so that he can see my breasts, and then my entire body. He lowers the camera, smiles, and strips off his clothes. Then he lies down beside me, and presses his toned, muscular, naked body against mine. Somewhere, a long way off, someone is shouting angrily in French ...

I awoke to find myself in my own bed and alone. I knew I'd been dreaming, but I still half-expected to see Alex's dark head lying next to mine on the pillow, and I felt very empty when I saw that he wasn't there. The dream had seemed very real. *Get over it, Anna, it was just a dream.* I realised that I could still hear a male voice, although it was too far away for me to make out what was being said, and it soon stopped. Alex must have been speaking to someone on his phone.

I sat up, yawning, and stretching. The short black halter-neck dress that I'd worn the previous night was draped across the back of a chair. There had been an appreciative glint in Alex's eyes when I'd appeared at nine o'clock wearing that dress, and his gaze had strayed to my legs before he'd told me that I looked great. I'd smiled and tossed my hair over my shoulder (Beth would have been proud of me), and told him that he looked great too. I almost said that the dark red colour of his shirt really suited him, but I thought that might be going a little too far.

'So which club are we going to?' I said.

'I thought maybe somewhere a bit different?'

'Different sounds good.'

'The last time I worked with Lou, she was raving about a new salsa club that's just opened round the back of Covent Garden.'

'You never wrote to me that you can salsa.'

'I can't right now, but I fully intend to be an expert by the end of the night. So what do you think?'

'What I think,' I said, 'is that the six weeks of ballroom dance lessons I took four years ago might be about to come in very useful.'

The salsa club was situated in one of those narrow pedestrian alleyways that run between Covent Garden's main thoroughfares. We were welcomed at the entrance by a Hispanic man who told us, in heavily accented English, that the first hour of the night was tailored especially for beginners. Once we were inside, a rickety staircase took us down to a bar with a dance area, where couples of assorted ages were already moving to the music of guitars, piano, drums, and maracas. Alex and I hastened to join them. At the far end of the room, on a small round stage, a pair of professional salsa dancers demonstrated the basic steps, which we and the other newcomers to the club copied with varying degrees of success. My limited experience of the waltz and the foxtrot (ballroom dancing had been a very short-lived enthusiasm of mine) wasn't much help when it came to mastering the fast-paced footwork of salsa, but Alex had no trouble picking up the sequence of movements, and once I relaxed and let him lead, neither did I. We danced until the musicians took a break, and then we sat at the bar, drinking caipirinhas (I made sure I sat at an angle which gave him a good view of my cleavage), until the music started up again. We returned to the dance floor, where we were now joined by the more advanced dancers, the women rotating their hips impossibly fast, the men swinging the women in the air and bending them over backwards so that their heads almost touched the ground. The dance floor was crowded now and it grew very hot, the whole club seeming to vibrate with the salsa beat. With my hand in Alex's, spinning away from him, spinning towards him, his arm sliding around my waist, our bodies moving to the sensual rhythms, I felt as though my blood was pulsing in time with the music. I yearned for Alex to kiss me, and to see where that kiss might lead us. I willed him to feel the same. But although we danced until well past midnight, as soon as we'd left the dance floor, he let go of my hand. His conversation on the way home was all about how much he liked salsa, that he was glad I'd enjoyed it too, and we should go back to the club before we forgot the steps we'd learned tonight. The only kiss I'd had from him was a brush of his lips on either side of my face as he wished me *bonne nuit*. I'd gone to bed wondering if he'd ever see me as someone other than a girl mate with whom he could have a good night out, if there was any chance that we might become a couple.

Perhaps I should just rip his shirt off like that model he brought home, I thought. I took a moment to picture Alex shirtless. These fantasies had to stop before I made a fool of myself. I got out of bed and hung up my dress inside my wardrobe. As I did so, I caught sight of the pad of notepaper that habitually sat on my dressing table. On impulse, I retrieved a pen from my bag, pulled on a jumper over my pyjamas sat down and began to write:

Cher Alex,

You and I have been friends for what seems like for ever. But now that you are in London, my feelings towards you have changed. When I look at you, I don't see a friend who happens to be male, I see a good-looking guy who makes my heart beat faster.

There was a moment yesterday when I felt sure that you were about to kiss me, but I was wrong. Maybe you've never thought of me as a girl you might want to kiss.

If you're not attracted to me, if you can only see me as a friend who happens to be female, that's OK. I'll understand. Just forget I ever wrote you this letter, and I'll forget it too. And I'll still count myself very fortunate to have your friendship.

Yours,
Anna

I read the letter through. I'd made my feelings towards Alex very clear, I thought, but I was far from certain if my words were enough to ensure our friendship would remain intact if those feelings weren't reciprocated. I read the letter again, but I was still undecided as to whether or not I should slide it under Alex's door. My stomach rumbled, reminding me that it was way past the time most people had breakfast, even on a Sunday. Folding the letter in half and putting it in a drawer, I headed off to the kitchen, and whatever repast I could scavenge from my kitchen cupboards before I went to the supermarket or did an on-line shop.

Looking along the hall and seeing that Alex's door was partly open, I went to check if he wanted to join me for breakfast. Not bothering to knock, as I would have if the door had been closed, I walked straight into his room, but then I froze. Alex was sitting slumped at his desk in front of his laptop, his head in his hands. Pieces of his mobile phone lay scattered across the carpet.

'Alex?' I said.

Slowly he raised his head, and swung around in his chair to face me. I'd never seen him look so pale and drawn.

'Anna,' he said, lifting a hand as though to fend me off. 'Anna, would you go – go away. *Laissez-moi –*'

'Oh. OK.' I felt as though I'd been slapped in the face, but I turned on my heel and took a step towards the door.

He said, 'No, wait. Don't go. I'm sorry.'

I turned back to him.

'I've done something stupid,' he said.

172

'Well, yes, you have.' I picked up what was left of his phone, and put the various parts, the battery and the sim card, on his desk. 'How did you come to drop it?'

'I didn't drop it, I threw it against the wall.'

'That was very stupid.'

'I wasn't talking about the phone.'

'What have you done? What's wrong?'

He raked his hand through his hair. 'I emailed that shot of you with the rose to my agent this morning. I was going through photos on my laptop, to see if there was anything else worth sending him, and I accidently clicked on an old file that contained pictures of Cécile.'

He angled his laptop so I could see the screen. It was filled by the monochrome image of a slender young woman wearing a black, long-sleeved top that hung loosely off one shoulder, and black leggings, sitting by a window, holding a glass of wine, one foot drawn up onto her chair. Her dark hair was shoulder length, with a heavy fringe that fell into her large, dark kohl-lined eyes, and her mouth was slightly open, the tip of her tongue just protruding from her lips. She wasn't classically beautiful, but she was very striking. If she looked at a guy the way she was looking at the camera in that photograph, I imagined he'd be unlikely to look away.

'I have so many photos of her –' Alex brought up a slide show of images of Cécile, posed portraits interspersed with shots of her laughing, lying on the grass in what looked like a park, walking by a river that I presumed must be the Seine. He said, 'I saw these photos, and I remembered when and where I'd taken each one, and how happy we'd been. And then, I called her. I'd got this idea in my head that it wasn't too late for us, that if only I could talk to her, I could win her back … All that happened was that we ended up yelling at each other.'

I thought of the shouting that had dragged me out of my realistic and very pleasurable dream.

Alex said, 'I told her that I still loved her, and I begged – I actually begged – her not to throw away what we'd had together, but she just laughed. She told me that she'd never loved me, that for months before we broke up, everything I did or said had annoyed her, and now she despised me. I said some things to her that I never thought I'd say to any woman ...' His voice trailed off.

I looked again at the photo of Cécile on Alex's laptop, and thought, she looks lovely, no denying it, but she is *not* a nice girl. To put it mildly.

Alex said, 'I never told you how Cécile broke up with me.'

'Tell me now, if you want.' I sat down on his bed.

'She left me a voicemail: "I cannot keep it from you any longer. I've met someone, a man who I want to be with, and who wants to be with me."'

'Oh, Alex, that's such a horrible way to end a relationship.' At least I'd told Nick to his face.

'I was on a shoot, so I'd switched off my phone. When I picked up her message after work, I didn't try to call her back, but went straight round to her place and let myself in. She was there and so was René – the director of a play she'd appeared in a few months back – the guy she's with now. When I walked in on them, he was massaging her bare feet. They looked so *intimate*.' He shook his head at the memory. 'When I saw him touching her – I'm not proud of myself – I took a swing at him.'

'You hit him!'

'Not very hard,' Alex said.

'Did he hit you back?'

'No, he ran and locked himself in the bathroom. And then Cécile started screaming at me to get out, and I kept asking her why she'd done this awful thing to me, how could she treat me this way, all the mindless clichés that everyone says when a partner cheats on them, and then, suddenly, I couldn't bear to be in the same room as her. I left her still screeching, phoned a mate, and he took me to a bar and got me very drunk. A few days later, another friend of mine, an actor who worked with Cécile, told me that since the summer she'd been staying over at René's apartment whenever I was away from Paris. I'd been

174

feeling very down, but knowing that the woman I loved had been having sex with another man made me feel worse.'

I said, 'Even knowing all that, you're still in love with her? You still want her back?'

There was a long silence, and then Alex said. 'Yes, I love her. Even knowing that she's going to marry René, and there's nothing I can do about it, I still love her. I thought I was getting over her, I've tried to move on, but I can't seem to get her out of my head.'

She lied to him, she cheated on him for months, he moved to another country to get away from her – and still he said he loved her? I was at a loss to understand how a detestable creature like Cécile could inspire such depths of passion. Despite the pain he was in now, there was a part of me that envied Alex. I should have liked to have known what it was to love – and to be loved – with such intense, all-consuming emotion.

I said, 'If you want to get over her, then phoning her and pleading with her to come back to you isn't going to help you do that.'

'I know. I won't call her again. *Mon Dieu,* she made me so angry. At least I only trashed my phone. It would have been worse if I'd taken my rage out on my laptop.'

'Or one of your cameras.'

Alex managed a wan smile. 'I don't think even Cécile could make me mad enough to destroy a camera.' He reached for his keyboard. 'I should never have looked at these photos. I'm going to delete the file. And then I'm going to delete every other photo of her that I have.'

'I'll leave you to it, then.' I suspected that if he deleted all his photos of Cécile, he'd probably come to regret it, but I wasn't about to suggest that he keep them. 'I'm about to have breakfast – can I get you anything?'

'No thanks,' he said, 'I've already eaten.' He added, 'This afternoon, I'll have to go and buy myself a new mobile, but later, shall we go for a drink at the Red Lion?'

'I think we should,' I said, 'It is our local, after all.'

Alex turned his attention to his computer screen. I went and stood behind him, putting my hands on his shoulders.

'Try not to be sad,' I said.

'I'm not – most of the time – when I don't think about Cécile. It was just seeing the photos unexpectedly, and then hearing her voice.'

I leant down and kissed the side of his face. 'I'll see you later, *mon ami*.'

I went back to my bedroom, tore the letter I'd written to him into small pieces, and threw it in the bin.

Twenty-three

I sat at my desk at Nova Graphics, my hands poised over my keyboard. At the other end of the studio, Alfie, his earphones clamped to his head, was singing tunelessly to a song that only he could hear. Another of the creatives told him to shut up, and when that had no effect, threw a scrunched-up piece of paper at him. Alfie took off his earphones, and looked around with a cheerful, lop-sided grin on his face. Failing to locate his assailant, he shrugged, replaced his earphones, and went back to work.

I completed the email I'd been writing before I'd been distracted by Alfie's singing, and pressed send. My mind drifted to Alex, and the letter I'd written to him and then torn up. I thought, Alex has never shown any sign of being attracted to me, and if I tell him how I feel, I could ruin our friendship. I live in London, and come the summer, he'll be living in Paris, so even if we did get together, there's no future in it. *And* he's still in love with Cécile. Having a casual hook-up with a guy who's in love with another woman – *really* not my thing. Thank goodness I didn't give him that letter.

I glanced at my watch. It was already mid-morning, and I'd got very little work done. I should start on my phone calls. Or I could fetch myself a coffee. I got up and went over to the drinks machine. Alfie, now minus his earphones, came and joined me.

'You're in a good mood today,' I said.

'Yes, I am,' Alfie said. 'Izzy and I finished the artwork for the prom at the weekend. I've just emailed it to you.'

'That's great, Alfie. Thank you. I'll take a look as soon as

177

I'm back at my desk.' I picked up the plastic cup containing my morning cappuccino.

'I'm happy with the artwork,' Alfie said, 'and I think your sister and her friends are going to like what Izzy and I have come up with – but that's not why I'm in such a good mood.' He lowered his voice. 'I asked Izzy if she'd come out with me, and she said yes.'

'Oh, I'm so pleased for you.'

'Yeah. Actually, I wanted to ask your advice. As you're a girl.'

I smiled. 'Go ahead.'

'I've booked us a table at one of those cinemas where you can have a meal while you watch the film. We're seeing a rom com. Do you think that's a good choice for a first date?'

'Absolutely,' I said.

'I prefer a good horror film myself, but I thought ... well, girls like all that romantic stuff.'

'Izzy certainly does.' He was taking Izzy to see a rom com? He must be *really* keen on her. Leaving Alfie by the coffee machine, I went back to my computer, clicked on the email he'd sent me, and downloaded the attached images. I looked at the posters and flyers with their background colours of pink, mauve, and pale blue, the black silhouettes of couples dancing, glitter balls and limos, and I thought, Vicky's Committee are going to love these.

Izzy got up from her work station and came and leant against the front of my desk. 'Alfie said he'd sent you the artwork for the prom – have you had a chance to look at it?'

'I'm looking at it right now.'

'What do you think of it?'

'It's great, Izzy. You and Alfie have done a brilliant job.'

'It was Alfie who did most of it. I just made a few suggestions.'

'Well, it's terrific. Thank you so much.'

'I saw you talking to Alfie just now – did he say anything about me?'

'He mentioned something about you and him going out.'

'We are.' Izzy said. 'On Saturday. He told me he's been wanting to ask me out for ages. He's such a sweet guy.'

'Yes, he is.'

Izzy's eyes were shining. 'I guess I should go and do some work.' She wandered back to the creatives' end of the studios. Alfie glanced up as she sat down next to him. They exchanged a look that could only be described as meaningful.

That was the prom project completed. And it'd certainly reached its target demographic.

I sat at my desk and drank my coffee. I wondered what Alex was doing while I was stuck in front of a computer screen. He'd said something about a shoot in Richmond Park. It was a sunny day, and I envied him being outside.

'What's that you're working on?' Unnoticed by me, Oliver had come out of his office and was standing behind my chair.

'Oh, this isn't work,' I said. 'It's a poster that Alfie and Izzy created at the weekend. It's for my sister Vicky's senior prom night.'

'Ah – that explains the colour scheme,' Oliver said. 'Designed to appeal to a teenage girl.'

'Yes, Alfie and Izzy are very good at following a brief,' I said, glad to be able to repay my friends for their hard work by praising them to the boss. 'They've designed tickets and flyers for the prom as well.' A few clicks brought the images up on my screen.

'They're excellent,' Oliver said. 'Have you had them printed?'

'Not yet.'

'Print them here.'

'At Nova Graphics? Really?'

'I doubt it'll bankrupt us to run off a few tickets for a school prom.'

'Thank you so much. Vicky and her mates will be very grateful. Their enthusiasm vastly outstrips their budget.'

'You're close to your sister, aren't you?'

179

'I am. Despite the ten-year age difference.'

'Are you close to your parents as well?'

'Oh, yes. My parents are great.'

'That's good. Family is important.'

'I agree,' I said.

Oliver regarded the scene in front of him, smiling benignly at the buzz of activity as his staff went about their work. 'Natalie and I could never have built up our business the way we have if our families hadn't helped us in the early days with childcare and all that sort of thing.'

Natalie appeared from behind her partition.

'Oliver?' she said. 'We should get going.'

'I'll be right with you, Nat,' Oliver said. To me, he added, 'We have a meeting with a potential new corporate client. We'll be back in a couple of hours or so.'

'OK.'

'You've got my mobile number, but don't call me unless the building's burning down.' He went over to Natalie and they left together.

I sighed. I wouldn't have minded getting out of the office for a couple of hours. Focus, Anna.

My phone vibrated.

Hi Anna, The Edge *entertainment dept has a bunch of comps for* A Tale of Two Cities, the Musical. *Tonight. 7.30. Would you like to come with me? Alex*

I texted back straight away:
Yes please. Shall I meet u at the theatre? Anna xx

He texted back the name of the theatre and a smiley face.

I sighed. Alex's friendship was important to me. I'd enjoy his company while he was in England, and then when he went back to France, we could go on writing letters to each other as we'd always done.

Alex would always be my friend, and that would have to be enough.

180

Twenty-four

'Can I get you another drink?' Oliver asked.

'Thank you, but no,' I said, 'I'm just about to go home.' Another week gone.

'I'll say goodnight, then. See you on Monday.'

'Night, Oliver. Have a good weekend.'

He went over to the bar. I drained my glass and said goodnight to Natalie and those of my co-workers who hadn't already left the pub. Izzy and Alfie were sitting together in a corner, away from the rest of us. I decided that the way they were gazing at each other (even before their official first date), they'd probably manage to have a good weekend without my telling them to, and headed to the door.

After the fug of heat and alcohol in the pub, the cool night air was very welcome. I weaved my way through the throng of people who'd chosen to bring their drinks outside, and headed towards the tube. It struck me, as I walked along Camden High Street, that I'd been working at Nova Graphics longer than any of my colleagues. Seven years I'd been there. Longer than anyone apart from Natalie and Oliver.

I reached the station, went through the turnstiles, and down onto the platform. Seven years was an awfully long time to stay in the same job, especially your first job after university. I wasn't quite sure how it had happened. I didn't *dislike* what I did for a living, but the idea that I might still be an account exec at Nova Graphics after ten years – after twenty years – didn't exactly fill me with joy. I was drifting along at work, just as I'd let myself drift along in my relationship with Nick.

A rush of wind and noise from the tunnel at the end of the platform heralded the arrival of my train. I got on and found myself a seat. Was it time I started looking for a new job? Maybe I should consider moving to a larger design company – or look around for something entirely different to do. A new challenge. And yet … Natalie and Oliver were so nice, and such considerate employers.

I should take some time to think about this. I thought. I don't need to decide anything in a hurry.

I put all thoughts about my job to the back of my mind, and started thinking about the weekend ahead. On Saturday night, I was invited to a friend's engagement party. On Sunday, Beth was bringing her children over to my flat, where Alex and Rob would join us for lunch, after they'd played squash.

By the time I reached home, it was getting on for midnight. My flat was in darkness. I closed the front door very quietly so as not to disturb Alex if he was asleep (if he was even home – he'd gone out every night this week), and started to creep along the hallway towards my room. From behind Alex's closed bedroom door came a snatch of female laughter – and the unmistakeable sound of a creaking mattress. My face grew hot. I backed away down the hall – and shrieked when a hand fell on my shoulder.

'Anna – it's OK. It's me'

I spun around. Alex, wearing just his jeans, was standing right behind me.

'Sorry,' he said. 'I didn't mean to scare you.'

'Oh – I thought you were in your bedroom – I heard – someone. A girl.'

He said, 'That would be Lou. Louise.'

'Ah. Yes. Lou. Your assistant.'

'Yeah. I was working with her again today. After we'd wrapped, I went out for a drink with her and her boyfriend, and we ended up back here.'

'Lou and her boyfriend are in your bedroom.' I felt ridiculously pleased that Alex wasn't in his room with a girl,

182

but here with me.

'They live miles out of town. I didn't think you'd mind if they stayed the night.'

'Of course, I don't mind. It's absolutely fine.'

'I'm going to sleep in the living room. I helped myself to your spare duvet.'

'That's fine too.'

He ran his hands through his hair. 'I know it's late, but there's something I'd like to talk to you about. It can wait 'til the morning if you're too tired.'

'No, I'm all good.'

We went into the living room. Alex picked up his discarded T-shirt, the muscles in his back rippling as he pulled it over his head. I sat down on the sofa, and he took a seat next to me.

He said, 'I have to go back to Paris.'

'W-what?' It was as thought someone had punched me in the stomach. 'But – I thought – your contract with *The Edge* runs until July.'

'It does. I'm only going to Paris for a few days.'

'Ooh.' Immediately, I felt a whole lot better. 'And the reason you're going is …?'

He smiled. 'I've been nominated for the Lécuyer Award.'

'I'm guessing that's really good news?'

He nodded. 'The Galerie Lécuyer is highly respected in the Parisian art world. They show contemporary and emerging artists, mainly those working in photography and video. To be nominated for the award is a great honour. To win would take my career to a whole new level.'

'Oh, Alex, I'm *so* pleased for you. This is really exciting.'

'It is – and completely unexpected. It was Marcel – my agent – who recommended me to the gallery as a nominee for the award. I only found out about it today, when he phoned me.'

'When will you know if you've won?'

'Not for another two weeks. The Galerie Lécuyer holds an exhibition of all the nominated artists' work, and the award winner is announced at the opening. It's an important event in artistic circles, attended by collectors and covered by the media.'

'This is amazing.'

'Yeah.' Alex hesitated, and then he added. 'One of the photos chosen for the exhibition is the picture of you with the rose.'

'I – an image of me – is going to be hung on the wall of an art gallery. In Paris?' Delight surged through me.

'Are you OK with that?' Alex said. 'Because I can tell Marcel to withdraw that particular picture –'

'Alex, I'm thrilled. A work of art like that photo should be in a gallery where it can be seen by people who appreciate just how beautiful it is.'

'I'm glad you feel that way, because I was wondering if you'd like to come to the exhibition with me.'

I gaped at him. 'The exhibition? But – it's in France.'

'I had this *wild* idea that we could go to Paris for a few days, maybe do a bit of sightseeing. We could stay at my place, if you don't mind sharing a one-room apartment. What do you think?'

I remembered a letter I'd once written to him.

... *Maybe one day ... I'll just jump on the Eurostar ... I would love to see Paris, and you of course ...*

'I'd love to visit Paris,' I said.

Alex smiled. 'It will be my great pleasure to show you my city.'

Twenty-five

'Shall I give you a hand with that?' Alex said.

I relinquished my large suitcase, and he hoisted it into the luggage rack, next to his small canvas holdall. 'Which way are out seats?'

Alex glanced at his ticket. 'This way, I think.'

I followed him along the train carriage. Our seats were facing each other across a narrow table.

'Oh, good,' I said. 'We both get a window.'

Alex's dark eyes glinted with amusement. 'I don't think I've ever travelled with anyone who finds a train journey as exciting as you do – at least not since I first came to England with my school.'

'I am excited,' I said. 'I don't mind admitting it.' For the last ten days, all I'd thought about was my visit to Paris with Alex. Anything else, particularly any decision about whether I was going to start looking for a new job, could wait until after our trip. 'Can I have the seat that faces the way we're going?'

'Of course,' Alex said. 'Although, I should probably warn you that for much of the way, the view out of the window isn't particularly interesting.'

'Maybe not for a blasé global traveller like you, but I'm sure it will be for me.'

We settled ourselves into our seats, and I arranged the provisions I'd brought for the journey – bottled water, chicken wraps, crisps, chocolate, a fat paperback, a guidebook – on the table in front of me.

'I hope I've brought enough food,' I said.

'You do know that it only takes two and a quarter hours to get from London to Paris on the Eurostar, right?'

'You're the one who's always hungry.'

Alex smiled, and ripped open a packet of crisps. 'I think we're just about to leave,' he said.

The train shuddered, and drew out of the station, and then gathered speed. Looking out of the window, I had to agree with Alex that the view was unspectacular. When we weren't plunging through a cutting, I saw a sprawl of factories, steelworks, and rusting metal girders, and as we left London behind, stretches of flat countryside, bisected by the concrete pillars of a motorway. Alex was scrolling through emails on his phone. I reached for the Paris guidebook that I'd bought at the station, and immersed myself in descriptions of Parisian landmarks and maps of the Metro. I peered out of the window again when we'd reached the Channel Tunnel, but the only thing to be seen outside the carriage was an impenetrable blackness. I went back to reading about the history of Montmartre, the area of Paris in which Alex lived. And then we burst out of the darkness into bright sunlight.

Somewhat unnecessarily, I exclaimed, 'We're in France!'

Alex, who'd dozed off before we'd reached the Tunnel, opened his eyes. He glanced out of the window, but didn't appear particularly moved to be back on his native soil. I supposed he went abroad so often, that the moment of return to his homeland no longer had any emotional impact. He picked up his mobile.

'I've a text from Hélène,' he said. 'She asks if you'd like to go shopping with her while you're in Paris? Perhaps the day before the exhibition, while I'm occupied at the gallery?'

'That's so kind of her,' I said. 'Please text her back that I'd love to.'

'I also have a text from my mother saying that she has been to my apartment to air it, and she has also stocked up my fridge.'

'The women in your family really spoil you, don't they?'

'*Mais oui*,' Alex said. 'They adore me.' He started to tap out replies to his doting female relatives.

I turned my face back to the scenery, but to my frustration, the train was now going through a whole series of cuttings, and all I could see were brief flashes of houses, electricity pylons, and a car park: not remarkably different from anything I'd seen as we journeyed across Kent. Then, suddenly, we were travelling through the open French countryside. I saw farmland, trees, and villages. I started to notice the subtle differences in the shape of the buildings, and that the cars were, of course, driving on the right hand side of the road. I looked at the square fields of bright green and yellow, and the tiny clusters of houses with their sharply pointed roofs, and thought how much it reminded me of some of the paintings I'd studied at university.

'The view looks like a landscape by Van Gogh,' I said to Alex.

'You're right,' he said. 'It does.' To my surprise, he reached across the table and took both my hands in his. 'I'm so pleased that I'm at last going to be able to show you my home, the place where I grew up. I love it that you're so excited to be visiting Paris.'

'I'm so glad that I'm going there for the first time with you.'

He gestured at the guide book. 'Have you decided what you most want to see?'

'No, I want to go to all the main tourist attractions, do all the things that first-time visitors to Paris do, but I thought I'd leave the actual itinerary up to you. I shall, of course, be taking a selfie of the two of us on top of the Eiffel Tower.'

'*Bien sûr*,' Alex said.

An hour or so later, we arrived at the Gare du Nord.

'*Bienvenue a Paris*,' Alex said.

'*Merci*,' I said. 'I can't quite believe I'm actually here.'

We got off the train and threaded our way through the crowds on the station forecourt – Alex insisted on taking charge of both our cases – and having bought a *carnet* of tickets, rode the Metro to Abbesses, the stop nearest his apartment. My guidebook had warned me that Montmartre was no longer the home of bohemian artists, musicians, and writers, but full of over-priced tourist restaurants and hordes of pushy souvenir sellers, but the Places des Abbesses, the square outside the station, was delightful, with pavement cafés, plane trees, and wrought-iron streetlamps. It was only a few minutes' walk from the square to Alex's home, but we took it slowly, giving me time to take in the sights and sounds of this historic part of Paris, the voices talking in French, the winding cobbled streets, the terraces and flights of steps, and the houses with shuttered windows and balconies. Eventually, we arrived at a typically Parisian apartment building. Alex produced a key to unlock the heavy double-doors that opened onto a paved interior courtyard. An archway on the far side of the courtyard led to a dim, narrow, twisting staircase.

'There's no lift, I'm afraid,' Alex said. 'Very few of the old buildings in Montmartre have lifts, but once we're on the fifth floor, I hope you'll agree the view is worth the climb.'

He hefted up my case, his holdall, and his camera case, and sprung lightly up the stairs, with me following rather more slowly in his wake. I was soon out of breath, and very glad when we reached the tiny landing at the top, and Alex's studio apartment.

'After you,' he said, showing me inside, and switching on a light.

I found myself in a small vestibule. To the left, the wall was completely taken up with a row of cupboards. A door on the right was open just enough for me to catch a glimpse of a cream-tiled bathroom. In front of me was an open-plan living area. It had a sloping ceiling, natural wood floors, white-painted walls, and French windows with iron railings across their lower half. It was furnished with a small round table and two chairs, a white, two-seater sofa with red cushions, and a double bed with a white wooden frame and a brightly striped duvet. On the side of the room where the ceiling was highest, a pair of folding doors had been left open to reveal a compact kitchen area. The overall effect was of a light, airy space, with just enough splashes of colour to relieve the monotony of the white walls and furniture. I went to the windows and looked out over the roof-tops of Paris, just as the sun was setting, streaking the sky with red and golden light.

'Ooh,' I said. 'I can see the Eiffel Tower. This view is amazing. The whole apartment's lovely. Not at all what I imagined.'

'What were you expecting?'

'You did write that you lived in an attic. I was thinking of peeling paint and threadbare carpets.'

'It really was an attic once, but about twenty years ago, the whole building was completely renovated. I still like to think that it was some impoverished nineteenth-century artist's shabby garret. And that he – back then it would have been a he not a she – set out each morning with his charcoal and his sketchbook to make drawings of Paris – just as I go out with my camera. Or maybe he painted the dancers at the Moulin Rouge or the Opera.'

'You've thought a lot about the artist that used to live in your flat, haven't you?'

Alex shrugged. 'If I'd been born in the nineteenth century I'd have been a painter, not a photographer.' His gaze travelled round the room. 'My home isn't large, but then I'm away so much, and I've accumulated so few possessions, that I don't need a bigger apartment – everything I own, including my clothes, fits into those cupboards in the hall. Anyway, now that you've seen my humble abode, shall we go out to eat or would you prefer it if I cook us something?'

'We should definitely go out,' I said. 'I can't possibly stay in – it's my first night in Paris.'

We went to a small restaurant, just around the corner from Alex's building, where the clientele were locals as well as tourists, and a young man played jazz on a piano while a girl sang. Alex and I sat at a rough wooden table which was barely large enough for the two of us and the single candle that flickered between us. We ate steak and *frites* and drank red wine, and Alex told me anecdotes about some of the less well-known artists and writers who'd once lived in his neighbourhood, stories that hadn't made it into my guidebook. His eyes were very dark in the candlelight, and when he reached for his wine-glass, and his fingers brushed mine, a shiver ran up my arm. I thought, enough, Anna, and reminded myself that nothing was ever going to happen between us.

Back at Alex's apartment, as soon as we got inside, I went straight to the window, and gazed out over night-time Paris.

'I can still see the Eiffel Tower,' I said. 'It's sparkling.'

'Yes, it does that once every hour,' Alex said. 'Shall we make the tower the first place we visit tomorrow? It's only a short walk from there to the Musée D'Orsay, so I could show you my favourite paintings.'

I remembered a phrase from a letter he'd once written to me:

One day I hope you will come to Paris, and I will show you my favourite paintings in the Louvre and the Musée D'Orsay.

'That,' I said, 'would be perfect.'

'We'll have to get there early to beat the crowds,' Alex said, 'so I suggest we call it a night. I'll get my sleeping bag –' He went out into the vestibule and returned with a sleeping bag which he spread out on the sofa. 'You're the guest – you get the bed, and you can go first in the bathroom.'

I opened my case, located my wash-bag, and my old baggy T-shirt, and went off to wash, change and clean my teeth. When I came back, Alex had stripped down to his boxers. He'd turned off the electric light, and was standing by the window, his muscular body, his broad shoulders, the sharply defined ridges of his stomach, bathed in moonlight and shadows.

He is so beautiful, I thought, And not for me. Aloud, I said, 'B-bathroom's free.'

'*Merci*,' he said, and headed off to perform his night-time ablutions.

I got into his bed – it was extremely comfortable – and whether it was the thrill of finally coming to Paris, the wine, or the effect of twice climbing the stairs to Alex's apartment, I fell asleep before he came back into the room.

Twenty-six

The first thing I did when I woke up was open the shutters –
Alex must have closed them the previous night – and take
another look at the Paris skyline. It was a gloriously sunny day,
with a blue sky and just a few white clouds. I took a photo of
the view on my phone, and then showered, dressed in a T-shirt,
jeans, and flat shoes suitable for exploring a city on foot, and
did my hair and make-up, all while Alex was still asleep. He
looked hideously uncomfortable on the sofa – he was too long
for it, and his legs inside the sleeping bag were hanging off the
edge – but he was sleeping soundly, so I didn't wake him.
Instead, I unpacked my case, hanging my clothes in one of the
cupboards in the vestibule. Then I made myself a cup of coffee
and sat by the open French windows, reading the book I'd
brought with me from England.

In a little while, Alex stirred, raising his tousled head from
the pillow, sitting up slowly and rubbing his hand along his
unshaven jaw.

'*Bonjour*,' I said. '*Du café?*'

'*Oui, s'il te plait.*' He got up and stumbled out to the
bathroom. I heard the sound of the shower.

I was still making him coffee when he came out of the
bathroom and went to the cupboard he used as a wardrobe. The
towel he'd wrapped around his waist suddenly fell to the floor,
and as there was no door between the living area and the
vestibule, I was treated to a full-frontal view of his completely
naked body. My stomach lurched, and to my embarrassment,
heat flooded my face. Hastily, before he realised that I'd seen

193

him, I looked away. I poured milk into his coffee and then went to the window, so that the breeze wafting in from outside could cool my flaming cheeks.

From the vestibule, Alex said, 'Last night, after you were asleep, I checked what provisions my mother left us, and I saw that we have baguettes.' He stepped into the living area, dressed now in jeans and a T-shirt, like me. 'That's one thing I've really missed living in London – you simply can't get good baguettes in England. They have them in the supermarkets, but they're just not the same as the ones you get from *le boulangerie*.'

Pulling myself together (I had, after all, seen a naked man before), I joined Alex in a typically French breakfast of baguettes, spread liberally with his favourite apricot jam.

'And now,' he said, when we'd both eaten our fill, 'I'm going to show you Paris.'

Alex told me that in his opinion, the most scenic way to approach the Eiffel Tower, and one of the best places for photographs, was from the right bank of the Seine, across the Pont d'Iéna. We took the Metro to the Trocadero, and walked through the gardens with their fountains and statues, to the river, and then crossed the bridge, stopping in the middle for Alex to photograph me with the tower in the background. The nearer we got, the more impressive the iconic landmark became, and when we were right underneath, all I could do was gape up at the massive structure and wonder how something so graceful from a distance could also be so majestic and monumental. Having arrived just before the tower opened, we didn't have long to queue at the entrance, and our climb up to the first level with its glass floors was unimpeded by the teeming crowds that Alex assured me would be there later in the day. From the first level, we took the lift, gliding up through the lattice of iron girders, catching tantalising glimpses of wide boulevards, palaces, and cathedrals, the blue of the river, the green of the Champs du Mars, until we reached the top, with its wonderful panoramic views of the whole city, including the hill of Montmartre, from where we had set out that morning.

'This is the ultimate tourist experience,' I said, 'so I have to do what every tourist does at this point –'

'Take a selfie?' Alex said. 'I was hoping you'd forgotten.'

I took several photos, and Alex took more on his camera – I suspected he didn't entirely trust in my ability to take a picture without putting my finger over the lens – and then we began the long descent down the stairs to the ground.

From the Eiffel Tower, we walked along the left bank of the Seine until we came to the arched façade of the former railway station, now art gallery, that is the Musée D'Orsay.

Alex said, 'My parents used bring me – me and Hélène – here when we were children. I was obsessed with those animal statutes.' He gestured to the bronze horse, rhinoceros, lion, and elephant that stood in front of the museum. 'Somewhere at home I still have the photos I took of them when I was about eight.'

I smiled to think of a skinny, eight-year-old Alex solemnly photographing works of art. 'Shall we go and join the queue?' I said, eyeing the line of people waiting to enter the museum.

'No need,' Alex said. 'I already have tickets. I bought them on the website while we were still in England.'

'I knew there was a reason why I hired you as my tour guide.'

Three hours later, I was still wandering awestruck amongst the masterpieces in the Musée D'Orsay, Degas' famous statue of a young dancer, paintings by Gaugin and Manet, Renoir and Cézanne, and Alex's particular favourite, *Women in the Garden* by Claude Monet.

'It's the way he depicts the play of light and shadow on the figure in the foreground of the painting that first fascinated me when I was a child,' Alex said. 'And the effect of the other figures' pale dresses against the dark green leaves.'

I studied the picture of the four women, one sitting on the grass, two standing behind her, and the fourth darting behind a tree. Most of the painted garden was in shadow, with a band of bright sunlight falling across the seated woman's voluminous white skirts.

'I think this painting influenced your photography,' I said. 'You have a lot of deeply contrasting light and shade in your work.'

'Not to mention that when I was a student I took a whole series of pictures of women dressed in white. My tutor once asked me if I was planning on becoming a wedding photographer.'

After the paintings and the sculpture, we looked at a display of early photographs – Alex's area much more than mine, and about which he talked very knowledgably and with great enthusiasm – before exiting the museum and finding a café down a side street, a little way back from the river, in which to have lunch. Eating my *salade niçoise*, drinking a glass of *vin rouge*, talking to my charming Frenchman about the view from the Eiffel Tower, and the paintings we'd seen, I felt sure that this trip was going to be every bit as wonderful as I'd hoped it would be. I listened to Alex telling me about the visits he used to make to art galleries with his parents as a child, watched as his fingers traced the route we'd taken that morning on the map, and thought, dreamily, I'm here in the City of Light with Alexandre Tourville – life doesn't get much better than this.

Alex said, 'And next, the kiss.'

I choked on my wine.

Alex half-rose from his chair in concern. 'Are you OK?'

'Yes, I'm fine. It just went down the wrong way. Sorry, what did you say?'

'Next, we should see *The Kiss*. The Musée Rodin is only a couple of streets away.'

'You're talking about *The Kiss*? The sculpture by Rodin?'

'*Bien sûr*,' Alex said.

We went to the Musée Rodin, and stood for a long time in front the sculpture of the nude man and woman, admiring the skill with which the artist had captured the raw emotion of their embrace. And when the image of Alex naked that morning floated into my mind, I quickly pushed it away.

By the time we left the museum, it was late afternoon. We strolled arm in arm along the left bank of the Seine, stopping to browse among the dark green *bouquinistes*, the second-hand bookstalls, that lined the pavement. I looked up at the blossom on the trees that grew beside the river, and decided that everything I'd ever heard about Paris in the spring, that it was one of the most beautiful cities in the world, was true.

We walked until we reached a point on the riverbank where we had a splendid view of Notre Dame rising above the Ile de la Cité – I was surprised to learn that the famous cathedral was built on an island – before deciding to head back to Montmartre. Our way to the nearest Metro led us past a number of souvenir shops, and although I'd spent the day looking at artistic masterpieces, I found myself irresistibly drawn to the garish T-shirts printed with badly drawn Parisian street scenes, the snow-globes containing miniscule models of the Moulin Rouge, and baseball hats with the logo *J'aime Paris* picked out in diamante.

'Shall I buy one of these?' I said to Alex, holding up a shiny, golden, foot-high statue of the Eiffel Tower. 'Do you think it would look good in my flat?'

'Absolutely,' Alex said. 'Because it really isn't one of those tacky souvenirs that seems like an ideal memento when you're on holiday, but as soon as you get home you wonder why you bought it.'

I took another look at my potential keepsake. 'You may be right.' With reluctance, I replaced the statue on the shelf, and contented myself with some postcards.

'So how did you like your first day in Paris?' Alex said, unzipping his sleeping bag.

'It was wonderful.' I climbed into bed. 'It really is a very beautiful city – and you know how much I like visiting art galleries.'

After we'd got back to his apartment, Alex had cooked us

197

mushroom omelettes, and then we'd sat by the French windows, eating, talking and drinking wine, looking out over the rooftops as the sun set, and the sky grew dark and full of stars. After the amount of walking we'd done that day, and with another early start planned for the next morning, both of us had been very ready to call it a night.

'Tomorrow, I'll show you more.' Alex turned out the lamp, and I heard a loud creak and a twang as he got onto the sofa. '*Bonne nuit.*'

'*À demain.*' I shut my eyes. I was tired, but pleasantly so, my mind and body relaxed. There was more creaking from the sofa, and then a loud thud. I flicked on the light-switch near the bed. Alex, tangled in his sleeping bag, was lying on the wooden floor.

'*Merde.*' With difficulty, he sat up.

'Are you hurt?'

'No. Maybe bruised a little.' He rubbed his elbow. 'All I did was turn over – and then I was on the floor.'

'You're just too huge for that sofa. Let's swap – you take the bed.'

'I wouldn't hear of it. You're my guest.' He kicked his way out of the sleeping bag.

'Alex, your feet hang over the side –'

'So would yours, if you were lying on a two-seater sofa.'

For goodness' sake. Too tired to argue, and now really, really needing to get some sleep, I said, 'Then let's share the bed.'

'You wouldn't mind?'

'No, of course not.' He could sleep in his sleeping bag on top of the bed – it was hardly any different to him sleeping a few feet away on the sofa.

'Are you sure?'

'We're friends aren't we?'

'Yes we are.' Alex walked over to the bed and before I could say anything, joined me under the duvet. 'This is such a relief. It took me hours to get to sleep on that sofa last night, and I've had a crick in my neck all day.' He rolled onto his side, with his back to me.

I was in bed with a gorgeous man who was wearing nothing but a pair of boxers. And I was only wearing a T-shirt.

He said, 'Goodnight, Anna.'

'G-goodnight.'

Alex's breathing changed to a soft gentle rhythm that told me he'd already drifted off to sleep. I slid over to the edge of the mattress, as far away from him as I could get without falling on the floor myself.

Twenty-seven

At some point during the night, Alex had turned over, and I awoke to find that we were lying spooned together, his arm draped across my waist. I could feel his steady breathing on the back of my neck. The shutters were closed, and the bed was soft, and it felt very good to lie there in the dim light and the warmth, with a man's strong arm around me. Then it struck me that when he woke up, it was going to be a whole lot less awkward for both of us – well, certainly for me – if our bodies weren't pressed together quite so intimately. Slowly, careful not to disturb him, I lifted Alex's arm off my waist, and slid out of the bed.

I showered and dressed, and when I came back from the bathroom, he was already up, wearing his jeans, and making coffee.

'*Bonjour*,' I said. 'Did you sleep better last night?'

'I went out like a light.'

'I slept well too.' Lying rigid on the edge of the bed, it had taken me a long time to actually fall asleep, but once I'd drifted off, I'd slept well and deeply. And now that I'd had a chance to think about it in the light of day, sharing a bed with a male who was a friend rather than a sexual partner actually didn't seem as outlandish as it had the previous night.

'So we can share the bed again tonight? I don't need to rush out and buy an air-mattress?'

'I'm fine to sleep in the same bed as you, *mon ami*,' I said.

Alex suggested that our first visit of the day should be to the summit of the hill of Montmartre, and so after breakfast, we joined the hundreds of other sight-seers climbing the steps and steeply inclined streets, up to the highest point in Paris and the domed basilica of Sacré Coeur. In the Place du Tertre, the main square, Alex steered me away from the portrait painters, the street hawkers, and the over-priced crêpe sellers, to the terrace in front of the church. The sun was shining and the air was clear, and the view out over Paris was, again, amazing.

'Let's walk straight down the hill from here,' Alex said, once I'd decided I'd taken enough photographs. 'Don't look back until I tell you.'

Steps and more terraces, thronged with camera-wielding tourists, took us down the hill. When we were roughly two thirds of the way down, Alex told me to look back up towards the summit, and when I saw the domes of Sacré Coeur, gleaming white against the clear blue sky, I actually gasped.

Alex, standing beside me, his thumbs hooked in the pockets of his jeans, said, 'It's impressive, isn't it? Despite the crowds.'

'It is,' I said.

'When I was a student, on summer nights, my friends and I would buy cheap wine, and come and drink it on these terraces. When it gets dark there are fairy lights. Sometimes, someone would bring a guitar.'

'That sounds magical.'

'It was. That was when I decided I wanted to live in Montmartre, although, as you know, it was three years after I left art school before I was able to afford it.'

'Selfie? If it won't offend your artistic sensibilities.'

Alex laughed, and got out his camera. He put his arm around me, and I leant against him while he captured the moment.

'Where are we going next?' I asked him.

'The Arc de Triomphe.'

We continued down the hill, skirting around the famous carousel (instantly recognisable from so many movies set in Paris), edged through the bottle-neck of tourist-jammed streets at the bottom (Alex firmly leading me past the souvenir shops) and took the Metro to the iconic monumental arch that looms over the western end of the broad, tree-lined Avenue des Champs-Élysées. We debated whether to go up to the viewing platform, but in the end Alex decided we didn't have time – and there are only so many aerial views a girl needs to photograph, even in a city as scenic as Paris.

From the Arc de Triomphe, we walked along the Champs-Élysées, past cafés, shops, and the Lido nightclub, taking a brief detour along the Avenue Montaigne, where the haute-couture fashion houses have their flagship stores (I gaped at the windows full of designer dresses, Alex talked about the time he'd photographed the backstage craziness of Paris fashion week). Continuing along the Champs-Élysées, we came to a large hexagonal square with a high stone obelisk in its centre, and cars and motorbikes roaring around its perimeter.

'This is the Place de la Concorde,' Alex said. 'Once we get across the road, you can take a photograph along the entire length of the Champs-Élysées, with the Arc de Triomphe in the distance. And over there, on the other side of the square, is the entrance to the Jardin des Tuileries.'

After the noise of the traffic in the Place de la Concorde, the Tuileries Gardens were a haven of quiet. We had lunch at a café under the trees, and then we walked along the dusty gravel paths, among the flower beds and manicured lawns, until we came to a circular pond with green metal chairs set all around its rim. Nearly every chair was already taken, but I spotted one that was free, Alex dragged another over from further around the pond, and we took a break from sight-seeing to sunbathe. I watched the people going past, some obviously tourists, laden with rucksacks, maps, and camcorders, others French, mothers pushing buggies or shepherding toddlers, a perspiring man in a business suit, students, and white-haired seniors. A French father appeared with two small boys carrying toy sailing boats, which they proceeded to launch, scurrying to meet the brightly painted wooden vessels as they drifted across the pond's smooth surface to the other side.

'Did you sail boats here when you were little?' I asked Alex.

'Yes, my father would often bring me here on a Sunday morning. Sometimes my mother and Hélène came too, but it was usually just the two of us.' He smiled, and stared off into the distance. Then he glanced at his watch. 'Are you ready to move on to the Louvre?'

The dark grey roofs of the Louvre were just visible from where we were sitting. A few minutes later, we were standing in the main courtyard of the museum, and I was asking Alex for advice on the best angle to take a photograph that included both the imposing royal palace that was the original building and the modernistic glass pyramid that was now its entrance. It was impossible for us to see all the works of art housed in the miles of galleries within the Louvre in one afternoon, but I saw the *Mona Lisa,* and despite the crowd gathered in front of this most famous painting, which limited where I could stand, I was able to verify that her eyes do indeed follow you as you move. For me, it was wonderful to see this masterpiece, and so many others that I knew from my studies, hanging on a wall instead of in the pages of a book or on the internet. Especially as I was able to discuss what I was seeing with Alex.

When we came out of the Louvre, the sun was low in the sky, and our shadows long on the ground, but it was still pleasantly warm. I didn't take any persuading to agree with Alex's suggestion that we take another walk by the Seine before returning to Montmartre. A broad ramp took us down to the stone quays that run alongside the river, Alex took my hand, lacing our fingers together, and we strolled by the water, enjoying each other's company without the need to talk. There were other people walking along the quays, couples holding hands or with their arms about each other's waists, and joggers and cyclists, but not many. More were sitting on the edge, soaking up the last rays of the afternoon sun.

'It's the golden hour,' Alex said. 'The best time of day for photography, when the shadows are no longer harsh.' He reached up and brushed a stray strand of hair off my face, and then he took a picture. And then, without my asking, he put his arm around my shoulders, held out his camera, and took a selfie of us both together.

I smiled at him and he smiled back, and then we went and sat on the edge of the quay, our feet dangling over the water. The sun sank lower, and the river grew almost too bright to look at. The Paris skyline, the Eiffel Tower just visible in the far distance, became a silhouette.

For a while we sat in silence, and then Alex said, 'When Cécile finished with me, I had to get away from Paris. Our lives here were so intertwined. We had the same friends, we were invited to the same events. Everywhere I went – restaurants, bars, clubs, and theatres – had an association with her. I thought I'd find it hard to come back here – but I haven't found it hard at all.' His eyes met mine. 'I'm over her, Anna. Over Cécile.'

Finally. 'I'm so glad, Alex. I've hated seeing you so wretched.'

'That last terrible phone call, when all we did was yell at each other, I think that was what made me accept that she really was never coming back to me – and I was finally able to let her go, and start to move on. And now, showing you Paris, I've remembered so much about my life, so many good memories of growing up, studying, working and living here, that the bad memories suddenly don't seem to matter. I'm no longer in love with Cécile. Talking about her now, all I feel is indifference. It's as though all the pain and hurt I went through happened to another person.' His mouth lifted in a smile. 'Thank you, Anna, for being there for me, for listening. Thank you for coming with me to Paris.'

Affection for him overwhelmed me. Sitting there with him in the golden light, the water gleaming beneath our feet, looking into his warm, dark brown eyes, I felt closer to him than I'd ever felt before. The longing to draw his head down to mine, to feel the touch of his lips on my mouth, became a physical ache, a craving for him that was so strong that I couldn't believe that he didn't feel it too.

'I'm always there for you, Alex.'

'And I for you, *mon amie Anglaise.*' He raised his hand to shade his eyes against the light, and gazed out over the river.

Mon amie Anglaise. My English friend. He was no longer hung up on his ex, but he still didn't see me as anything other than a friend. Between us, nothing had changed.

Alex said, 'Time we started for home, I think. We'll pick up a bottle of wine and something to eat tonight on the way. And then, I'll need to call Marcel – it shouldn't take long. Later, I thought we'd go to Le Cave, a bar I like on the Rue Oberkampf. I'll ask a few people to join us … Luc, Henri, Marthe. If that's OK with you, Anna?'

'Sounds good,' I tore my gaze away from Alex's full, sensual mouth that I was never going to kiss, and made myself focus on his plans for a night out in Paris.

Twenty-eight

'Ah – there's Luc and Édith.' Alex stood up and waved his arm above his head. The man and woman who'd just entered the bar started to make their way over to our table.

Alex's friend, Henri, a tall lanky man, with a pleasant, amiable face, said, 'Did Alex ever mentioned Luc or Édith in his letters?'

I thought for a moment. 'I don't think so. You're the only one of his friends here tonight that I remember reading about.'

Henri had known Alex since they were students. His name had at one time, cropped up regularly in Alex's letters. Usually in such comments as

Henri and I got wasted ...

or

Henri and I met two American girls studying at the Sorbonne ...

'Obviously, I'm Alex's most interesting acquaintance,' Henri said.

Like many of the bars in Paris, Le Cave, situated in a vaulted stone cellar, became a club after dark, with live music. Alex and I'd found ourselves a table in an alcove, far enough away from the stage and the dance floor to hold a shouted conversation. Before we'd left his apartment, he'd texted a number of his friends, asking if they wanted to join him for a drink in the Oberkampf district, and sitting with us were Henri, a guy named Léon, and a couple whose names were Marthe and François. Chatting with a group of people in French meant that I'd had to concentrate far more than when I was only talking to

Alex, but I'd been pleased to discover that I understood almost all of what they said about the merits of this or that Parisian restaurant, the films they'd seen, the books they'd read. I'd tried to memorise any idiomatic or slang expressions I didn't recognise, so that later I could ask Alex for a translation. Henri had complimented me on my French accent – or lack of an English accent – and expressed surprise that this was my first visit to France. Like my friends in England, he'd been amazed to learn that Alex and I actually wrote letters to each other.

'*Salut tout le monde.*' Luc and Édith arrived at the table. They greeted Alex with air kisses each side of his face, exclamations of pleasure at seeing him back in Paris, and congratulations when he told them the reason for his return. He introduced me as his friend from England.

'Having your work shown at the Galerie Lécuyer is an achievement in itself,' Édith said, taking the seat on my right. 'Let alone being nominated for the Lécuyer Award. You must be thrilled'

'I am,' Alex said. 'I admit it.'

Luc fetched a chair from another table and sat down beside Édith. 'We'll go and see the exhibition, of course,' he said. 'Whether you win or not.'

'The photos you're exhibiting are portraits?' Édith said.

'Yes,' Alex said. 'There's a shot of Anna that I'm particularly proud of.'

I smiled at him. He raised his glass to me, and drank.

'Are you a model?' Henri said.

'Not professionally,' I said. 'Only for Alex. I work for a graphic design company.'

'My round,' François said, getting up from the table. Luc went with him to the bar. The live band finished their set, and were replaced by a DJ playing club anthems.

Henri said, 'Would you like to dance, Anna?'

'Oh, I –' I didn't particularly want to dance with him, but there wasn't any reason why I shouldn't. It seemed mean to refuse him in front of all these people that he knew. 'Yes, I'll dance with you.'

I followed Henri onto the dance floor. While he wasn't nearly as good a dancer as Alex, he did at least lurch and shake in time to the music, and didn't stamp on my toes. A slow track came on. I'd have been happy to go back to the table at that point, but Henri put his hands on my waist, confining his dance moves to an occasional sway. I put my hands on his shoulders, making sure I kept plenty of space between us.

When the slow track came to an end, I dropped my hands to my sides, smiled, and said, '*Merci,* Henri.'

He looked a little disappointed, but didn't try to detain me.

We went back to the others. Alex was having an intense conversation with François and Léon, and Henri joined them. Luc was talking to Marthe.

Édith moved her chair close to mine and said, 'So how long have you and Alex been together?'

'Oh – No – We aren't together. It's like Alex said – we're friends.' As I needed to keep reminding myself.

Édith arched her eyebrows. 'You do surprise me. When you were dancing with Henri, Alex couldn't take his eyes off you.'

'I don't know why.' I glanced over at Alex. He seemed entirely absorbed in whatever Léon was saying to him.

Édith smiled. 'I can think of several reasons – Oh, I love this song! Shall we girls go and dance?'

Calling for Marthe to follow, Édith dragged me back to the dance floor. The three of us strutted our stuff for a while, and then the guys came and joined us, and we all danced together, with much raising of arms in the air, and vocal accompaniment. The tempo of the music changed. Alex caught hold of me and pulled me close. Slow-dancing with his arms about me, I thought how good it was to have a night out with him in Paris, to meet his friends, to be a part of the life he'd described to me in his letters.

'One more drink?' he said. 'And then we'll go back to mine?'

'*D'accord.*'

The others had already abandoned the dance floor. Alex steered me back to the alcove, Édith giving me a very knowing smile when she saw his hand on the small of my back. I decided that if she was determined to believe that I was more than his *amie*, there wasn't much I could do about it. Alex bought a final round of drinks, and after everyone had drained their glass, we all left Le Cave together. Amidst a throng of students and twenty-somethings bar-crawling along the Rue Oberkampf, Alex said *á bientôt* to his friends. They all wished him the best for the exhibition, hoped that I'd enjoy the rest of my stay in Paris, and then we went our separate ways.

Alex and I reached his apartment at around one in the morning. We discussed the arrangements for tomorrow – he had to go to the gallery, I was to go shopping with his sister – and then he took first turn in the bathroom, reappearing in about two minutes. I took far longer, scrupulously removing my make-up, and brushing my hair. I took off the jeans and top I'd worn to Le Cave. Then I put my baggy T-shirt on over my bra and thong. If I'd known I was going to be sharing a bed with Alex, I'd have brought something less revealing to sleep in.

I went back into the living area. Alex was already in bed, his head resting on one hand. With his other hand, he pulled back the duvet, and gestured to the mattress.

'Are you happy sleeping on this side of the bed?' he said. 'I didn't think to ask you last night, but most people have a preference.'

'I don't mind.' I wondered if he lay on that side of the bed when he slept with other women? My face flushed. All the awkwardness I'd felt the previous night came rushing back. Hoping Alex hadn't noticed my unease, I lay down on the mattress, making a conscious effort not to position myself right on the edge, and covered myself with the duvet. My body jerked involuntarily when Alex's foot brushed against mine.

'Are you OK?' he said.

'Yes, I'm fine, but could you move your foot – it's freezing.'

'*Pardon.*'

'No worries. *Pas de quoi.*'

He switched out the light. I turned onto my side and shut my eyes.

He said, 'Was Henri hitting on you tonight?'

'No,' I said. 'At least – I didn't notice.'

'He seemed very taken with you.'

'He was just being nice – I think.' I thought back over the evening, unsure now whether Henri had been flirting with me or not.

'Maybe I was mistaken,' Alex said. 'Not that I'd blame him if he'd hit on you. You're a very beautiful girl, Anna.' He also turned over so that we were lying back to back.

I was in bed with Alex and he'd just told me that I'm beautiful. I was intensely aware of him, almost naked, so close to me. If I turned to him, and kissed him right now, I couldn't see him pushing me away. My stomach clenched.

'*Bonne nuit,*' Alex said.

Having sex with Alex would be a really bad idea. He was barely over his ex. He'd never shown any sign of wanting a relationship with me. It would be casual sex and nothing more. I lived in London, he lived in Paris, so there was no future in it. Having sex with Alex could – would – ruin our friendship.

'*Bonne nuit, mon ami,*' I said.

Twenty-nine

'Do I look all right?' I twirled around so that Alex could inspect my denim shirt-dress, caught in at the waist with a wide leather belt. Mindful of the number of cobbled streets we'd walked down the day before, I'd made the reluctant decision to stick to my flats rather than the ankle boots I usually wore on shopping expeditions. Luckily, my shoulder bag matched my belt and my shoes. 'Is this smart enough for me to wear to go out with Hélène, do you think?'

Alex, sitting crossed legged on the bed in his jeans, going through the photos he'd taken yesterday on his camera, looked at me blankly. 'I've no idea. Why would you care what you wear to go shopping with my sister?'

'Frenchwomen are known to be effortlessly stylish. I don't want Hélène to think that just because I'm English, I don't know how to dress. What sort of clothes does she usually wear? Smart or casual?'

'I don't take much notice. She usually looks OK, I guess.'

'Alex! How can you not notice your sister's clothes? You do fashion shoots all the time.'

'But I don't choose the garments. All I do is turn up in the studio and photograph them on the models. And try to keep the peace between the client, the art director, and the stylist.'

A thought struck me. Hélène worked as a book illustrator. She'd been to art school. Perhaps her style of dress was bohemian. Would she come floating into Alex's apartment, trailing patterned scarves and a long skirt?

I said. 'Maybe I should change back into my jeans.'

The front door bell rang.

'No time now,' Alex said. 'Anyway, you look great. You always look great, by the way. Just saying.' He went to the door and opened it to let in his sister.

'*Bonjour*!' Hélène stepped into the vestibule and flung her arms around her brother. 'It's good to see you, Alexandre.'

'*Bonjour*, Hélène. *Ça va?*' He air-kissed each side of her face.

'*Trés bien, merci*.' She came further into the apartment, and immediately I saw the resemblance between her and Alex. They had the same very dark hair – hers curling past her shoulders – and dark eyes, and like him, she was very good-looking. She was tall for a woman, as tall as me, enviably slender, and dressed very elegantly in a pair of well-cut, cropped, light-tan trousers and a loose white shirt. I decided I'd made the right choice of outfit for a day out shopping with a *Parisienne*.

'*Bonjour*, Hélène,' I said. 'I'm Anna Mitchel.'

'Anna! *Bonjour*. It's so lovely to meet you at last.' We also exchanged air-kisses.

'I'm very pleased to meet you, too,' I said, speaking in French as she had. 'Alex has told me so much about you in his letters.'

'Knowing my little brother,' Hélène said with a smile, 'that is just a tiny bit worrying.' Her gaze travelled around the apartment, lingering on the un-made bed, glancing back at Alex, standing there nonchalantly without a shirt, his hands hooked into the pockets of his jeans, his feet bare. I knew exactly what she was thinking. I tried to think of a way to let her know that Alex and I weren't sleeping together – well, we were sleeping together, but not *sleeping together* – without saying it straight out, but decided that was a conversation best left until I knew her a little better.

Alex said, 'Whereabouts are you thinking of going shopping?'

'That rather depends on Anna.' Hélène turned to me. 'Paris has so many different shopping districts. There are the big department stores, of course, and I'd recommend the Left Bank if you're after vintage. And for all the best European chains, the Rue du Commerce.'

'Oh, I'm definitely a chain store girl,' I said. 'I'd love to buy a dress or shoes by a brand I couldn't get in England.'

'Sounds good to me,' Hélène said. 'What time shall I return Anna to you, Alex?'

Alex thought for a moment. 'I should be finished at the gallery by four. Why don't you both come and meet me somewhere for a drink?'

'As the Galerie Lécuyer is in the Marais,' Hélène said, 'let's meet in front of the Pompidou Centre. If you're delayed, Anna and I can watch the street performers in the piazza'

'*D'accord*,' Alex said. 'You go and bond over the clothing rails and I'll see you after I've seen my photos hung.'

Leaving Alex in the apartment, Hélène and I walked down the five flights of stairs to the street.

'This really is so kind of you to volunteer to entertain me while Alex is working,' I said, as we headed to the Metro.

'It's my pleasure,' Hélène said. 'There's no way accompanying you to the Rue du Commerce can be considered an altruistic gesture on my part. I'm only too delighted to have an excuse to hit the shops. Oh – I meant to ask you if you'd prefer to speak in French or English. Your French is so good that I forgot.'

'I'm happy speaking French,' I said. 'I'm glad to have the chance to practise.'

'Then we'll speak French,' Hélène said. 'Out of interest, which language do you speak when you're with Alex?'

'When he first came to England, we spoke English most of the time,' I said, 'but lately we seem to drift in and out of English and French.'

'It was a bit like that in our house when Alex and I were children,' Hélène said. 'We and our parents talked to each other in both languages – although when our mother told us off it was always in English. Alex and I knew that was a sign that she was really angry. People tend to express strong emotion in their first language, I think.'

The Rue du Commerce was situated not far from the Champs du Mars, but at the opposite end to the Eiffel Tower. We got off the Metro at the La Motte-Picquet-Grenelle stop – Hélène told me there was an excellent farmers' market there on Sundays – and she led me down a narrow, one-way street, much less crowded than any of other shopping streets I'd walked along in Paris. There were some fashion and make-up stores that had made the journey across the Channel from Europe to the British high street, but there were others whose brand names were unfamiliar to me, as well as small, quirky boutiques. Almost all the voices I heard were speaking French – the Rue du Commerce, it seemed, catered more for Parisians than tourists.

Hélène and I spent a very enjoyable morning flitting from shop to shop. Like her brother, she was very easy to get on with, and our talk – about the clothes we were trying on, the places Alex had taken me in Paris, my job, her job – never faltered. In one small shop, I found a pink shift dress that I simply couldn't resist ('What do you think, Hélène?' 'It was made for you, Anna, you look *trés chic.*'), and a little further along the street, I found the ideal pair of shoes to go with it. Hélène bought herself a silk shirt and two of the cutest dresses ever for her daughters. By then we were both in want of refreshment. As the Rue du Commerce was the site of numerous eateries, we had no trouble in finding a café with an empty table.

'How old are your girls?' I asked Hélène, as we ate our *assiettes parisiennes*.

'Véronique is eight, and Élodie is six. I have a photo, if you would like to see them.'

Hélène fished in her bag and eventually extracted a wallet containing a photo of two extremely sweet little girls standing by a fountain.

'They're delightful. So pretty. And that's a lovely photo. Did

Alex take it?'

'Yes. He's the only photographer who's ever managed to get Véronique to smile for the camera. She's a very quiet, serious child, while Élodie is very talkative, and never sits still. Alex and I were also very different as children. I was the outgoing one – he was shy.'

'I remember. He's changed so much since he was a boy.'

'You and Alex have become very close since he has been living with you in London, I think?'

Seizing the opportunity to correct any false impressions that Hélène may have received at Alex's apartment, I said, 'I'm not his girlfriend, but we are very close friends.'

Hélène regarded me thoughtfully. 'Has he told you why he left Paris? Do you know about Cécile? What she did to him?'

I nodded.

'Anna – I have to ask you – Do you think he's still in love with her?'

'He's over her,' I said. 'He told me so himself only yesterday.'

'Oh, I'm so relieved.' Hélène sank back in her chair. 'We – his whole family – have been so anxious about him. That *bitch* broke his heart.'

'He was sad when he first came to London,' I said. 'But not all the time. And I really do think he's fine now.'

'I suspect much of that is down to you,' Hélène said. 'That night I rang him to tell him that Cécile was getting married, I felt so much better knowing that you were there and he wasn't on his own.'

'All I've done is listen when he needed to talk,' I said, 'as any friend would do.'

'Well, I'm grateful – and I know my parents will be very reassured when I tell them that he's over Cécile. I'm under strict orders to report back to my mother as soon as I get home. Alexandre may be a grown man, but he's still her son, and she worries about his emotional well-being. And to me, he's still my little brother who I feel I have to look out for – which is

217

totally ridiculous, of course, but that's families for you.'

Alex, I decided, was as fortunate in his family as I was in mine.

Hélène said, 'I never liked Cécile. I tried to like her, really I did, particularly when it became obvious that Alex was serious about her, but she always gave me the impression that my conversation bored her. I'm sorry that my brother had to suffer all that pain, but I'm not sorry that Cécile is out of his life. Anyway, we've talked about her quite enough, I think.' She drained her coffee. 'We've another hour before we need to go to the Pompidou Centre – let's shop.'

It was when we were making our way back along the Rue du Commerce to the Metro, that Hélène announced, 'Last year, I bought a wonderful jacket in that little shop opposite – we must go in. If we're late meeting Alexandre, I'll tell him it was all my fault.'

I laughed. 'I'm sure he won't mind waiting.'

We went into the tiny boutique – there was barely room to move for all clothing-rails and the tables in the centre piled high with jumpers and shirts. Hélène immediately swooped on a sundress ('This would be perfect for picnics in the Jardin du Luxembourg') and went to try it on. I wasn't intending to buy another outfit, but I couldn't resist leafing through the assorted dresses, every one unique, that were on a rail at the back of the shop. Amongst the bright primary colours and the pastels, I found one dress made of white cotton, with inch-wide shoulder straps, a tight bodice with tiny pearl buttons all down the front, and a calf-length skirt with deep tiers. There was something timeless about the design that really appealed to me. I was still looking at it when Hélène returned.

'That would look lovely on you, Anna,' she said.

'Oh, I'm not thinking of buying it. I never wear white – I'm too pale.'

'At least try it on.'

'*D'accord.*' I went into the changing room, changed into the dress, and surveyed myself in the mirror. To my surprise, the dress really suited me. An image flashed before my eyes of me sitting in a garden, sunlight falling across my white skirts, just like the woman in the Monet painting that Alex liked so much, and of him taking my photograph. I pulled back the changing room curtain.

'What do you think?' I said to Hélène.

She smiled. '*Charmant.*'

'*Merci.*' I checked the price tag – the dress was very reasonably priced. And buying two dresses in the same day wasn't so very extravagant. I was, after all, on my first trip to Paris.

'You should definitely buy that dress,' Hélène said.

'I'm very tempted to buy it, but I'm not sure when I'd wear it.'

'You could wear it to the gallery tomorrow,' Hélène said. 'You must buy it,'

'You know,' I said, 'I really think I must.'

'It really is an extraordinary construction,' I said, looking at the photo I'd taken of the Pompidou Centre, with its brightly coloured utility pipes and air ducts on its outside wall, and its external elevator.

'Yes, it isn't often that you see a building turned inside-out,' Alex said.

Hélène and I had arrived at the Pompidou Centre half an hour after our appointed meeting time with Alex, but he'd been perfectly content watching the street performers entertaining the people gathered in the piazza. The three of us had wandered amongst the crowds, admiring the skill of the unicyclists, jugglers, mime artists, and contortionists, and had then gone for a drink at a nearby café. Hélène couldn't stay long as she had to pick up her daughters from a friend's house. Alex and I'd had a meal, and lingered over a second glass of wine, before going back to Montmartre.

'I wish we had longer in Paris,' Alex said, lying stretched out on his bed, his arms behind his head. 'These last three days have gone so fast. There are so many things, so many parts of the city that I still want to show you. Not just the famous sites, but the places the tourists don't see. Once I move back here in the summer, maybe you could come and stay for a couple of weeks.'

'I'd like that.' I didn't want to think about the time Alex would no longer be living in my flat, when I wouldn't see him all the time, and we'd go back to being penfriends, writing each other letters, telling each other about our lives, rather than doing things together. 'This trip has gone very quickly, but we still have one more day before we go back to London.'

Alex nodded. 'Tomorrow morning, I thought we'd go to the Musée du Montmartre. It focuses on the *belle époque,* and I think you'd find it interesting.'

'And in the evening, we have your exhibition. I'm so looking forward to it.'

'Me too,' Alex said. 'I'm very pleased with the way my photos have been hung. Edouard Geroux, the director, may have been running the gallery for only six months, but he certainly knows his job. The picture of you with the rose is placed exactly where the light is perfect for it.' He added, 'I've given it a title: *Anna Awakening.*'

'I like that.' I smiled. 'It's going to be strange seeing myself on the walls of an art gallery after looking at so many famous works of art in the last couple of days – Sorry, Alex, tomorrow isn't about *me*, it's about you.'

'It does have something to do with you – you're my favourite artist's model.'

'Do you think the artist who used to live in your apartment had a favourite model?'

'I know he did. She was very beautiful.'

'Did she come to this room to pose for him?'

'*Bien sûr.* He was too poor to rent a studio, but the light up here was ideal for him to work by. His easel was in that corner, and she posed in front of that window. One day, I'll be browsing in a flea market, and I'll see an old oil-painting of a girl in an attic room with a view over the rooftops of Paris, and I'll know it's her.'

We both laughed.

'What happened to them?' I said. 'The artist who used to live here and his model?'

Alex shrugged, and then he yawned.

'Are you tired?'

'Yeah. I know it's not late, but would you mind if we called it a night?'

I was wide awake, my head full of the artist who used to live in Alex's apartment and his beautiful muse, but I said, 'Of course not. You need to get a good night's sleep. Tomorrow is an important day for you.'

'It is. If this show goes well, I can see Edouard and I having a very successful creative partnership.' He stood up, reaching behind his head, the way guys do to pull off his T-shirt. Then he took off his jeans. 'Do you want to go first in the bathroom?'

'Ye-es.' I went to the bathroom, taking my baggy T-shirt with me. However irrational it might be, considering we were friends sharing a bed, I felt far too self-conscious to casually strip off in front of him, the way he'd just done in front of me. I told myself I was being ridiculous, that I wouldn't think twice about getting changed in front of Beth, that Alex had already had an eyeful, but it didn't make any difference.

Make-up removed, teeth cleaned, and wearing my T-shirt over my underwear, I went back into the living space, and slid under the duvet. Alex padded off to the bathroom. I was already drifting off, when he came and got into bed next to me.

'Goodnight, Anna.'

'*Bonne nuit, mon ami*,' I said. And fell asleep.

Thirty

From outside the bathroom the next morning. Alex said, 'I'm starving, and we're completely out of anything remotely edible.'

'Won't they be feeding us at the reception?'

'They only ever serve hors d'oeuvres at these events. I'm going to run down to the *boulangerie*. I won't be long.'

'*D'accord*.' I finished blow drying my hair. Having by now memorised the layout of Alex's neighbourhood, I knew that he wouldn't be back for a least another ten minutes, so I felt able to leave the bathroom wearing only my lace-trimmed, ivory silk bra and thong. I fetched the two dresses I'd bought in the Rue du Commerce and the dress I'd brought from England from the cupboard in the vestibule, and laid them out on Alex's bed. The deep blue wrap-around was one of my favourites, and I always felt good when I wore it. The pink shift was, as Hélène had said, very *chic*. But I knew immediately that it was the white dress, simple and summery, that I was going to wear to the photography exhibition. With my wide leather belt, and the ankle boots I'd rejected the day before, it would make me look just slightly bohemian, I thought. I'd even brought a bag and jacket with me that would match the rest of my ensemble. I stepped carefully into the dress, slid the straps onto my shoulders, and started to fasten the bodice. The buttons were tiny and the holes were very stiff, so I went and stood by the window to see them better in the bright, early afternoon light.

'Anna, I've bought bread, and cheese to go with it –'

I looked up to see Alex standing just a few feet away,

holding several large paper bags, his dark eyes staring at me intently. Instinctively, I clutched the dress closed over my bra.

'I didn't hear you come in,' I said.

He said, 'Anna, please don't move. I – I have to take your photo.'

'What? *Now*? But, I'm not wearing any make-up. I haven't straightened my hair –'

'That doesn't matter. *S'il te plait,* just stay where you are by the window.' Distractedly, he tossed the paper bags he was carrying in the general direction of the kitchen and picked up his camera. 'Could you let go of your dress – put your hands the way they were, and look down – as though you're doing up the buttons, as you were before.'

I did as he asked. I heard the now familiar click and whirr of his camera as he took shot after shot.

'If only I had time, and the right equipment – and Lou to hold a reflector – to do this properly,' he said. 'There – that'll have to do. The light's changing already.'

I relaxed and let my hands fall. And then, realising that the open front of the dress was exposing not only ivory silk and lace, but a fair expanse of my breasts, I hastened to do it up.

Alex sat down on the bed. 'Anna, you have to see these photos.'

I sat beside him, and looked at the screen on his camera. I saw myself caught in the act of fastening the bodice of my white dress, my hair uncombed, my feet bare, light streaming in through the open window, the rooftops of Paris behind me.

'Ooh,' I said. 'It's the picture you talked about last night – the oil-panting of the artist's model.'

'*Mais oui,*' Alex said. 'When I walked in and saw you standing by the window in a ray of sunlight, dressed in white, it was uncanny. I felt as though I'd stepped back in time.' He showed me the rest of the photos. Naturally, the images were much smaller and therefore had much less impact than if they were on a computer screen, but I was still impressed. He zoomed in so that I could see my face more clearly.

'You've made me look amazing – again,' I said.

He smiled. 'As I have told you before, you are extremely photogenic.'

'Thank you. But it's your skill that creates a picture.'

'Thank *you*. These shots are nowhere near as technically proficient as if I'd taken them in a studio – I could never exhibit them – but sometimes, you just have to seize the moment. And I hope I never become so pretentious about my *art* that I stop taking photos for pleasure.' He pointed at my dress. 'You've missed a button – actually, you've missed several. Here, let me.'

I sat very still while he fastened my dress. The sun had moved, and the light was now falling on the bed. I wondered what Alex would do if I sank back onto the cotton sheets. Would he lie down beside me? And undo all those tiny pearl buttons?

His hands dropped to his lap. 'If we're going to eat before we head over to the Marais, it's going to have to be soon – I can't arrive late at the gallery.'

I realised that I'd been holding my breath. Enough, Anna. I thought. Focus on your friend's photography exhibition which is really important to him and to his career. 'No, you really can't be late. You go and shave. I'll make you a sandwich.'

He went off. I stood, and smoothed my skirts. When I'd looked up, my dress half-undone, and seen Alex's dark eyes watching me, I'd been sure he was looking at me in the way a man looks at a woman who is *not* a female friend – or a photographic model. Apparently, I was once again mistaken.

Alex was expected at the exhibition an hour or so before the reception, to meet the gallery owners, the guests who were important enough to have a relatively private viewing, and to be interviewed by the media. I travelled across Paris with him to the Marais, so that he could show me exactly where the Galerie Lécuyer, formerly a large residential house, was situated amongst the maze of twisting lanes and cobblestone alleyways that made up this district of Paris. While he networked, I intended to do some more sight-seeing.

'This area has some of the oldest streets and buildings in the city,' Alex said, as we stood outside the gallery. He pointed to an archway leading to a narrow alley 'If you walk that way, you'll even see some medieval timbered houses.'

'I won't go very far,' I said. 'I don't want to get lost.'

'Yeah, I'm kind of counting on your being there as soon as they start letting people in.' He ran a hand through his hair, and straightened the sleeves of his black, collarless shirt.

I looked at him more closely. 'Are you OK? You seem a bit tense.'

He shrugged his shoulders. 'Knowing my work is about to be seen and judged by some very knowledgeable art critics is somewhat daunting. I feel like I'm a student again, just before my graduation show.'

I put my hands on either side of his face. 'You're a great photographer, Alex. An artist.'

'Not that you're biased or anything.'

'I should perhaps remind you, monsieur, that I have a degree in the History of Art. I know how to judge a visual image. Even if I'm also your greatest fan. And your very good friend, of course.'

He drew me close and I slid my arms around his waist. As we held each other, I felt his body relax.

'I should go,' he said. 'Wish me luck.'

'*Bonne chance.*' I kissed his cheek, and looked up into his eyes. He trailed a finger along the line of my jaw. Then he let go of me, and took a step away.

'*À bientôt, mon amie,*' he said.

'See you later.' I watched as he walked to blue-painted door of the gallery. He looked back over his shoulder and raised a hand, and then vanished inside. I consulted my map, marked the position of the Galerie Lécuyer with an 'X' – I wasn't taking any chances on letting Alex down by being unable to find it again – and made my way through the arch he'd indicated. The alley brought me to a courtyard, where I did indeed spot a timber-framed house. I walked across the square, through a covered passageway, and into a labyrinth of crooked, narrow streets. Keeping a track of where I was going on the map, I strolled past art galleries and bars, boutiques, and *patisseries*, old ivy-covered apartments and design stores. Catching sight of my reflection in a gallery window, I thought I looked as though I belonged in this trendy area of Paris. I may have given away my tourist status when I took a photo on my phone.

My circuitous route through the Marais brought me back to the Galerie Lécuyer in good time. Seeing that the blue doors were now standing wide open, and people were going inside, I followed them. I found myself in a bright, white atrium with a metal staircase leading to an upper floor. To my left, a square archway provided a glimpse into a large room displaying a cobweb of light fibres and a colossal pyramid of brown cardboard boxes – Alex had told me that the ground floor of the gallery was used for installations, not really my thing, but I hoped I could appreciate its intentions. In front of me, two women, one in a multi-coloured mini dress (think paint splatters) that was a work of art in itself, the other in unrelieved black, were welcoming invitees to the exhibition, and directing them up the metal staircase. I went over to them, my invitation clutched in my hand.

Without looking at my invitation, the woman in the colourful mini dress gave me a broad smile and said, 'Welcome to the Galerie Lécuyer. The award exhibition is on the first floor.'

'*Bonsoir, mademoiselle.*' The other woman, the one dressed in black, ushered me to the staircase. 'At the top, please turn to the left and you will see the entrance to the exhibition.'

'*Merci.*' I followed her instructions, climbing the stairs and turning left into a long, light-filled room, divided into a succession of smaller exhibition spaces, by high partitions. Looking around the first section, I saw that its white walls were hung with close-up photographs of people. Although they were portraits, I knew immediately they weren't Alex's work. He

227

was interested in capturing the personality of his subject, but these shots had been edited so that the faces were distorted. Wanting to find him and let him know I'd arrived, I scanned the knots of viewers gathering in front of the photos. They were of various ages, some younger than me, others considerably older. A middle-aged couple, the woman wearing the sort of dress I'd seen in the shops on the Avenue Montaigne, were talking to a young man in scruffy denim, his long hair tied back in a ponytail. A grey-haired man, standing close enough to one photo to make a nearby gallery employee rather nervous, was writing in a spiral notebook. I wondered if he was an art critic. As there was no sign of Alex, I went into the next section of the gallery.

Here there were more people, many of whom seemed to know each other, and the level of conversation was considerably louder. There was also a bar: a trestle table, behind which a waiter was pouring champagne. I went and helped myself to a glass. The waiter gave me what I thought was a very searching look. For a moment I worried that I'd breached some unspoken rule of exhibition opening etiquette, but other people were helping themselves to champagne, so I decided I was imagining things. Moving away from the bar, I found myself looking at a group of randomly hung monochrome photos no more than a foot square. At first I thought they were abstracts, but as I walked further into the exhibition space, I saw that each individual picture was part of a whole, and if they'd been moved around and fitted together like a jigsaw they would have made a cityscape, a bleak urban wasteland of high-rise tenements and flyovers.

A man standing next to me said, 'It's clever, but also alienating, and ultimately depressing. I can't look at it for very long.' He was about forty-five, with longish brown hair, and smartly dressed in a linen suit.

'I find it a very desolate piece of artwork,' I said, 'but I presume that's the response the photographer wanted to evoke.'

'It seems she has succeeded.' He added, 'I'm Marcel

Guilleroy, Alexandre Tourville's agent. And you, I believe, are one of his models. I recognise you from his photograph.' He held out a hand.

I shook it, and said, 'I'm Anna Mitchel.'

'I'm delighted to make your acquaintance, mademoiselle. Have you seen Alexandre's pictures? They are already receiving a great deal of favourable attention.'

'No, not yet. I've not seen him yet either.'

'His photos are hanging in the next room. I believe you'll find him there also.' He gestured towards the far partition. '*Á bientôt, Mademoiselle Mitchel.*'

'*Á bientôt, Monsieur Guilleroy.*'

Marcel Guilleroy turned away, and began talking to the elderly, distinguished-looking man standing on his other side. I took a sip of my champagne, and made my way past the throng now swarming around the bar, and into the next section of the gallery.

I saw Alex straight away, deep in conversation with a man in his thirties, who was listening to whatever he was saying with rapt attention. I managed to catch his eye and he smiled at me, before resuming his discussion. I was about to go up to him when I remembered that while for many of the guests, the opening was a social occasion, for Alex and the other exhibitors, it was work. Rather than interrupt him, I looked around the room for the picture of me. From where I was standing, it was impossible to see any of the photos as each one was hidden behind a cluster of spectators. I went over to the nearest group, and by standing at the side, managed to get a partial view of the photo they were looking at, which turned out to be a portrait of my favourite author, Verity Holmes. I remembered that Alex had photographed her for *The Edge* not long after he'd arrived in England – and given me that novel. In the picture, she was sitting at her laptop, her brows drawn together in concentration.

I heard a woman say, 'It is as though Tourville has photographed the actual creative process.'

Her companion said, 'I am usually bored by figurative art, but this – this is different. This is *good*,'

A stout matron speaking American-accented English, the one person I'd heard not speaking French, said, 'Only a Frenchman could photograph a woman who has reached her half-century and make her look so magnificent. I must have this Tourville guy photograph me for my fiftieth birthday.'

This was my friend Alex they're talking about. I turned away from Verity Holmes – whom I happened to know was in her seventies – with a smile on my face, and moved on. Walking past two young men, I was aware that both of them were nudging each other and openly staring at me, which I thought very unsophisticated behaviour considering the venue and the occasion. Deciding that I was flattered rather than annoyed – they were very young, probably photographic students – I ignored them, and headed across the room to a photo which for the moment had only one other viewer. It turned out to be a shot of a little girl sitting on the branch of a tree reading a book. A small plaque gave the title of the photo as *Véronique Reading*, and I recognised Hélène's elder daughter from the picture she'd shown me the day before. Given the angle at which the photo had been taken, I couldn't see how Alex could have got the shot unless he too had climbed the tree – before common sense told me that he wouldn't have sat a child up so high, and that it was his skill that had created the illusion of height. I studied the picture for some time, noting the dreamy expression on the little girl's face, the way she seemed to float between the sky above her head and the ground, seemingly a long way beneath her. I thought about how it felt to lose oneself in a book, particularly when you're young and the stories you read are almost as real to you as everyday life. Alex had precisely portrayed that feeling in this photograph. I wondered how he could capture such emotion through the lens of a camera.

Aware that a number of viewers were beginning to gather behind me, and conscious that I was in the way of those who might be potential customers or curators of Alex's work, I moved away from the photo.

By now, people were streaming into this part of the gallery, many of them gravitating toward the group that had collected in front of a photo hanging on the far wall. Seeing that Alex was currently surrounded by about a dozen men and women, all talking animatedly and with many wild gesticulations, I too made my way to the far end of the room. Hovering on the edge of the crowd, I heard snatches of conversation, words like '*formidable*', '*extraordinaire*', '*merveilleux*', '*incroyable,*' and '*exquis*' and, in an American accent, 'awesome' Edging my way forward, I finally managed get through the crowd, and stand in front of the artwork that Alex had entitled *Anna Awakening*.

I'd thought the photograph beautiful when Alex had first showed it to me on his laptop, but now, seeing the picture blown up and hanging on the wall of an art gallery, I felt its impact anew. The play of light and shadow over the girl's body – over my body – the expression on the girl's face as she first caught sight of the rose, the emotions and the narrative that the image conveyed, all of this combined to make an extraordinary visual image. I heard a male voice say, 'The photograph obviously depicts a sexual awakening' and a female voice say, 'No, it is more than that, it is a picture of a young girl awakening to all the possibilities of life and love.' When Alex came to London, I thought, he woke me up. I was sleep-walking, and I didn't even realise it.

I became aware that someone was standing very close behind me, and I caught an oh-so-familiar masculine scent.

I said, 'Hey, Alex.'

He moved forward so that he was standing next to me. He took my hand, and it was as though an electric shock passed between us. I felt his breath on my neck as he put his mouth close to my ear.

In a low voice he said, 'Here we have *Anna Awakening,* by the French photographer Alexandre Tourville. A nude female

231

figure lies on a bed. The artist has captured the moment she awakes after a night of love. The picture is one of a number of photographs that Tourville took of his friend Anna Mitchel while he was living and working in London.'

I said. 'Is the girl in this photo actually *me*?'

'What do you think?'

'You created the image.'

'But I don't want to tell you how to respond to it. All I'll say is that the original title of the picture was *Woman Awakening*, but the photographer changed his mind.' His mouth lifted in a smile. 'If you've looked at this photo long enough, there's someone I'd like you to meet.'

'Sure,' I said. 'I can come back and admire myself later.'

Alex led me around the partition on which *Anna Awakening* was hung, and into the next white-walled room. Here, there were fewer people examining the photographs. Several heads turned as we walked past.

'People are staring at you,' I said to Alex. 'The *renowned* French photographer Alexandre Tourville.'

'No,' Alex said. 'They are looking at you – the photographer's beautiful model.'

I laughed.

'Seriously, Anna. Almost all the people who've been talking to me about my work this evening, including the gallery staff, have been more interested in the photo of you than any of the others. Obviously, they recognise you.'

'Actually, now you come to mention it, your agent introduced himself and said that he recognised me from the photo. And I've noticed other people looking at me ever since I came into the gallery.'

'Do you mind?'

'Not right now. I can see that it might become tiresome if it happened all the time. Not that *that's* very likely – I'm not about to take up modelling as a full-time career.'

We continued walking until we came to the final section of the gallery, where a woman with short iron-grey hair was studying a spectacular landscape of snow and ice, large enough to cover half the wall. Hearing our approach, she turned around, and I saw that she was in her mid-forties, with piercing blue eyes.

Alex said, 'Caroline, may I introduce you to Anna Mitchel, my childhood penfriend, and now my model. Anna, this is Caroline Gauthier, who in the year I was her assistant, taught me everything I know about photography.'

'Not everything,' Caroline said firmly. 'The shot of Mademoiselle Mitchel hanging in the next room shows me that your photographic skills have progressed considerably since you worked in my studio. Your photographs have an emotional and intellectual depth that I find lacking in the other images I've seen this evening. I'll be extremely surprised if the Lécuyer Award isn't yours.'

'*Merci*,' Alex said, quietly. 'Your good opinion means a lot to me.'

Caroline gave me an appraising look. 'I can certainly see why Alexandre chose to photograph you, and why he chose to show *Anna Awakening* in the exhibition.'

'It's a great photo,' I said. 'But only because Alex is such a talented photographer. I usually look awful in photographs.'

'Do you really? You surprise me.' Caroline glanced at her watch. 'I'd love to stay for the presentation, but I have a plane to catch.'

'I know you have a crowded schedule,' Alex said. 'I really appreciate your taking the time to come here tonight.'

'My pleasure, I assure you, to see the work of one of my former assistants on the walls of the Galerie Lécuyer. I always told you that you'd go far. It's good to be proved right.'

They exchanged air-kisses, and Caroline swept off.

'So,' Alex said, 'what do you think of my mentor?'

'She's very direct,' I said. 'but I liked her – and what she said about your work.'

'She's had an extraordinary career.'

'So have you.'

'Not like Caroline. Not yet.'

From behind us, Hélène's voice said, 'There you are, Alex. We've been looking all over for you.'

Alex and I swung around to see his sister, with a man of around her age and an older couple.

Alex's face broke into a delighted smile. 'Anna, these are my parents, Caitlin and Guillaume, and my brother-in-law Raymond. Hélène, you know already.'

We exchanged the usual greetings – in a mixture of French and English – and Caitlin Tourville gave her son a hug.

'It's so good to see you,' she said. 'And looking so well. London obviously agrees with you.' She turned to me and smiled. 'After all the years that you and Alex have been exchanging letters, and it's only now that you have come to Paris. It's wonderful to meet you at last.'

'I'm so pleased to meet all of you,' I said. It was, I thought, very easy to see where Alex got his good looks. His mother was a beautiful woman, dark-haired, tall and slim, and although I knew she was in her late fifties, she could have been a decade younger. His father was an older version of Alex himself, with glasses, and hair that was still thick, if shot through with grey. They were an exceptionally attractive family.

Alex said. 'Have you seen my photos?'

'We have,' Caitlin said. 'And we're all very impressed. The picture of Anna is one of the best you've ever taken. Everyone at the exhibition is talking about it. I feel quite sorry for the other photographers.'

'I was inspired when I took that shot,' Alex said, smiling at me.

'As anyone looking at the photograph can see,' Guillaume said.

At that point a gallery employee approached, and informed Alex that the presentation of the Lécuyer Award would shortly be taking place in the atrium.

'Now it gets serious,' Guillaume said.

'No pressure, Alex,' Hélène said.

Along with everyone else at the exhibition, we made our way through the white-walled gallery and down to the lower floor. Alex went and stood with the five other nominated photographers, two men and three women, at the foot of the stairs, while I stood with his family at the front of the assembled crowd. Whatever he was feeling inside at that moment, he appeared calm and relaxed, chatting easily with his rivals. He's brilliant and talented, I thought. He *has* to win this award. I let my gaze travel round the atrium, spotting Marcel Guilleroy, the American woman who'd wanted Alex to take her birthday photograph, and the elderly man with the notebook. A number of people cast interested glances in my direction, and more than once I heard someone nearby mention the name 'Anna'. We'd only been waiting a few minutes, although it felt like much longer, when two men and one woman emerged from a side-room and joined the photographers.

'The guy with the beard is Edouard Geroux, the gallery director,' Hélène said to me. 'The others are Monsieur and Madame Lécuyer, the gallery owners.

'Do you know them?' I said, surprised. As far as I was aware, Alex was the only one in his artistic family to have made any inroads into the inner circles of the Parisian art world.

'Oh, no,' Hélène said, 'I googled them before we came out.'

The hum of conversation in the room gradually faded into silence. Edouard Geroux, holding a microphone, stepped forward, and made a short speech, thanking everyone for their support of the gallery, and of the artists whose work was displayed within its walls. My heart started hammering in my chest.

'But you haven't come here to listen to me talk all evening,' Edouard said. 'What you want to hear is the name of the photographer who has been awarded the Lécuyer Award.'

Everyone in the gallery held their collective breath.

'It is my very great pleasure,' Edouard said, 'to tell you that the recipient of this year's award is ... Alexandre Tourville.'

The atrium erupted into loud applause. Alex looked

completely stunned. The gallery owners shook his hand, as did Edouard and the other photographers, but he stared at them as if he either hadn't heard what the director had said or didn't understand. Then his eyes met mine, and suddenly his face broke into a dazzling smile. He beckoned me forward. I shook my head, but he nodded and mouthed 'yes'. Aware that people were looking at me, and that his family were smiling at me encouragingly, I went to him. He took my hand in his, raising it to his lips and kissing it, before sliding his arm lightly around my waist. A flashbulb exploded as someone took a photo of both of us. I smiled up at Alex, my extraordinarily talented friend, and clapped my hands so hard that they stung.

Thirty-one

'You have a lovely home,' I said to Hélène, looking around her state-of-the-art kitchen, and smiling at the children's paintings taped to the fridge. 'Have you lived here long?'

'Nearly nine years,' Hélène said. 'We moved here when I was pregnant with Véronique. Before that we lived in a place that was even smaller than Alexandre's.'

'His studio apartment is tiny,' I said, smiling across the table at Alex, 'but I love it. It's wonderful to wake up in the morning, open the shutters, and look out over the rooftops – and I adore Montmartre. Alex once wrote to me that living there is like living in a village, even though it's in the heart of a city, and I know exactly what he means.'

Caitlin, sitting next to me, said, 'Your first visit to Paris has been a great success, I think?'

'It's been everything I hoped it would be and more. Alex winning the award has made it absolutely perfect.'

After the presentation of the Lécuyer Award, once the applause had finally died down, Alex had been besieged by any number of people wanting to congratulate him. I stood next to him while he accepted their compliments, thinking how handsome he looked, and feeling ridiculously proud and pleased for him. Eventually, with the woman in the paint-spattered dress wishing them *au revoir* and a safe journey home, people started to drift out of the gallery's open doors. Alex, after one final conversation with Edouard Geroux and Marcel Guilleroy, joined his thrilled and delighted family. They hugged him, each other and me, before we all headed out into the night. There was some discussion about whether we should go to a bar, but Hélène and Raymond had to get home to relieve their child-sitter, and so Alex and I, and Alex's parents, went with them.

Back at their stylish apartment in a leafy residential avenue in Montparnasse, Véronique and Élodie were still wide awake, and very excited to learn that Uncle Alexandre had won an award, Hélène explaining that it was the same as winning a prize for coming top of the class at school. They were also very interested to meet 'Anna, who is from England, just like your *grand-mére.*' Véronique had asked me shyly if I'd seen the photograph of her sitting in a tree and smiled happily when I told her that I had indeed. Élodie, talking non-stop, had dragged me by the hand to see her room, where I duly admired the dolls' house made for her by her *papa.* Once the children had been sent off to bed, the adults sat around the kitchen table, the talk flowing as freely as the wine with which Raymond kept topping up our glasses.

'The first time I visited Paris,' Caitlin said, 'was just after I'd graduated from art college. I was sitting at a table outside a pavement café, sketching the other customers and passers-by, when this very good-looking Frenchman, also carrying a sketchbook, sat down beside me and asked if he could draw me. That was how I met Guillaume.'

'That's so romantic,' I said. 'How come you've never told me that story, Alex?'

'Have I not?' Alex said. 'I guess I've heard one or other of my parents tell it so often, I never thought to put it in a letter.' He and his sister exchanged amused smiles.

'We still have that drawing, framed and hanging in our dining room,' Guillaume said. 'Of course, when I sat down next to Caitlin that day, the only thought in my head was to chat up this very pretty English girl, and hopefully persuade her to meet me later for a drink. I'd no idea that she was going to turn out to be the love of my life.' He reached across the table and took his wife's hand. 'It took me a whole week to figure that out.'

'It took me a little longer,' Caitlin said, 'but before the end of my holiday, I was smitten.'

'So what happened after you went back to England?' I asked Caitlin. 'Did Guillaume visit you? Did you write letters to each other?'

'I never went back to England,' Caitlin said.

'*Never*? Not even once?'

'I had no reason to go back. My brother and his family, my only living relatives, had emigrated to New Zealand the year before. My few close English friends, girls I'd known from school and college, were scattered all around the country. When Guillaume asked me to stay with him in France, it wasn't a hard decision to make. I soon made friends here and found myself a job. Paris very quickly became my home.'

'It was a brave thing to do all the same,' Guillaume said. 'At the time I didn't realise quite how much I was asking of you, *ma chérie*.'

Caitlin smiled. 'It was crazy, but we were both very young.'

I wanted to ask Caitlin more about her early days in France, but the conversation moved on, talk about work, gossip about friends, the sort of discussions close families have around a kitchen table. I looked at Alex's mother, with her husband and adult children, and tried to imagine how it must have been for her as a young woman, starting a new life in a new country, with a man she'd only just met. It struck me that if I ever wanted to experience living and working abroad, now while I was still young, would be the time to do it. If I did decide to move on from Nova Graphics, maybe I could get a job in Paris, just as Alex had done in London. Not that I wouldn't miss my friends and family in England, but going back and forth across the Channel was a lot simpler now than when Alex's parents were my age. For the first time in years, I found myself remembering how after I'd graduated, I'd tried to get a job in an art gallery – without success. I thought of all the small galleries I'd seen this afternoon in the Marais and wondered if any of them were looking to take on an assistant …

Alex's voice broke in on the half-formed thoughts tumbling

around my head. 'We're catching an early morning train tomorrow, and neither of us has packed. We should be getting back to my place – if you're ready, Anna?'

'I'd love to stay longer,' I said, 'but you're right – we do have to get up early tomorrow.'

With many hugs and promises that I'd come and see them the next time I was in Paris (and promises that they'd come and see me if they ever came to London), Alex and I said goodbye to his relatives. Caitlin accompanied us to the front door, giving me an extra hug, telling me once again that she was delighted to have met me at last. She stood watching Alex and I from the open doorway until we were inside the lift.

'I do like your family,' I said, as we walked to the Metro. 'They all made me feel so welcome.' Unlike Mrs Cooper. I had a sudden vision of Nick's mother standing in front of *Anna Awakening*. Somehow, I doubted that she would appreciate its artistic merits. I spared a thought for Nick, wishing him well, hoping that he was over me, and that he'd soon meet someone who would make him happy.

Alex said, 'My family like you. While Élodie was showing you her toys, your complete and utter wondrousness was all my parents talked about. I did point out that it was me, the *award-winning* photographer, who should be getting all the praise and attention, but they told me not to be so up myself, and that I was very lucky to have you as a friend. Which is true enough.'

I laughed. 'They're all very proud of you – as you well know.'

'Yes, they are.'

'As am I,' I said. 'I'm *so* proud of you, Alex.'

Alex's eyes shone. 'It was a good night, wasn't it?'

'It couldn't have been better.'

'I think it's only now that it's all sinking in.'

Suddenly, he pulled me to him, and danced me around and around, and along the pavement. Despite my protests, he didn't let me go until we'd reached we reached the old iron *Metropolitain* sign that marked the entrance to the station.

Laughing, hand in hand, we ran down the steps onto the brightly lit platform of *ligne* 12 that would take us back to Montmartre.

Thirty-two

We came up out of the Metro into the Place des Abbesses – just as we had on my first night in Paris. I looked round the pretty square, golden light spilling out of its cafés and bars, and thought how familiar it seemed, even after just four days. Alex, declaring that although we did need to pack, there was no reason why we shouldn't have another drink while we were doing it, went into a bar and re-appeared carrying a bottle of champagne. Once we were away from the square, he opened it, the cork flying very satisfactorily through the air. We walked through the winding streets of Montmartre, passing the bottle back and forth between us. I looked up at the stars and the full moon overhead, and I'd never felt more alive.

We arrived at Alex's building and he unlocked the communal front door. Inside, the courtyard was dark and silent. We picked our way through the shadows, both of us warning the other not to make too much noise, smothering our laughter.

'Wait, Alex,' I said, when we came to the staircase. 'I need to take off my heels or I'll never make it up all those steps.'

'I could carry you up,' Alex said. 'At least – I could try.'

'Or maybe not.'

'I'll have you know, I'm an award-winning photographer. There are very few things I can't do.'

'But carrying your model up five flights of stairs is likely to be one of them.' I sat on the stairs and took off my ankle boots. Alex hauled me to my feet, and I straggled after him up the staircase, collapsing breathlessly against the wall when we reached the top.

243

'What you need is more champagne,' he said, opening the door to his apartment.

'Oh, yes, more champagne is definitely required.' I went into the living area, tossing my boots on the floor, and my jacket over the back of a chair. Alex poured the last of the champagne into two glasses, and handed one to me. He opened the French windows and the shutters, and then he switched off the lamp, so that the room was flooded with silver moonlight. I went and stood beside him, and we gazed out over Paris. A cool breeze stirred my hair and the skirt of my white dress. I sipped my champagne. In the distance, I saw the glitter of the Eiffel Tower. Alex draped his arm around me, his fingers warm on my bare shoulder. Then his hand moved to the back of my neck, and slowly down my spine, and it was as though his fingers left a trail of flame. It was not the touch of a friend.

My heart racing, scarcely daring to believe what had just happened, I turned to look at him. He was staring at me, his eyes black in the moonlight. He took the empty champagne glass from my hand and put it on the dining table. Then he reached up and brushed a strand of hair back from my face. Suddenly I was finding it hard to breathe.

'Tonight would have meant nothing to me if you hadn't been there to share it,' he said.

He rested both his hands on my waist, drawing me close, so that I could feel his heart beating against mine. He bent his head so that our faces were almost touching, and I knew that whatever happened now, everything between us, what we were to each other, had changed for ever.

'Anna,' he said, 'Oh, Anna –' And then he kissed me.

At first it was just a brush of his lips, a butterfly's wing, a soft caress that melted my insides. Then it was demanding, and fierce, as he crushed me to him, enfolding me in his strong arms, exploring my mouth with his tongue. My senses reeled, and if he hadn't been holding me, my legs would have given way. When he lifted his head from mine, we staggered apart, both of us wide-eyed and breathing hard.

I said, 'Y-You kissed me.'

'I want you, Anna.' His voice was hoarse.

I looked at him standing there, this tall, strong, handsome man who I knew so well, and I wanted him. All the reasons I'd given myself for not doing this no longer seemed important. Or if they were, I simply didn't care. The taste of him was in my mouth. Desire, hot and insistent, was spreading like wildfire through my body.

Alex had kissed me.

He stepped towards me, and then he was kissing me again, and I was kissing him back, my arms about his neck, my hands in his hair, his hips pressed against me so I could feel that he was hard. He started unbuttoning the front of my dress, and in his haste, several pearl buttons went flying off and across the room. At that precise moment, I really didn't care. The dress fell to the floor. Our mouths still locked together, I unhooked my bra, and my stomach lurched as his hand cupped my breast. Then he was tearing off his shirt, and I was frenziedly undoing his belt, fumbling with the stiff leather, unzipping his trousers, tugging them and his boxers down over his rear, flinging away my thong, both of us naked, as we fell onto the bed. I clung to him, gasping as he kissed my throat, writhing with pleasure at the touch of his lips and tongue on my breasts. His mouth sought mine again, and he kissed me hungrily, his hand between my legs, and then he rolled away from me, and I heard the sound of tearing foil.

He turned back to me, his hands parting my thighs so that he could lay his body along mine, taking his weight on his elbows. And then he was inside me, his body rising and falling above me, and the sensations coursing through me were so deliciously intense that I moaned aloud. I locked my legs around his hips, and he thrust himself deeper, again and again, his breath coming in ragged gasps. I was light-headed now, waves of pleasure surging and receding, as he moved within me, as we moved together, my head thrown back as he took me to the height of passion, feeling his body grow taut and then shudder, as he found his own ecstasy.

Slowly, I came back to myself, smiling up at Alex, as he lay on me, our bodies still joined. He smiled also, and kissed me lightly on my mouth.

'This has to be one of the best nights of my life,' he said.

'And mine.' I felt him slide out of me. He kissed me again, and then eased himself onto the bed beside me, pulling the duvet over both of us. He gathered me in his arms, and with my head on his chest, we fell asleep.

When I woke up, early morning sunlight was streaming in through the open shutters. Alex was still sleeping. I lay next to him, watching him, inhaling the scent of his skin, warmed by the heat of his body. Very gently, I brushed his hair off his forehead. Then I traced the line of his jaw, shadowed now with dark stubble. I touched his mouth and then my mouth, where he'd kissed me. Suddenly, I felt such a rush of affection for him that it left me dizzy and breathless.

I loved him.

My heart started pounding. I sat up, hugging my knees. Alex stirred, but didn't wake. I gazed at him, the beautiful man asleep beside me, and knew that I'd fallen in love with my male friend. I thought of all the times over the past few weeks when I'd longed for his kiss. My head whirled as I realised I'd been in love with him even before we came to Paris.

Then the thought came to me that while my feelings towards him had changed, I'd no idea how he felt about me. Last night had been incredible, but I wasn't so naive as to believe that our sharing one night of passion meant that he'd want us to have an on-going relationship.

I whispered, 'I love you, Alex. I so want you to love me.'

I lay down again, my head next to his on the pillow. He shifted onto his side, and his eyes flickered open. When he saw me, his smile lit up his whole face.

'*Bonjour*,' I said.

'*Bonjour*.' He kissed me very gently, on my forehead, on my eyelids, and on my lips and the hollow in my throat. Slowly, he lifted back the duvet so that we were lying together on top of the sheet, naked in the sunlight. I stretched, raising my arms above my head, luxuriating in his appreciative smile.

'You are so beautiful,' he said, stroking my face, trailing a finger between my breasts and along my side. He kissed my shoulder, and my neck. I moaned and sighed, and he moved leisurely down my body, his hand softly caressing me as he kissed my breasts and my stomach, sending delectable shivers across my bare skin. Then his mouth was on mine again, a long deep kiss, our tongues entwined, his arms holding me close, my breasts pressed against his hard, unyielding torso. When we broke apart, I slid my hand between us, running the tip of a finger along the length of his erection. He groaned and then smiled, twisting away from me to get a condom out of the nightstand.

I lay on my back, and he knelt between my thighs, lowering his body until he was poised above me. He kissed me softly, tenderly, and then he reached down and guided himself into me, smooth and slow, moving rhythmically, gliding in and out and in, looking down at me with half-shut eyes. I raised my hips to meet his, exquisite heat growing within me, my blood singing, my body quivering, Alex whispering my name, as we lost ourselves in each other.

Afterwards, he rolled off me and stretched out beside me, one arm behind his head. I turned to face him, drinking him in, my body languid from his caresses, a pleasurable ache between my legs.

He said, 'How did I sleep in the same bed with you for three nights without touching you?'

'Did you ... want me before last night?'

'I'm only human, Anna.'

I willed him to say more, to give me some sign that he thought of me as more than a friend he'd had sex with one night in Paris, to kiss me again and tell me that he loved me. Instead, to my disappointment, he sat up, swung his legs off the bed, and

247

sprang to his feet.

Looking at me over his shoulder, he said, 'Don't go back to sleep. We have to catch the Eurostar – and we haven't packed.' He headed off to the bathroom. A moment later, I heard the sound of the shower.

I got out of bed and went to the open window, relishing the warmth of the sun on my skin. The sky was cloudless, and the city shimmered in a haze of heat. I gazed out over the rooftops, and thought, What happens to us now, Alex? I was still staring at the view, when he came back into the living area, naked, towelling his hair. At the sight of him, my heart soared, brimming over with love.

I stepped towards him. 'Alex, I – Last night – This morning – I –'

'Ssh.' He rested a finger against my lips. 'I need – *We* need to talk, I know we do. But when we're back in London, not now.' His dark eyes searched my face. '*D'accord*?'

I'd almost told him that I loved him, but now, under the intensity of his gaze, all I said was, '*Oui, d'accord.*'

'I don't mean to rush you, but we do need to catch that train –'

'Oh, yes, the train –' I hurried off to shower. I blow-dried my hair, and packed my wash-bag. Alex had seen me without make-up often enough over the past few months, but I took the time to put on some mascara and spray myself with perfume. In the vestibule, I scanned the outfits I'd hung in his cupboards, picking out a white top and a floral skirt. I got dressed, and carrying the rest of my clothes, went back into the living area. Alex, also fully dressed now, was sitting on the sofa, texting on his mobile. He put down his phone and retrieved my suitcase from under the bed.

'I've made you coffee,' he said.

'*Merci.*' I dropped my clothes on top of the duvet, folded them one by one, and put them in my case. Last to go in was the white dress I'd worn to the exhibition, rescued from the floor where it had fallen the previous night. Many of the tiny pearl buttons were missing and there was a small tear in the cotton that I'd have to repair, but the memory of Alex undressing me was enough to make me smile as I stowed the dress away.

'I'm done,' I said, closing the case and zipping it shut. Alex wheeled it into the vestibule, and left it with his small holdall next to the front door. I gulped down my coffee, rinsed out the mug, and put it on the draining board.

'Ready to go?' he said.

'Just about.' I checked my shoulder bag for my passport and my Eurostar ticket.

The doorbell rang.

Alex rolled his eyes. 'Who calls at this hour on a Sunday?'

'One of your family perhaps? Come to see us off?'

'Unlikely – we did all the fond farewells last night.' With a sigh, he went to the front door and opened it.

A girl, wearing a short black dress, was standing on the landing outside. Her hair was longer and more unkempt, and her face was thinner than in her photograph, but I recognised her immediately. Her kohl-rimmed eyes were feverishly bright.

'Alexandre,' she said. '*Mon* Alex.'

'*Cécile?*' Alex's whole body tensed. 'How did you get into the building?'

'Your neighbour was just going out and she let me in. She's seen me here often enough.'

'Who told you I was back in Paris?'

'No one *told* me – there are photos of you at the Lécuyer Award all over the internet.' Alex's ex, the girl who'd broken his heart, stepped over the threshold and into the apartment.

'What do you want, Cécile?' Alex said. 'Why are you here?'

'I've come back to you.'

Alex stared at her.

Unbelievable.

Cécile said, 'René and I are over.'

Alex opened his mouth as if to speak, and then shut it again.

A single tear ran down Cécile's face. 'Oh, my Alex … When I left you I made the worst mistake of my life. The two of us are meant to be together.' Without warning, she flung herself at him, burying her face in his shirt. 'I know I've wronged you, and I'm so very sorry, p-please f-forgive me.'

Her hands snaked over Alex's chest and around his neck. His face was an expressionless mask. I waited for him to disentangle himself from her grasp and tell her to leave, but he just stood there. Then, to my dismay, he put his arm around her, and ushered her through the vestibule and into the living area. The shutters were still open, and the sun still shone, but for me, it was as though all the light had gone from the room.

Why didn't he just tell her to get lost?

Alex cleared his throat. 'Cécile, this is my friend Anna.'

Cécile sank onto the nearest piece furniture, which happened to be the bed where Alex and I had so recently made love. She glanced vaguely in my direction, and then she started crying in earnest, throwing herself full length on top of the duvet, her whole body wracked with heaving sobs.

'*Mon Dieu*,' Alex said, 'she's becoming hysterical. Cécile, you have to stop this.'

'I c-can't s-stop. I'm s-so unhappy.' Cécile continued to cry, but more quietly. I regarded her with distaste. Then I thought to look at my watch.

'Alex,' I said, 'we have to check in for the Eurostar in less than an hour.' I gestured questioningly at Cécile. Alex took me by the arm and drew me across the room.

'I'll have to get a later train,' he said, his voice low so that only I could hear.

What? 'Why would you do that?'

'Cécile – I can't leave her, not like this.'

I looked at Cécile lying on Alex's bed. A leaden weight settled in my chest. 'I'll get a later train as well.'

'I don't think so, Anna.'

He didn't want me to stay with him. Why?

'Do you remember how to get to the Gare du Nord? Do you have a ticket for the Metro?'

I heard myself say, 'Ye-es.'

'I'll carry your case downstairs.' Raising his voice, Alex said, 'Cécile –' He went closer to the bed. 'Cécile, listen to me. I'm going to take Anna's suitcase down to the street. I'll be right back.'

Cécile sat up, her face wet with tears. 'I'll be here waiting for you, Alex.' She spared me one dismissive glance, before turning her head away.

This wasn't happening.

Alex was in the vestibule, opening the front door, wheeling my suitcase out of his apartment.

I said, 'Alex, don't do this –' But he was already on the stairs, leaving me no choice but to go after him. On shaking legs, I followed him down to the ground floor and across the courtyard.

Outside on the street, he said, 'I may still be able to make our train. If not, I'll see you in London.'

Mechanically, I repeated, 'Yes, I'll see you in London.'

'*À bientôt.*' He kissed me as friends do in France, on both sides of my face, and then he went back inside his building. The door closed, and he was gone. I pictured him running back up the five flights of stairs and going into his apartment, where Cécile was waiting for him. I could picture her too, tragically dishevelled, sprawled on his bed: her short black dress, her long pale legs. It was all too easy to imagine Alex lying down beside her.

My throat constricted, but I made myself start walking down the hill to the Place des Abbesses, my bag on my shoulder, dragging my suitcase behind me. The wheels kept jamming on the cobbles, but eventually I reached the entrance to the station. I man-handled my case down the short flight of steps that led to the elevators and the ticket barriers, and finally I was standing on the platform. As always seemed to happen on the Metro, I only had to wait a few minutes for a train, but it felt like an eternity. I hefted my case into a carriage and got off again at the Marcadet Poissonniers stop to change from *ligne* 12 to *ligne* 4. When I'd done this journey in reverse with Alex it had seemed very quick and easy, but now it seemed unnecessarily complicated. My arms ached from the weight of my case.

I arrived at the Gare du Nord with half an hour to spare. I went through security and passport control, and found myself in a crowded departure lounge. All the seats were taken by other travellers, tourists discussing the sights they'd seen in Paris and spending the last of their euros at the bars and food counters, businessmen and women tapping away on laptops, harassed parents trying to amuse lively toddlers, a school party of bored teenagers welded to their iPhones. Resigning myself to standing until it was time to board my train, I found a space where I could lean against a wall. It grew hotter, and the noise levels rose. I was desperately thirsty, but couldn't face the thought of fighting my way through the crowd to buy a bottle of water. More people came into the waiting room. Alex was not among them. A few minutes later, I heard an announcement that the check in was now closed.

There was a sudden flurry of activity as people started to round up their children and their belongings. I joined a ragged queue going through the doors that led to the platform, lugging my suitcase, following the throng. I walked alongside the train, counting off the carriages until I came to mine. I put my foot on the first of the steps leading up to the carriage door, but struggled to lift my case off the ground. On the outward journey to Paris, Alex had carried my case. Tears pricked my eyes. Behind me, a group of people waited impatiently to mount the steps into the train.

A boy of about twenty said, '*Puis-je vous aider, mademoiselle?*'

'*Merci*,' I said, pathetically grateful.

He was shorter than me, but wiry, and he had no trouble in hoisting my suitcase into the carriage, and placing it in the luggage rack.

'*Merci*,' I said, again. '*Merci beaucoup*.'

'*De rien*.' My rescuer shrugged, in a manner achingly reminiscent of Alex, and slouched off down the aisle between the seats.

My seat was next to the window, not far from the entrance to the carriage. I slid into it, and put my bag on the empty seat next to it. The seat where Alex would be sitting if he hadn't stayed in Paris with Cécile. Misery overwhelmed me. I'd fallen in love with a man who loved another girl.

Alex didn't love me. Our first kiss and the torrid night that followed, the way he'd looked at me, his gentleness as he'd made love to me again this morning, had made me think he must have feelings for me, but I was wrong. For him, it was just sex, and nothing more. Given his reluctance to talk to me, apart from telling me to hurry and pack my case, I should have realised that.

A couple, a man and a woman in their thirties, sat in the seats opposite mine, talking in soft Yorkshire accents about a restaurant they'd been to in Paris, smiling at me. I shrank into the corner, avoiding eye contact. I couldn't have made conversation with anyone at that moment, let alone strangers. To my relief, the guy got out an iPod and she started reading a Kindle. There was a burst of laughter from the seats across the aisle as a girl showed her friend something on her phone. Further along the carriage, a child wailed. I sympathised – I felt like wailing too.

The train started to move out of the station. I stared unseeingly out of the window, pressing my forehead against the glass. Cécile cheated on Alex. She left him. She told him she never loved him. How could he still love her? And how could I live with him now?

I thought about the three months Alex had shared my flat, how much I'd liked having him around, and knew that I couldn't go back to that, couldn't live with him as though I looked on him only as a friend. I'd have to ask him to find somewhere else to stay. If he ever came back to London, now that he had Cécile. The thought that Alex might not return to London made my heart ache. No, he would come back. He was too much of a professional to break his contract. At least, I assumed he was. If he could take Cécile back after the way she'd treated him, maybe I didn't know him as well as I thought. I couldn't decide what would be worse: having Alex living in my flat, seeing him every day, knowing that he would never love me, or not seeing him ever again.

Suddenly, outside the window of the carriage, there was nothing but opaque darkness, as the train entered the Channel Tunnel.

Thirty-three

The first thing I saw when I started walking along the platform at St Pancras, was the famous bronze statue of the man and woman locked in an embrace. It was separated from the passengers disembarking from the Eurostar by a glass panel, but as I drew closer, I could see the exact spot where I'd met Alex when he'd first arrived in England. My eyes filled with tears. I dashed them away with the back of my hand. Somehow, I got myself together, and followed my fellow passengers down the escalator that led to the arrivals hall and out onto the station concourse. I'd only been away for four days, but the sudden onslaught of English voices all around me was strangely disorientating. Tightening my grip on my suitcase, I followed the signs to the underground, and the Piccadilly Line train that would take me home. I was back in London. Alex was in Paris. With Cécile. I *would not* cry.

Encumbered as I was with my luggage, dragging my ridiculously heavy suitcase up and down steps and escalators, and on and off the train, my wretched bag sliding off my shoulder, the journey home took on the quality of a nightmare. When I finally emerged from the underground into daylight, it was to find that the sky was overcast, and it was beginning to spit with rain. A fresh wave of misery hit me. Shivering in my thin summer T-shirt and flimsy skirt, I trundled my luggage along the uneven pavement as fast as I could, but the rain grew heavier, and I was drenched by the time I reached my building. Gritting my teeth, and with many stops on the way to catch my breath, I managed to haul my case up the stairs and onto the landing. I unlocked my front door and stumbled into my flat. I let go of my case. It toppled over and burst open, spilling its contents out onto the carpet. I dropped my shoulder bag beside it.

I loved Alex. I went into the kitchen and drank some water. Then I went into my bedroom, stripped off my sodden clothes, and put on jeans and a jumper. I lay down on my bed. Alex didn't love me. He'd kissed me and slept with me, but he'd never told me that he loved me. He'd made me no promises he couldn't keep. I wanted more from him than he was able to give.

I will always be your friend. I'd said that to him once. Before I'd fallen for him. How could I go on being his friend, when I was in love with him and he didn't want me?

That was when I cried. I lay on my bed, curled myself into a foetal ball and cried, hot tears pouring down my face, until I had no tears left, and I fell into an exhausted sleep.

I opened my eyes. For a moment, I was blinded by afternoon sunlight streaming through my window. Then I gasped. Lying on my pillow was a long-stemmed red rose. Next to it was a tiny metal statuette of the Eiffel Tower, less than an inch high, and a pale cream envelope with my name written on the front in Alex's handwriting. Alex was sitting on the end of my bed.

He smiled. '*Bonjour*, Anna.'

'Alex –' My voice caught in my throat. I sat up, reaching for the rose and holding it close to my face so that I could smell its scent, scarcely daring to hope that I knew why Alex had put it on my pillow. I picked up the tiny statue, balancing it on my hand.

'I wanted to give you a souvenir of your first visit to Paris – I thought this was less tacky than that gold statue you nearly bought –' He broke off. 'Anna, have you been crying?'

'I – Yes –'

'But why?'

'Cécile.'

He frowned. 'What about her?'

'I – I thought – you were still in love with her.'

'*Quoi?* Why would you think that? No, I am *not* in love with Cécile. I have no feelings left for her at all.'

'You let her into your apartment –'

'The state she was in, I couldn't turn her away.'

'I thought you were sending me away, so that you could be with her.'

'Is that how it seemed to you? *Je suis désolé.* I didn't want to deal with my hysterical ex-girlfriend in front of you. And you did have a train to catch. So, much as I didn't want to be parted from you, I didn't ask you to stay with me. After I'd taken your case downstairs, I went back up to my apartment, and made it clear to Cécile that there was no chance of us ever getting back together. There were some harsh words said – by her – and then she left. She's no longer a part of my life.' He reached up and trailed a finger down the side of my face. 'There's no reason for you to be sad.'

'I know that now. Now that you're here with me.'

Alex leant towards me, his finger tilting up my chin. And then he kissed me. The rose and the statue fell from my hands, and I melted against him. Still kissing me, he put his arms around me, and together we sank back onto the bed.

I said, 'If you knew how many times I wondered what it would be like to kiss you – even before we went to Paris.'

He laughed. 'There were occasions when I caught myself thinking about doing a lot more with you than kissing. I'd never have made a move on you, of course.'

'Why not?' I was genuinely curious.

'You and I were *friends*. Before we went to Paris.'

'And now …?'

'Anna – you haven't read your letter.'

I picked up the cream envelope, tore it open, and read the letter inside. Suddenly, I couldn't stop smiling.

He said, 'There was a moment at the Gallery Lécuyer – we were looking at *Anna Awakening* – that was when I realised that you were more than just a friend to me.'

'I don't know exactly when it was I fell for you,' I said, 'but it was long before this morning, when I woke up next to you in your bed.'

'I want to wake up next to you every morning of my life. Which is why we need to talk.' He took my hand. 'I can work anywhere, Anna. If you'll have me, I won't go back to France in July. I'll stay in London with you. Unless – would you consider living with me in Paris?'

I smiled at him. 'Alex, I would love to wake up next to you every morning in Montmartre. I would love to live with you in Paris. *Je t'aime.*'

He kissed me again, for a very long time. And then I re-read my letter. The shortest – and best – letter he'd ever written to me.

Dear Anna,
I love you.
Alex xx

Abi's House

Newly widowed at barely thirty, Abi Carter is desperate to escape the Stepford Wives lifestyle that Luke, her late husband, had been so keen for her to live.

Abi decides to fulfil a lifelong dream. As a child on holiday in Cornwall she fell in love with a cottage – the prophetically named Abbey's House. Now she is going to see if she can find the place again, relive the happy memories … maybe even buy a place of her own nearby.

On impulse Abi sets off to Cornwall, where a chance meeting in a village pub brings new friends Beth and Max into her life. They soon help Abi track down the house of her dreams … but things aren't quite that simple. There's the complicated life Abi left behind, including her late husband's brother – a man with more than friendship on his mind …

Will Abi's house remain a dream, or will the bricks and mortar become a reality?

People We Love

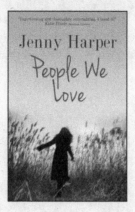

**Her life is on hold – until an unlikely visitor climbs in
through the kitchen window**

A year after her brother's fatal accident, Lexie's life seems to
have reached a dead end. She is back home in small-town
Hailesbank with her shell-shocked parents, treading softly
around their fragile emotions.

As the family business drifts into decline, Lexie's passion for
painting and for her one-time mentor Patrick have been buried
as deep as her unexpressed grief, until the day her lunch is
interrupted by a strange visitor in a bobble hat, dressing gown
and bedroom slippers, who climbs through the window.

Elderly Edith's batty appearance conceals a secret and starts
Lexie on a journey that gives her an inspirational artistic idea
and rekindles her appetite for life. With friends in support and
ex-lover Cameron seemingly ready to settle down, do love and
laughter beckon after all?

A Perfect Home

Claire appears to have it all - the kind of life you read about in magazines; a beautiful cottage, three gorgeous children, a handsome husband in William and her own flourishing vintage textile business.

But when an interiors magazine sends a good-looking photographer to take pictures of Claire's perfect home, he makes her wonder if the house means more to William than she does.

This is the beautifully observed and poignant love story of a woman who has to find out if home really is where the heart is.

The SW19 Club

What would you do if you were told you could never have children?

Faced with this news, Gracie Davies is at an all-time low. But with the support of some new Wimbledon friends, an unorthodox therapist, her hippy-chick sister Naomi and Czech call-girl Maya, she sets up The SW19 Club and begins her rocky journey to inner peace and happiness. Add in a passionate fling with handsome landscaper Ed, a fairytale encounter with a Hollywood filmstar and the persistence of her adulterous ex, life is anything but predictable…

What would you do if you were told you could never have children?

Faced with this news, Chloe Davies begins an unlikely love affair with the woman next door, Wu, the glamorous a...

For more information about **Lynne Shelby**

and other **Accent Press** titles

please visit

www.accentpress.co.uk